NEW HORIZONS

NEW HORIZONS

Visit us at www.boldstrokesbooks.com

By the Author

The Broken Lines of Us

New Horizons

NEW HORIZONS

by

Shia Woods

2024

NEW HORIZONS

ISBN 13: 978-1-63679-683-3

THIS TRADE PAPERBACK ORIGINAL IS PUBLISHED BY
BOLD STROKES BOOKS, INC.
P.O. BOX 249
VALLEY FALLS, NY 12185

FIRST EDITION: OCTOBER 2024

CREDITS
EDITOR: BARBARA ANN WRIGHT
PRODUCTION DESIGN: SUSAN RAMUNDO
COVER DESIGN BY INK SPIRAL DESIGN

Dedication

For my brother, my favorite person to watch on stage.
Sorry I broke your ThunderCats fort in 1995.

CHAPTER ONE

D ammit, Quinn. Can you please hurry up? This is a commercial flight. It won't wait on your highness!"

Quinn laughed as her manager, Mikey, shouted from the other room, and she could picture him pacing as he looked at his watch for probably the twentieth time. Sometimes, she wondered if his arm ever felt sore from so much exertion. "Oh, I like that one. Please only refer to me as your highness going forward," she said as she skipped into the room.

"Well, aren't you in a good mood. Come on, *your highness.* The car is loaded, the driver's ready, and the plane literally won't wait for us." He walked straight to the front door. "What are you doing? Come on."

She ignored his pestering as she bent next to the large tank lining the far wall of her apartment and pointed at the fish. "Okay, Leo, I want you to be nice to your brother while I'm gone. Uncle Henry will be here to check on you later. And while I'm gone..." She paused so she could look between the fish in the tank. She pointed at the smallest one in the corner. "Donatello is in charge. No arguments, Raf. You lost your privileges."

"If you're done giving orders to the Ninja Turtles, can we please get this show on the road?" Mikey looked at his watch again like he didn't know the exact number of seconds that had passed since the last time he checked.

Quinn rolled her eyes as she stood up straight. "Family is super important, Mikey. Had to say good-bye. Now, stop scowling.

It'll make your Botox wear off faster." She moved past him in the doorway and playfully flicked the lapel on his designer suit, humming as she made her way down the hall that would take her to their waiting car.

Mikey followed, growling things under his breath about punctuality the whole way.

Quinn preferred to be the last passenger to get on a flight, but Mikey insisted they board as soon as first-class entry was announced. She tried to ignore the looks other passengers directed her way as they shuffled onto the plane and past her seat.

It wasn't that she disliked people as a rule. She was rather sociable and usually got along with most people. It was the confused stares she hated. People who recognized her face but couldn't place her. It wasn't unusual for someone to come up to her in public assuming they had met her at some point in their life.

But that was the reality for someone who briefly found her face splashed across the tabloids due to a relationship gone wrong with someone who *was* recognizable. She knew it wasn't her past modeling or even her book that caused people to take a second look. She had rarely been recognized for any of her modeling work.

As she sat back in her seat, she tried to relax and remind herself that this plane was taking her to a new beginning. One that would take her out of LA and to a city that didn't automatically link her name with Jenna Matthews.

The fact that she was going to debut her show that she was incredibly proud of made it that much better. She had hoped the success of the book would curtail some of the attention from that ill-fated affair. But all it had done was make people google her more, and when someone googled her, they got Jenna.

Mikey must have noticed the emotions flitting across her face because he gently placed his hand on her leg, keeping his palm lightly resting on her knee. He was often all business, and he got stressed at the drop of a hat, but he had been Quinn's manager since she was fifteen, and they had grown up in the fashion industry together. Mikey had been there for her most important milestones and was her emotional rock throughout her career. There was nobody she felt safer with than him, even if half the time, he annoyed the hell out of her with his meticulous scheduling and nagging.

But he never judged her. Not even when she made some terrible decisions. He was the one who'd picked her up off the ground when Jenna had left her in a whirlwind of regret and media attention. He'd wiped her mouth when she'd drank herself to sleep for an entire year, and he'd convinced her to seek help when it was clear she'd needed it.

Mikey and his overly priced suits, his penchant for older rich men, and his obsessive need to be early *everywhere they went* were just part of who he was. And she loved him like a brother.

"You nervous for this, sweetie?" he asked her gently, taking her hand.

"You know I leave that job to you. I'm excited. I just want to start. When is that happening again?"

"We have a meeting with Horizon Theater's managing director the day after tomorrow. She'll give us a tour. On Friday, you have a meet and greet with Simon Anders."

"The big dog," she replied with a small smile. She knew how anxious Mikey was to get all this going, but she couldn't help but tease him a little. She was never one to get intimidated by successful industry people like he did, especially so far into her career.

But she also knew how much work he had put in to making her New York debut a success. Not that this was really her New York debut, per se. She'd done that when she was sixteen in a small fashion show for an up-and-coming designer. And again when her show opened in the New York Fringe Festival last year.

But this felt different. This wasn't modeling other people's clothing. This was something she'd written, and it was as personal as a piece of work could get. She was self-aware enough to know that it wasn't Shakespeare or any of the other heroes she'd grown up reading, but Quinn had managed to secure her name in a Playbill. And not just because her figure could sell a dress.

She was lucky that the early buzz and reviews from the festival last year had secured interest from some of the bigger Off-Broadway companies. But choosing the right theater was vital. Mikey and her agent had worked for six months to make sure everything was perfect for her New York premiere.

"Simon Anders is the artistic director of Horizon Theater," Mikey said. "He's a notorious bull. He's made a name for some of the biggest stage actors in New York and has broken down an equal amount of wannabe stars. He's as old-school theater as they come. Not your typical Hollywood type who will schmooze and flatter you. We need to impress him to make this easy."

"Why would he even want my show if he's so old-school?"

"His daughter is handling the programming for their winter series, when they present new works. So I'm guessing she made the push. She's the person I've been dealing with."

Quinn nodded but didn't add anything else as the plane began to taxi down the runway. She had learned years ago that her physical appearance made people treat her like an idiot. She had stopped trying to join meetings with Mikey after enough men had made more eye contact with her chest than her face.

Still, it annoyed her a little that the artistic director of Horizon was most likely against her show before she had even gotten into rehearsals. "Does he at least know what it's about? I'm not going in there just to be told I need to make my show less gay or swear less, am I?"

"Alex said he's on board. Plus, it's the theater. Everybody's gay."

"Alex?"

"Alex Anders. Simon's daughter and the theater's managing director. Keep up. Anyway, she will go through everything with us, including your schedule with Diego." When Quinn just stared back at him dumbly, he sighed loudly. "Diego. *Your director*."

She laughed. "I know, I know. I just wanted to see your annoyed face again. It's been too long."

He gave her a disbelieving look, but she really did remember who Diego was. The person who directed her show was one decision she didn't leave for Mikey or anyone else. She had a list from the theater, and Diego was the person she'd connected with most when they'd spoken.

"Stop worrying," she said, squeezing his hand. "I'll be there. Bells and whistles all securely attached. I'll even wear underwear."

He scrunched his nose and looked at her lap, seemingly trying to determine if she had any on now. "Please just be there on time. In fact, I'll be picking you up."

"My constant savior. Where would I be without you?" She leaned her head against his shoulder and batted her eyelashes.

"Probably auditioning for soaps," he replied and gently pushed her off.

She scoffed at that. "That's my mother's dream. Not mine."

"You have offers coming in left and right. Not just for soaps."

"If you're going to try to convince me to get into the adult film industry again, the answer is still no."

"Speaking of Diego," Mikey said, ignoring her comment to bring them back to business like usual. "We need to send him the new pages soon. He'll want them before rehearsals start."

"We weren't speaking of Diego. We were speaking of porn."

"Could you not say *porn* so loudly?"

The engine was loud, and she could barely hear herself, but Mikey's natural state was concerned, so she patted his arm like a child. "Calm down. And I have new pages to send. But I wanted to finish the whole first act, so I still need a couple days."

"Have you thought more about Rachel's suggestion?" He dropped his voice so low, Quinn almost couldn't hear him.

But she didn't have to strain too hard. He probably figured she would have a harder time deflecting when stuck on a plane. She sighed. She and her agent had gone back and forth about this ever since the show had done so well in the festival last year. "The show isn't about my personal life, Mikey. It's hard enough not naming people in all the stories I tell. It's way too complicated adding personal relationships into that mix too."

"If this is about that letter from Jenna's team, you know it means nothing. She has no power over you anymore."

"Maybe not, but I've finally made a name for myself as something other than *that* girl. I'm not going to talk about it just to sell a few seats and make Rachel's job easier."

Mikey took her hand in his again. "I get it, Q. I'll talk to her. You just finish your script. How you want it."

She brought their hands up and gave his knuckles a quick kiss. "Thanks, Mickey Mouse."

"I'm only letting that awful nickname slide because you're all vulnerable."

"Noted." Needing to lighten the mood and determined not to start thinking about the dark corners of her life, she said, "Should we come up with a code name for 'porn'?"

"I'm ignoring you now." He put in a pair of earbuds, closed his eyes, and she knew he'd sleep like a baby until they landed in New York City.

Sleep wouldn't come as easy to Quinn. She could never understand people that could sit for an entire flight without getting antsy. That was why she had always preferred the runway to a photo shoot. Or perhaps all the times she'd had to sit for a photographer was the reason she *did* hate to be still. She glanced over at Mikey fondly. As different as they were, he was her brother. And she was never one to pass up a good sisterly prank. As he continued to sleep, Quinn took out her phone. She flipped open her camera and moved close to his face so she could take a selfie of her tongue lightly touching his nose.

She leaned back, giggling to herself as she reviewed the handful of shots. "That will teach you to sleep on me," she said to herself. She was planning on saving the photo to use as blackmail later. But as she looked at the silly image, a much better idea crossed her mind. Before the plane took flight, she quickly opened her Twitter app and posted a new tweet.

Heading to a new adventure with this Sleeping Beauty. Get ready New York! #NYCDebut #HesBoringMe #WhatElseShouldIDoToHim? #RunwayQueens

She laughed to herself again as she put her phone away. He was going to kill her when they landed.

CHAPTER TWO

This meeting was more of a formality than anything else, but that didn't stop a burst of nerves from rolling around Alex's stomach as she walked toward her father's office.

He was rarely at the theater. He only spent two or three days a week there. Producers knew how deep his pockets ran, and he often had his hand in other investment projects, including a handful of Broadway shows. If Alex needed to meet with him, she had to carefully plan it around his schedule, and this meeting had already moved twice.

She knocked on the door but moved in before he could reply. "Hey, Dad," she said as she took the chair across from his desk. She suppressed a smile at the small grimace that crossed his face. He had always said the word made him feel too normal, and Simon Anders prided himself on being anything but normal. He was an artist, and artists were not just *dads*.

"Hello, Alexandra. Let's get started. Where are we with the final signatures on the Quinn Collins show? I won't sign anything that promises a full run. If that hasn't changed, this meeting can end now."

She took a deep breath. It was typical of her father to not even ask how she was and then to act as if she wasn't on top of things. After all, he had been the one avoiding her that week, not the other way around. "We've updated the contract. It's a strict three-week run in the winter series, just as we discussed. And it's a done deal. Quinn is on her way to New York as we speak."

"Good, good," he said as he looked at his phone, obviously not paying attention.

"We can sign the final contract today if there aren't any more issues from our side."

He glanced up from his phone and seemed almost surprised to see her still there. "I already told you I would sign." He narrowed his eyes. "Just remember, this is on your shoulders. If this little experiment doesn't pan out, I will not have it impact my theater."

"I know, Father, and I also know it will be a success. If you watched some of the videos I sent you, you'd understand just how much she—"

"Alexandra. Please don't ramble."

She took another deep breath while she decided what she could say to give him some confidence in her decisions. She had sent him plan after plan as to how they would execute a production in such a new format for them. Everything from how they would integrate the multimedia aspects of Quinn's show to how they were going to leverage the subject matter to reach new audiences. None of that really mattered, and she wasn't even sure her father had read any of it.

"I have full faith in the winter series and what you've chosen to do," he continued. "I just hope this one little show you're pushing isn't due to your own bias."

She was taken aback before she schooled her features. "Bias?"

"Don't act obtuse."

"You think I would put my name on the line for a show because the artist is gay?"

"Don't make this about that. You know I never cared who found their way into your bed."

Alex was used to comments like that from him, but it never failed to make her angry. "No. I don't pretend to think you care about anything I do."

"On the contrary, I care about everything you do. As it reflects on me and the theater. I care about the messes I have had to clean up."

She urged her body not to recoil. He had an innate ability to make her feel like she was still a child and not the successful woman she had become. A woman who'd gotten a degree while taking care of her sick mother and who had single-handedly kept her parents' theater from turning into a museum.

"You know that wasn't my fault," she said, barely over a whisper.

He smiled in the way he did when he thought he was being fatherly. Alex knew they bore a striking resemblance with their bright blue eyes and dirty blond hair, but she hoped she never looked as cold and detached as he did when he smiled.

"Let's not dwell on the past," he said and put his hand up as if she was trying to cut him off. "I won't deny you've had some good ideas. You have. But this theater is successful because of its legacy. For me to see you as leadership, I need to see that you understand that."

Alex took three long breaths through her nose, a coping mechanism she'd used as a child and into her teens to stop from snapping back at him. It had always annoyed her how he talked about theater. As if he invented it. Theater was something they should share, but somehow, it was the thing that caused the most tension between them.

"I understand, Father," she responded, standing. She needed some space, and there was nothing useful she could get out of him at this point. "I'll send the final contract soon. Please sign when it comes in." She left without waiting to see if he had a response. She knew he didn't truly care that she was gay, considering most of his friends were gay. This was about perception and embarrassment. He would prefer Alex had no personal life since that alleviated any possibility of a scandal within his theater.

After making one mistake, he'd acted as if she was a walking time bomb for another. That situation wouldn't have even happened if her last name wasn't Anders.

As she made her way down the hallway of the administrative offices, Alex decided against going back to her own office. She wanted to be alone without the threat of interruption, so she headed to the elevators that would take her to the lobby and into the theater. Given the fact that it was early September, the space would be free of rehearsals and production teams.

She entered one of the wings and took a moment to stand at the back row, taking in the quiet familiarity of the room. Theaters, especially dark and empty ones, had always felt like her sanctuary, and it was the place she had experienced her highest highs and lowest lows.

The ghost light on the stage shone bright enough that she could make her way down the aisle and choose a random seat. She closed her eyes and breathed in the familiar scent that only a theater could produce. This place felt more like her home than her actual childhood home. She had spent endless precious moments sitting on her mom's lap in these very seats as they'd watched her father direct.

It was also in these seats that she'd watched her mother perform. Sitting in the empty theater, staring at the stage, she could almost see her mother now. The vision danced before her eyes like a distant memory. She was Ophelia, lost in the depths of her own sorrow. Her mom hadn't only been one of New York's premier Shakespearean actresses; she'd been a vision to behold. Alex pushed a lump from her throat as she looked away.

Horizon Theater wasn't huge, but it was a pretty good size for an Off-Broadway space. It also wasn't as glossy as some of the new venues, but Alex had always loved the old Vaudeville feel of the place. As she ran her fingers down the dark fabric of the seats, she opened her eyes and let them settle on the lush red of the carpet up middle aisle. Like so many times before, she thought about the performers who had worked there when the building was first constructed in 1890.

The irony wasn't lost on her that the same theater that felt like an escape from her father was the very one he owned. He had started it with her mom, but somehow, even though they were co-artistic directors, he had always viewed this place as his. And after Alex's mother had passed, her father had made it clear that Alex's place was in the admin offices, far, far away from the artistry of the stage. But even after she'd given up performing, she still felt safest in these seats.

As her mind returned to her father, an old familiar anger surged through her, tensing her muscles. Anyone on the outside would assume that a man who'd spent his life building the careers of actors would cultivate the talent under his own nose, but in all her years, her father had never seen one performance. Every show she did was viewed as just another attempt to ride his coattails.

He had never been particularly warm to anyone outside her mom, but he seemed to hold a special disdain for Alex. When she thought back on it, she couldn't even remember him ever acting like a father.

He considered himself a director first and foremost. Being the artistic director of one of New York City's most renowned Off-Broadway theater companies would be next on the list. Years ago, he had also considered himself a husband, but since her mother's death during Alex's junior year of college, he rarely even mentioned being married. What wouldn't be on that list was being a father, and most of the time, Alex felt like an inconvenience at best.

Performing isn't right for everyone. Find what's right for you. She repeated his words in her head. He had been careful never to say anything like that around her mom, who had been nothing but supportive. Peggy Anders had been in the front row of every show. Even when Alex was just playing a tree in an elementary school production.

She choked back the emotion that threatened to take over. She rarely allowed herself to think about her mom these days. Or about being onstage. She needed to focus on what was important, which was the winter series and assuming Horizon's executive director role at last. She needed to prove to her father that she would take Horizon into an era that didn't rely on subscribers who were on their death beds.

Alex had been meticulously working on the winter series since spring, when she'd heard that their current executive director was leaving. She knew it was the perfect chance to prove that she could manage the business of the theater while also having an eye for artistic programming.

Quinn Collins was her missing piece. The other two shows were more traditional pieces that would do well with their demographic, but Quinn's show was special. Not only did Quinn bring her own level of fame, but the show itself offered the perfect chance to diversify their ticket buyers.

New York audiences would eat up the chance to see the beautiful ex-model sharing eye-opening stories of an industry that eluded most people.

A small, familiar vibration moved through Alex's body as she thought about Quinn, something she couldn't deny was happening more and more the closer they got to meeting. Ever since she'd seen her show in a New York festival last year, she couldn't get the work, or the woman, out of her head.

For someone who desired to control everything in her life, seeing beautiful dark eyes every time she got in bed and closed her eyes was an inconvenience beyond confusing. But it wasn't just her beauty. There was something else that drew Alex to Quinn's show beyond her looks.

Quinn was unassuming onstage, yet had the ability to engage an audience with her dynamic energy and sexy, sultry voice. The writing was witty and self-aware, and the stories were enlightening, heartbreaking, and raw. Her ability to weave stories in and out of her personal experience in the fashion industry, to impersonate those she had come across, to integrate her own sense of style into each section was simply unlike anything Alex had seen.

She thought back to the jab her father made about Quinn's sexuality. She knew Quinn had gone through a messy breakup with Jenna Matthews not too long ago. But as far as Alex was concerned, the only part that was intriguing about Quinn's Hollywood "scandal" was that it involved another woman. She'd had her own she said, she had experience and knew not to believe anything that the tabloids or even another woman might say.

Alex didn't feel the need to go online sleuthing for anything about Quinn. She had seen her show, and that was enough for her to feel confident in her decision to sign the contract.

Hopefully, it wouldn't be a huge mistake.

CHAPTER THREE

You sure you don't want me to stay tonight, sweetie?" Mikey asked from Quinn's new couch.

She leaned back against the cushions and sighed dramatically. "Go, *Dad*. I'll be fine. In fact, I don't think I'll ever leave this couch again." She sank deeper into the large cushions, sighing again. "Who decided on this couch? I will propose to them right now."

"Who else do you think would decide on these pillows?" Mikey tossed one over to her as he stood against the end of the couch.

"Yeah, those are a nice touch. Henry really is a doll. You *should* propose to him."

"Your *assistant* is too young for me," he replied as he pretended to dust something off his suit.

"He's literally three years younger than you are. And don't be a snob."

"Let's talk about tomorrow." He always deflected when it came to his personal life, and Quinn often wondered how she'd ended up with the most prudish gay best friend in the entire world.

"It's just a meeting, Mikey."

He gazed at her quietly for a moment. "I'm just proud of you. For doing this. This is going to be big. I know it."

His sudden tenderness was touching. She knew how much he cared for her, but it was rare for him to be so effusive. "For us both."

"I'll be here at eleven. I need you to have pants on. And socks. Hopefully shoes that match. We're out the door by eleven thirty."

"Noon with socks on. Got it," she replied with a loud yawn.

"*Quinn.* Eleven o'clock. And please don't be naked when I get here."

"As you know, people have offered big sums of money to have this body naked on their covers." She stretched out, dramatically posing.

"Not lately," he replied with a wink as he moved toward the front door, narrowly avoiding the pillow thrown at him.

"See you tomorrow at noon, loser," she shouted as the door closed behind him.

A few minutes after he left, she heard her phone ping on the coffee table. She had been tagged on Twitter from Mikey's rarely used account. *Who's Sleeping Beauty now? #Payback #HelloNYC*

Attached to the tweet was a photo he must have taken of Quinn sleeping on the couch earlier when she had dozed off after unpacking. Mikey had strategically placed the pillows Henry had bought around her while she slept. She laughed at herself surrounded by the four faces of the Teenage Mutant Ninja Turtles.

She smiled and pressed the reply button on Twitter. *Game on.*

To be fair, the photo wasn't as bad as the one she'd posted. At least she'd inherited her mom's way of sleeping, unlike her sister, Eve, who, like their dad, always fell asleep with her mouth hanging open. She had hundreds of photos locked away in her phone in case she ever needed to blackmail her sister later in life.

Not that she'd ever need to use anything against her. Eve was the kindest, most good-hearted person Quinn had ever met. It would have been easy for someone on the outside to think Quinn was the favored sibling by the way her mom bragged about her career and global adventures. But it was more complicated than that. Most people didn't know about the constant nagging she'd endured as a kid when her parents had tried to get her to excel in anything other than what she wanted: to sit in her room and read. Eve was only two years older, but their parents had always let her do her own thing.

When they were younger, Eve had been the leading example of a good kid. She'd consistently brought home good grades, was involved in all the clubs and sports, had friends and boyfriends, and had graduated with honors. She went on to get a teaching certificate.

Wild from day one, Quinn had never had much interest in school or sports. She didn't intentionally break rules or get into trouble; she just didn't connect with her peers, especially the girls who were mostly interested in boys.

She wasn't expecting the sudden surge of homesickness. She missed seeing Eve's kind and understanding eyes each day. She picked up her phone to check the time. It was still early on the west coast. She pulled up her sister's name and set her phone on speaker so she could rest it on Michelangelo's pillow face.

"Hey, Quinney," Eve said after a few rings, her light and easy voice warming Quinn at once.

"Hey, yourself. How's my favorite sister?"

Eve laughed. "Only sister, you mean?"

"I just got settled in my apartment and figured you'd be missing me right now. What with me being on an entirely different coast."

"How sweet of you to check in. How's the apartment?"

Quinn carried the phone back to the bedroom so she could stretch out while they chatted. "It's really nice. Pretty big for New York, I guess."

"Well, only the best for Manhattan's newest celebrity."

Quinn snorted. Her sister wasn't being snarky. She really did think Quinn deserved all the accolades in the world. "More like Manhattan's newest D-lister."

"Don't talk about yourself like that."

Quinn decided to change the topic. "How's Will?"

"He misses you. He upgraded his Super Soaker thingy thing for next time you come."

"It's not a thingy thing. He has a Freezefire 2.0. What did he upgrade to?"

"I don't know. A different one. It has green on it."

"You're useless. Tell him I expect a text."

Quinn missed her brother-in-law almost as much as her sister. Will and Eve had begun dating during their junior year of college, and Quinn had hit it off with him immediately. Probably because they both tended to act like children. But Will was a good man and treated her sister well.

"When do you start rehearsals?" Eve asked. She had always been one of Quinn's biggest supporters, even if their parents didn't really care outside of the prestige she could bring to the family.

"In a couple weeks. Tomorrow, I go into the theater for a tour." She rolled her face into the nearest pillow. It felt like a cloud. She really needed to send her assistant a thank-you text. Or a fruit basket.

"By the lack of any sarcastic comment or lude statement, I'll take it you're nervous," Eve replied.

"I just don't want to come across as some bimbo model who knows nothing about theater."

"There's my little drama queen. Quinney, you are the smartest woman I know. You wrote a book. You made that book into a show. You are totally awesome."

Quinn smiled. Between Mikey and Eve, she felt unbelievably lucky. After years of people kissing her ass to sell a magazine or a line of clothing, having someone like Eve in her corner meant the world. "Thanks, Evie. I'll text you tomorrow and let you know how it went with the theater meet and greet."

"You better. And Quinn?"

"Hmm?"

"Please call Mom. I can't keep her at bay forever. Just let her know you're there and safe, and you'll call her soon. Okay?"

Quinn sighed. "Yeah, okay. Love you. Give Will a kiss for me."

"Will do, talk later. I love you."

Quinn stared at her phone for a moment before resigning herself. She knew that sending her mom a text now would save her a world of pain later. Maggie Collins could be a formidable force.

The moment after she sent the text, she silenced her phone and set it on her nightstand. Her mom tended to answer a text with a call, and Quinn wasn't about to get into an hour-long, passive-aggressive conversation.

Her mom's favorite thing to hassle Quinn about was her looks. Unless she was talking to her friends. Then Quinn was the most beautiful thing to ever grace *Vogue*'s pages. Their mom and Eve had straight, light brown hair with appealing, gentle features. Quinn looked more striking like her dad. Dark hair, dark eyes, and high cheekbones.

She felt exhausted after the long day, but instead of putting away more clothes, she decided to give her new bed a good sleep test.

As she lay there, the nerves she had pushed aside since landing in New York began to form in her belly. With her modeling career over, the run at Horizon meant more to her than she was willing to let on, even to the people closest to her.

When sleep didn't come, she opened her phone and pulled up her browser. She figured she might as well do some research before tomorrow's meeting. As she scrolled through the first results on Horizon, she smiled thinking about how shocked Mikey would be if he could see she was prepping.

After going through a few show reviews and articles on the theater, she made her way to YouTube and typed in the theater's name. As she scrolled though the list of videos, she saw that most were sizzle reels promoting various shows. But halfway down the page was a video titled "Spring Gala 2019" that she clicked on.

The beginning was boring, and Quinn was about to click out when something caught her eye. Or rather, *someone*. Three people were on a stage for what looked like an announcement. She paused the video and stared at the static image. A blonde was standing next to two men with her hands clasped behind her back and a regal, almost bored look on her face. Quinn's eyes fell to her tight skirt, the front of which was partially covered by a sleek black blazer.

Her dark blue eyes weren't like any Quinn had ever seen, but it wasn't the color as much as the movement behind them that pulled her in. They reminded Quinn of the ocean. As if there was a constant wave moving through them, betraying her otherwise stoic features.

Quinn pressed play, and small type appeared below each of the people with their name and title. She leaned closer so she could read the screen.

Simon Anders: Horizon Artistic Director, Rick Weston: Horizon Executive Director, Alexandra Anders: Horizon Managing Director.

Quinn swallowed hard. *That* was Alex Anders? Mikey could have at least mentioned she was drop-dead gorgeous. A moment later, the video cut to more sizzle reels for the season and fast-forwarding didn't produce any additional views of the blond beauty. Not able to stop herself, she left the video and went back to the browser. *Alex Anders* might have another video that included more than just one shot.

More search results came up than she was expecting for a managing director, but it was the second video titled, "NYU Workshop: *A Streetcar Named Desire*, 2009," that she clicked on.

The description on the page read, "Part one of *A Streetcar Named Desire*, performed by NYU's all-women theater group led by Alexandra Anders and Courtney Powers."

Quinn was enthralled. The video had obviously been taken on someone's cell, so the quality wasn't great, but they'd filmed the entirety of the play and uploaded it into parts. She watched every second of it.

She'd read the play in college. And she would never watch anyone play the role of Blanche now that she'd seen Alex do it. Her talent was so subtle, Quinn almost forgot she was watching an actress. Besides the fact that Quinn was still reeling over how beautiful Alex was, she also couldn't wrap her head around the fact that she was the *managing director* of a theater company. Why wasn't she starring on every stage in New York?

She turned back to her browser to see what else she could find out, but other than a few reviews, most results focused on her dad and Horizon Theater. Once she sufficiently felt like Alex Anders's stalker, Quinn locked her phone and put it aside, finally laying her head down to sleep.

But sleep still didn't come. She couldn't shake the image of those deep blue eyes and the beautiful face that accompanied them. She was in serious trouble.

CHAPTER FOUR

W hen's the last time you actually watched a show?"
Alex glanced up from her computer but not with
annoyance or even surprise. She was used to Courtney barging into
her office without warning. They had known each other for more
than twelve years when they'd met at an NYU college audition.
Neither of them landed that role, but Alex had landed in Courtney's
dorm that night. Once they'd figured out that they didn't fight as
much if they took sex out of the equation, they became best friends.
These days, Courtney was Alex's *only* friend.

Alex smiled, choosing to ignore the question. "It's late. Done
with rehearsal?"

"Finally." Courtney ungracefully fell into a chair across from
Alex's desk, sighing as she tossed her red curls out of her eyes. "And
I was going to come kidnap you for reasons of alcohol consumption,
but you've got that concentrated furrowed look you always have
these days."

"I've always furrowed my brow when I concentrate."

"Yeah, but lately, you've looked slightly in pain."

Alex knew she was right, but it was also the start of a new
season, and the summer months had been their usual grind. Between
rental contracts, finalizing the upcoming season, and constant
meetings with her father, she felt depleted.

"You're just as talented as anyone out there," Courtney
continued, nodding toward the direction of the theater. "You're

wasted behind that desk." She paused to give Alex a once-over before lowering her voice and raising an eyebrow. "Even if you do look exceptional in those business suits."

"No, Court. What I know is that I've been told by people who matter that I'm *not* as talented." Alex's tone had more bite to it than she meant, but she and Courtney had been down this road before, and she didn't feel like revisiting the same conversation again.

"Your dad is not people. Your dad is an asshole."

"Be that as it may, he's a talented asshole who owns this theater and has the ear of almost every director in town. He's made it clear where my talents lie." Courtney looked like she was going to argue, so Alex put up a hand to stop her. "I love you and how protective you are. But I'm happy, I promise. I like my work, and it's fulfilling." She stood, hoping to indicate that the conversation was over. "Let's go get a drink. I can't look at these contracts anymore."

"Blanche, darling, you had me at 'drink.' Let's roll."

Alex smiled at the use of the nickname, which was an old callback to the all-women theater company they'd started at school. As much as they teased each other, she knew how lucky she was to have Courtney in her life. Though she didn't like to talk about it, Courtney's not-so-subtle disdain for her father made Alex feel less alone. Courtney knew more about Alex's family than anyone. She had briefly gotten to see the tenderness of Alex's mom before her death and witnessed the shrewd father who had taken over after.

As she gathered her coat from the back of her door, she pushed those thoughts from her head. Drinking with Courtney was a much better option than wallowing in the past. When she turned, Courtney had stood, but her eyes were glued to the book sitting on Alex's desk. A book she should have put away before her gossip-prone best friend came into her office.

"Well, now I know what you were doing in here," Courtney said, a playful smile growing on her lips. "Doing some light reading, are we?"

The book was facedown so Quinn's author's photo was peering up at them, and even in that moment, when Alex was trying to act blasé, the image again caused something to stir inside her.

She moved over to the desk and flipped the book over. "Stop, you perv. We're bringing her show here." She lifted a warning finger. "Do not repeat that. I'm serious. We need to keep this under wraps for now. My father is anxious enough about producing it."

"Wait, you're serious? You're producing Quinn Collins's show? At Horizon? An edgy, one-woman show that your father would never, ever approve of for his precious, pretentious theater? Okay, spill." Courtney sat and looked up at Alex expectantly.

Alex sighed but didn't join her. She had been meaning to mention this to Courtney for a while, especially since she was the one who'd made Alex go to the festival featuring Quinn's show in the first place. But this reaction was the exact reason why she hadn't said anything. Courtney wasn't ever calm about anything. She had a way of adding a dramatic flair to even the most mundane bits of information, and the negotiations had to be completely confidential until the signatures were signed. "I'm pretty sure I heard you mention alcohol. Can we continue this while I sip something strong?"

"Fine," Courtney replied, standing. "But we're talking about this the second a drink is in your hand. I know you have a lady boner for her."

"You're absolutely disgusting," Alex replied, but she had a smile on her face. Courtney had a special talent for making inappropriate comments, and Alex was used to them. She put her arm around her waist as they left the office. "Come on, Stella, the bar awaits."

❖

Alex and Courtney's go-to spot around the corner of the midtown theater was still relatively empty. On most nights, the place didn't fill until the various Broadway and Off-Broadway shows let out since most of the customers were stage managers, techies, and others who worked in the industry.

Horizon was technically an Off-Broadway house, but due to the prestige of her father's name and the success of the company itself, their location was in the thick of the Broadway houses. They headed to their usual table that was set toward the back of the dingy space next to a jukebox nobody had used in twenty years. The whole place had a retro vibe and could have used a bit of a facelift, but there was also something familiar about it that she loved.

Courtney nodded toward the bar and pointed at their table, indicating to someone that they needed a drink. Alex hadn't even sat before she felt Courtney nudging her in the ribs. "Uh-oh. Incoming... the Ghost of Girlfriend Last."

Alex looked up to see a bartender not-so-subtly swaying her hips as she walked to their table. "She wasn't my girlfriend. It was a casual fling."

"Said every lesbian since Joan of Arc."

Alex grabbed the nearest menu to avoid making eye contact. "Hey, Gabby," she said, looking down.

"Hey, Alex. Haven't seen you in a bit," Gabby responded with a hint of flirtation in her voice. "How are you?"

"Good. Fall has arrived. New season, busy times, and all that," Alex rattled off as she pretended to read the menu she didn't need. Her drink order never changed.

"I'm doing well too. Thank you for asking," Courtney volunteered, even though Gabby hadn't even looked at her yet. "My application just got accepted for this new high-rise in the Flat Iron district. Exposed brick along each wall. *It is to die for.*"

Alex couldn't stop the quick laugh that bubbled out of her at Courtney's unsolicited update, but when she saw the expression on Gabby's face, she tried to brush it off as a cough.

Gabby glanced between them, clearly not understanding the joke. "Uh, right. Congrats. That's awesome."

"One bourbon neat and a glass of red, please," Alex added, trying to put Gabby out of her misery and hopefully make her leave.

Gabby grabbed the menus, leaning down slightly so she was eye level with Alex. "If there's anything else you need, let me know. I'm over there," she said, pointing to the bar. "Until eleven and then, I'm being cut loose early."

She turned and left without waiting for a response, which Alex was grateful for since she couldn't control whatever came out of Courtney's mouth next.

"Unnecessary," Alex chided once Gabby was safely out of earshot.

Courtney narrowed her eyes. "I don't get you. You refuse to date any of the gorgeous women that go in and out of your theater, then you go and spoil our favorite watering hole by sleeping with the bartender? Don't think I've forgotten about our long-lost Jamba Juice. I miss my peach perfection."

"First of all, when have you ever before used the phrase, 'watering hole'? Secondly, that forbidden Jamba Juice isn't even the closest one to your apartment. A peach perfection is a block away from where you sleep."

"Not the point," Courtney replied, holding up a finger. "The point, my dear friend, is that you have been holding out on me. *Quinn Collins*. Her book strategically placed on your desk with the photo up so you can ogle it all day. Now, spill."

"That is not remotely the point you were making a minute ago," Alex replied, but she knew she wouldn't get out of this one. Not with Courtney. Instead of responding, she quietly watched Gabby approach with their drinks. This wasn't a conversation she wanted her to hear. Not because Quinn's show meant anything personal, but until they announced it, she needed to be careful. Or at least, that was what she had been telling herself every time her eyes found that book cover, and she was caught by those beautiful eyes staring up at her. Alex gave herself a mental shake, knowing Courtney would pick up on even the smallest amount of daydreaming.

"One bourbon," Gabby said with a wink as she put the drink in front of her. "And one glass of wine." She set Courtney's glass down without looking at her.

As Alex took her first sip, she noticed Gabby still standing there, and the hopeful expression on her face sent a pang of guilt to her stomach. Gabby wasn't a bad person at all. Alex just wasn't interested in anything serious with her or anyone.

After seeming to realize that Alex wasn't going to say anything else, Gabby turned and headed back to her spot at the bar.

Courtney snorted quietly before taking a sip. "You've got to start letting these women down, you know. You leave them in this limbo, and I get to watch sad puppy eyes over the rim of my wineglass."

"I don't like closure. It never leaves room for anything else," Alex replied, quietly watching Gabby. Her eyes lingered on Gabby's back as she bent slightly to shake a new customer's drink. Maybe she had been too rash about her.

"Ah. I see."

Alex's eyes snapped to Courtney's. "Oh, really? And what do you see?"

"Nope," Courtney said, shaking her head. "I'm not taking your angry bait. Forget about Gabby and tell me about Quinn's show."

Alex sighed. It was as if Courtney could read her mind sometimes. Most people quaked when she turned on her "don't fuck with me" voice, but Courtney had never let her get away with what worked on others.

She studied Gabby's profile as she took another sip. "Pretty basic. Her book sales went through the roof after her little stint at the festival last year. Now everyone in New York wants the *Times* best-selling author on their stage. We won the bid."

"Meaning you won. How surprising. Go on."

"Her team wanted a small downtown theater since they didn't think she was ready for a huge media splash. But we pitched it anyway. Well, I did. I put together this whole proposal on why I was so moved by what I saw at the festival. How I thought Horizon could help elevate the work. Anyway, I thought it was a long shot. But I got a call from her manager and agent, and they wanted to see the space."

"Did she come with them?"

"No, her manager handles a lot of the business side of things for her. And I imagine she's busy. She just finished a book tour too."

"Did you actually read the book, or are you just using the cover to get off on?" Courtney scrunched up her nose as if Alex had been the one to say something so crude.

Alex flung a napkin at her. "Court! Jesus. What is wrong with you?"

Courtney put her hands up innocently. "Don't be a prude. I know you're not one."

"Yes. I read the book. It's different than the show. Not as personal. Way more focused on the intricacies of the fashion industry." She took the last sip, letting herself feel the burn of the liquor against her throat before she continued. "Anyway, after weeks of back-and-forth on the contract, the union negotiations, media negotiations, and so forth, we secured it. I met with my father today to finalize our side."

Courtney's eyebrows shot up. "And how does Daddy-Doo feel about this? I can't imagine how you got him to agree to a one-woman show. It doesn't exactly play to the boomer crowd. She literally shows Instagram comments in her show. Does your dad know what Instagram is?" Courtney gasped dramatically. "Does he even know what the internet is?"

Alex laughed. It was, after all, a miracle that her father was allowing her to bring this show to the theater, let alone for their winter series, which was generally one of Horizon's most successful annual programs. She looked around, making sure nobody had arrived at a nearby table. She already felt like talking about this could jinx things, but she had been wanting to tell this additional piece of news to Courtney for months.

"Rick is stepping down," she said in an almost whisper. "I heard him talking to my father about it at the spring gala."

Courtney looked at her for a second before understanding showed in her eyes. "Al, wait. Does that mean what I think it means?"

"No, it doesn't. It's my father. He'd never just hand me the role without making me jump through fire hoops with nails in them. But that's why they offered me the winter series. It's a final 'test,' so to speak."

"Test?" Courtney asked in a shout.

Alex put her hand on her leg. "Court, please. Shh."

"Sorry, but come on. Horizon was an ancient relic when you joined. With a subscription base equally as old. You completely revolutionized the programming. Plus, you've brought in actual revenue. Both those assholes should be kissing your beautifully talented feet."

Alex squeezed her leg again, but this time in affection. She appreciated Courtney's protectiveness of her. She had, in fact, worked her ass off, and it was nice someone noticed, even if her father chose not to.

Rick Weston was Horizon Theater Group's executive director. He'd been part of Alex's life since she was a little girl. He was basically the gay version of her father. As pretentious about the art and equally as old-school.

When Alex was promoted to managing director from the production office, she immediately had her sights set on Rick's job. Sweet or not, he was as lazy and uninspiring as a head of a theater could be. She had always suspected that part of why her father loved him in that role was that he was pliable. And she knew that was also why he was reluctant to have his overly stubborn daughter take the reins.

"You know exactly why he's doing this," Alex said.

"That was five years ago. Not to mention complete and utter bullshit. You were a pawn."

Alex put her hand on Courtney's arm to quiet her again. For an actor, Alex always marveled at Courtney's lack of volume control or any awareness of how loud she could be. "I know that. You know that. Rick knows that. And, yeah, my father knows that. But it's still a mark on my record, even if it wasn't fair."

"If Simon doesn't give you this promotion, I will create a Voodoo doll out of him, and I will use it."

Alex smiled. "Please marry me."

"Two tops do not make a right," Courtney replied dryly. "And don't think I've moved on from the real bit of juiciness here. Quinn. Collins. The sexy model turned author turned actor turned Alex Anders bedwarmer. And I know you have a thing for her. So is rule number one going out the window?"

"Rule number one remains. No intermingling in the theater."

"You and your damn rules."

"I like my rules."

"Oh, I remember very clearly how you like them."

"Not the kind I was talking about. Though I like those too." Courtney knew why she couldn't mingle in the theater. Alex had already made that mistake, and her father would never let her forget it. "Enough about me," she said. "Still seeing the stage manager?" When Courtney uncharacteristically blushed at the change of topic, she leaned forward and smiled. "Oh, do tell. It's not often I get to see your face the same color as your hair."

Courtney flicked a coaster at her, but it fell short. "It's going well. I don't know. I think I like her?"

"Was that a question?"

"Maybe." She dropped her head onto her arms. "Ugh. I don't know. I want her to be just with me, I guess. All the time."

Alex's smile grew. "Courtney Powers flustered over a woman? You should tell her all that. She'd be beyond lucky to have you and just you."

Courtney lifted her head and returned the smile. "I think I will. I'm heading over there tonight."

"Oh, so you double-booked on me then?"

She knew Courtney would understand that she wasn't really upset. During their friendship, they had both ditched each other for women more times than she could count. And as that thought flitted through her brain, she found herself gazing back at Gabby, who was interacting with someone at the bar.

"Well, it doesn't seem like I'm really leaving you completely alone." When Alex's eyes moved back to Courtney, she was smiling in that annoying, best friend kind of way.

Courtney began pulling some money out of her pocket, but Alex put her hand on her arm. "Stop. Go. Be merry. Get laid. Tell me about it later."

"Fine, but I need to know what happened here," Courtney responded as she motioned between Alex and the bar. "I'll stop by your office after rehearsal tomorrow."

Alex was overjoyed that Courtney would be around the theater so much this fall. Getting cast in Horizon's fall show had nothing to do with Alex and everything to do with the fact that she had been killing it in the New York scene. "You'll know everything. Because you'll drag it out of me."

"And you love me for it," Courtney replied as she stood. Once she had her coat on, she leaned in to kiss Alex's cheek. "Have fun tonight. Don't break too many hearts before sunrise."

"No promises."

As Courtney left, Alex let her gaze linger over Gabby. She shouldn't even think about being with her again, considering how it might confuse things. After all, Alex was never going to give her what she really wanted: a commitment.

But the temptation was too much, and she selfishly needed to forget about everything and control a situation for a few hours. Control a woman writhing under her. As if Gabby could hear her thoughts, she looked over and held her heated gaze. Gabby's darkened eyes made it clear she knew exactly what Alex was thinking.

After setting cash on the table, Alex swiftly walked to where Gabby was pouring a drink for one of the customers.

"Alex. Hey. Are you leaving?" she asked as she looked at the clock behind the bar.

"I am. I'm heading home to shower. I'll see you after your shift." She didn't wait for Gabby's response before she headed out. She knew she'd be there the second she could.

CHAPTER FIVE

Alex took another gulp of coffee and glanced up at the conference room clock. One more hour. There was nothing she loathed more than meetings with Horizon's public relations agency. She knew publicity was a part of the business, but talking to the PR people always made her feel numb and as far away from the art she cared about as she could get.

She was also hyperaware that Quinn arrived at the theater in two hours, and concentrating on anything else was futile. She tried to remind herself that this wasn't different to any other artist meet and greet, but the butterflies rolling around in her stomach betrayed that logic.

"That takes us into the winter series. We'll want to do the norm for that this year. After the shows are announced at the gala, we'll pitch for a feature that focuses on all three shows to the *Times* and elsewhere. But we should talk about Quinn Collins as well." Janet Jameson, the owner of the successful PR firm the Jameson Group, rattled off her orders to a team of professionally dressed women silently typing on laptops.

Hearing Quinn's name finally caused Alex to pay attention. Normally, she didn't bother with the agency's work on behalf of the theater since it was always the same process. Her measure of success wouldn't be based on ticket sales. After all, the winter series always sold well. Her father would judge her on the artistry and whether he and Rick deemed the performances worthy of their precious stage.

"What do you want to do differently with Ms. Collins's show?" she asked Janet.

"Oh, hello, Alex. So happy to have you here," Janet replied. She was used to Alex zoning out toward the end of meetings, so her sudden interest probably wasn't subtle. Janet was also hard to fool, considering how many years she had known Alex. Not only had she been best friends with Alex's mom, but it was hard to go anywhere in the New York theater scene without running into Janet. "Quinn's show is likely to garner a lot of interest," Janet said and paused for a moment, her gaze piercing. "We think the story around her show has legs, and we'd like to pitch a larger brand piece around it." She folder her arms, causing the dozens of metal bracelets she always wore to jangle loudly. Her sense of style had always been expensively flamboyant, and as a kid, Alex had always thought it was funny how loud she was when she walked.

"What do you mean by a brand piece?" Alex hated PR mumbo jumbo, and the lack of sleep over the past two days was making itself known against her eyelids. Staying up all last night with Gabby was probably a bad idea.

Janet continued enthusiastically, not hearing—or pretending not to hear—the annoyance in Alex's tone. "We'd like to pitch a story around *you*. Wait, let me finish please." Alex hadn't even tried to interrupt, but Janet put her arm up as if she had. "Picture this," she said excitedly and put up her hands as if reading a headline in front of her. "*The lady boss behind Horizon's latest surge of edgy programming shakes up the winter series with a modern look at fashion, beauty, and the darkness behind the lens.*" Janet gestured in the air as each new "headline" idea came to her. "*The daughter of powerhouse Simon Anders steps out of her father's shadow to team up with ex-model darling, Quinn Collins. LA bad girl teams up with NYC's enigmatic stage maven. Hollywood drama meets New York grit.*"

After rattling off her last headline, Janet turned to Alex, who couldn't help but laugh at the absurdity. But the others around the table didn't seem to think what Janet had done was even in the realm of odd, and as soon as Alex realized Janet wasn't joking, she stopped laughing. "Lady boss? Enigmatic stage...what was the word you used?"

"Maven," one of the women around the table eagerly supplied.

"Right. Maven. Okay, so, Janet." Alex turned her best polite smile at her. "Your enthusiasm is noted. Thank you for whatever that was. But I am not the story. Quinn Collins and her show are the story here."

Janet returned the smile, apparently unmoved by the protest. She was one of the best theater publicists in New York, and Alex was lucky to have her. But the fact that Janet had watched her grow up made it hard for Alex to get her to take her opinion seriously sometimes.

Before she spoke again, Janet looked around the table. "Thank you all so much for today. I'd like a moment alone with Alex. I'll follow up with you on next steps." The others nodded and left. Janet waited until the door closed and turned back to Alex. "I know Rick is leaving."

Alex sat up straighter. That was not what she'd thought Janet was going to say.

"Your mom's favorite thing in the world was to see you onstage," she continued. "And I know I'm overstepping here, but your father has kept you in his bubble for too long. You deserve to break free. A brand story like this could set you up to do that."

Alex felt like the air was being sucked out of her. She worked so hard to keep her emotions at bay and felt a flash of anger at the mention of her mom. But before she could respond, Janet put her hand on her arm.

"Alex, she was my best friend, and she knew how I felt about that father of yours. I know you want Rick's job. You've been working toward it since you joined the theater. But I also know your father, and backing him into a corner is the best way to get what you want."

That last statement caused her head to snap up. This was probably the first personal conversation she'd had with Janet since her mom had passed. They'd had frequent dinners and talked at each opening night, but they hadn't really *talked* since her mom had died.

Their conversations usually revolved around Horizon. That wasn't too surprising since Alex didn't really talk to anyone outside of Courtney, and even with her, she could probably count on one hand the number of times she had discussed her mom in the years since she'd passed.

"I never knew you felt that way about him," Alex responded in a quiet voice.

"Your mother loved him. Fiercely. But she also loved you. The story we're planning will be about Quinn. That *will* be the focus. But with you at the helm of her New York debut. Trust me, dear. I won't embarrass you. But I do think this could help solidify you as the driver of Horizon's future. Just like your mom would have wanted. Will you please trust me on this?" She squeezed Alex's hand gently, and the contact felt almost comforting.

Janet was nothing like Alex's mother, but they had somehow worked as friends. Just like Alex did with Courtney. But Janet was wrong. Her father would only see this as some ploy to get media attention away from his company. "Let me think about it."

"Good enough for me." Janet smiled and let go. "Call me this week and let me know what you've decided. We've been in touch with Quinn's publicist and have a call with her next week to iron out the media plan. It would be good to know by then."

They stood, but as they got to the door, Janet paused and did something else unexpected; she hugged Alex. A few beats went by before Alex slowly brought her hands up to Janet's back, returning the gesture.

"You go get 'em, kid," Janet said before pulling back and opening the door for them.

Alex looked at the time as she left the office. She had just over an hour before Quinn arrived. She took a deep breath of the stuffy New York air as she left the building and willed her ever growing nerves to calm.

CHAPTER SIX

S o," Quinn said as she settled into the back seat of the cab with Mikey, yawning widely. "Tell me what you know about Alex Anders." She had stayed up way later than she should have, but she couldn't stop thinking about Alex. Images of her gliding across the stage so effortlessly as Blanche flitted across her eyelids every time she closed them.

"Not much. She's been easy to work with so far. A bit intense and serious, which makes sense, I guess, considering her pedigree."

"She's not a dog, Mikey."

"It's a thing here on the east coast, Quinn. As I understand it, the Anders family is royalty here. And not just within the theater scene. Simon Anders's grandfather comes from old New York money. She seems to take that legacy seriously."

"She sounds super fun."

"She doesn't need to be. She just needs to be good at her job."

"Too bad you're gay. An intense woman who takes her job too seriously sounds perfect for you."

"Well, as elusive as Ms. Anders may be, I *have* heard through the gay grapevine that she's family," he replied, uncharacteristically raising his eyebrows.

Quinn held up a finger. "First of all, I want to know more about this gay grapevine. I never got the memo about that in my coming-out welcome package."

"It's more for us queens, love."

"That feels les-phobic not to share the vine, but whatever. *Secondly*, how and why have you been hearing things about Alex Anders?"

"Don't forget, I've been spending many a week here securing this precious deal for you. One of my east coast gentleman callers is a producer on Broadway with Simon. He happened to mention that Ms. Anders is quite the lady-killer about town."

Quinn gasped and grabbed his arm. "You never mentioned any producer! Now I have questions."

"I don't feel the need to tell you about every dalliance, unlike you. It was brief, not important," he said, waving to dismiss the topic. "Next question better be quick. We'll be there soon."

"Don't pretend you don't love stories of my sexual escapades."

"I assure you, I don't."

"Not even the story about the girl with the sticky fingers from the ice cream cone who—"

"Quinn! Stop. Gross. No."

She couldn't help but laugh. "Prude." As their taxi made its way down the congested morning traffic, she questioned their decision not to walk. She turned to suggest it when she caught Mikey staring at her quietly, an amused look on his usually expressionless face. She hated when he did that. He could always read her way too well. "What?"

"Why so curious about her anyway?"

"About whom?" She couldn't play dumb with him, but she also wasn't about to admit she was mainly asking about Alex because she'd watched two hours of her the night before.

The amused expression didn't leave his face. "The only person we've talked about on this ride."

"She holds our future in her hands. Of course I'm curious."

He simply hummed under his breath. Luckily, their cab had slowed in front of the theater on 52nd street.

Quinn looked up at the building that held her future, trying to convince herself that the butterflies that just erupted in her stomach had everything to do with this new step for her career and nothing to do with the sexy blonde she was about to meet.

Horizon's lobby was larger than she expected. There were three entrances to her left that directed audiences into the theater with an area for merchandise nestled in between. To the far right of the expansive room were two winding staircases that led up to what she assumed was the balcony.

While beautiful inside, the building was not modern. Intricate designs led all the way up the wooden railings on the staircase, and the whole room had a feel of modern upkeep and historic elegance. She had seen photos; that was one of the main reasons she'd chosen it. She wanted to *feel* like she was working in the theater, not as if she was on another set. Horizon obviously took care to maintain their venue, but a lot of care also went into honoring the past.

"Wait until you see the theater itself," Mikey murmured as he came up next to her.

"It's beautiful," she replied quietly, continuing to look around.

"I'm so glad you think so," a confident voice joined them from behind, causing Quinn to spin around. A woman had silently entered from a door to the right that said *Staff*.

Quinn's tongue felt heavy as she stared at the stranger. Well, *technically* a stranger, but Quinn recognized her from the videos she'd watched all last night. That college production had been more than twelve years ago, but Alex didn't appear to have aged at all. A spark of surprised amusement shone in her eyes as she seemed to take in Quinn's lingering gaze.

"Ms. Collins, Mr. Rubio, I'm so happy to have you here." Alex reached out to Mikey first but kept her eyes on Quinn.

Quinn sighed in relief when her body seemed to be able to do more than her mouth, and she reached to take Alex's offered hand.

"Ms. Anders, the pleasure is all ours," Mikey said. "But please, it's Mikey and Quinn."

"I quite like the sound of Ms. Collins. It makes me feel sexy and mature," Quinn blurted before mentally face-palming. Alex simply smiled. Her easy confidence only made Quinn want to fidget.

"I assure you, you can call her Quinn," Mikey said flashing a confused look.

Alex continued to smile, not even glancing back at Mikey. "And I can assure you, Quinn, that you look mature and sexy from here. And please, call me Alex. Why don't you both come with me so we can sit in my office?" Without waiting, Alex turned and went back to the door she'd come through.

Mikey leaned close to Quinn's ear. "What is wrong with you?"

She shrugged. She knew exactly what was wrong with her, and it was swaying its hips ten feet in front of them.

CHAPTER SEVEN

A lex chided herself as she opened the door to let Mikey and Quinn enter her office. Flirting with Quinn two minutes after meeting her—in front of her manager, no less—was not keeping things professional and friendly. She just hadn't been prepared for how beautiful Quinn was in person. Even more than she was onstage or splashed across magazine covers. She was simply perfect. She reminded Alex of a prima ballerina with her long limbs, high cheekbones, and pale composure.

Quinn's eyes were such a dark brown that they looked black. Alex knew she had been staring, but she had trouble looking away from them. "Mikey, I have a handful of paperwork I need you to go through and sign so I can take you to a conference room. While you do that, I thought I could start by giving Quinn a tour of the space. Then, we can figure out the final rehearsal schedule. As I understand it, Diego will be here by the fifteenth to start with you?"

Part of Quinn's contract negotiation was that she got to choose her own director. Luckily, Diego Ruiz was the man ultimately chosen for the job, and he was a familiar and respected face around Horizon. Alex knew he would protect the integrity of Quinn's original work while also tightening it for the more experienced New York audiences. It was why she had subtly mentioned him to Mikey a few months prior when she had given him a list of approved directors.

Quinn sat back and distractedly looked around, settling her gaze on a show poster hanging on the wall behind Alex's desk.

When Quinn kept staring, Alex glanced up at it before looking back to her. But whatever was going through her mind was unreadable.

"Yes, Diego gets here on the fifteenth, and we start with him on the twentieth," Mikey said. "That gives Quinn time to settle in the city before rehearsals begin."

"Do you know a good bagel shop?" Quinn asked, her eyes finally leaving the poster.

The question wasn't what Alex was expecting. "Uh, bagel shop?"

Quinn leaned forward, a small smile playing on her lips. "New York is famous for them. I figured it would be good to know some around here since this is my new neighborhood and all."

Alex stared dumbly for a moment before answering. Whatever she was expecting the cool, chic model to be like, this playful woman asking about bagels wasn't it. "George's. Down two blocks on 50th. Yellow awning out front. His are the best."

There was a silent pause before Mikey chimed in again, obviously trying to get things back on track. "Point me to the conference room, and I'll dig in while Quinn checks out the theater."

"Great. Follow me. I'll take Quinn to the rehearsal rooms."

"This is our rehearsal space where you, and Diego will spend most of your time," Alex said, pushing open a door that connected to backstage. She led Quinn down the hallway, but rehearsal for the fall show must still have been going because the space was absent of the usual shuffle of actors and crew. They were both quiet until they reached a new door.

"We have five different rehearsal rooms of various sizes," she said as she moved into the room. "Each map out to mirror the stage floor, and your rehearsal schedule will specify which room you're in each day. Most likely, you'll be in the same room for each rehearsal for consistency, but sometimes, things shift." Quinn quietly walked around. Without Mikey's presence or any other prying eyes, Alex was able to take her in without feeling creepy.

She was dressed more casually than Alex's own skirt and blouse. Sporting black skinny jeans that seemed sculpted to her body and a light grey pullover hoodie, Quinn made overly casual look stunning. She turned. "But this is just a room."

Alex tried to school her features but knew she couldn't hide her confusion. "Well, yes, it's a rehearsal room."

"Exactly. It's not the stage," Quinn replied, taking a step closer.

"All of our productions use the rehearsal space until it's time to move into the theater. We have other shows before yours." She spoke slowly, hoping she didn't sound like she was speaking to a child.

"I need the *stage* to inspire my art." Quinn stepped closer again.

Alex was at a loss for words. She hadn't thought the conversation would veer this way and hadn't pegged Quinn for the diva type. But before she could answer, Quinn burst into laughter.

"I'm so kidding. This room is great. But you really should have seen your face. You looked like you wanted to hit me."

"I'm not in the habit of hitting our artists. Unless they ask me to, of course." She immediately regretted adding that last part, especially when she saw a quick spark of surprise cross Quinn's features. She needed to get herself under control, but Quinn was nothing like she'd imagined.

"But you do if they ask?" Quinn was somehow standing in front of her now.

Alex hadn't even noticed that she'd advanced that far into her personal space. She could feel heat coming from Quinn's body that she could have easily touched if she so much as reached out with a finger. "Only if they ask nicely," she replied in a low voice.

The air around them felt hot as Quinn leaned closer. Alex had to put a stop to the blatant flirtation. She needed to focus on the prize at the end of the season. Not the expression in Quinn's eyes that resembled desire.

Before she said anything else that she would regret later, she stepped back, putting some much-needed distance between them. "Let's keep going." She walked to the door, leaving Quinn with the same clouded look in her eyes.

Alex took a breath as soon as they left the room. Rehearsal for the fall show must have just gotten out since the hallway was peppered with actors laughing and horsing around. The noise steadily increased as more people filed out of the rehearsal room at the back of the hall.

Quinn's eyes widened, and she smiled as she joined Alex in the hallway. Someone called Alex's name from the other direction. She turned and groaned as Courtney bounded down the hall.

In simple black leggings and an oversized T-shirt, Courtney had her red hair tied in a messy bun atop her head, though the headband struggled to tame her unruly curls. She gave Alex a sweaty kiss on the cheek, pushing in to avoid getting hit by the rush of people going past.

"Ugh, you're gross," Alex said as she pushed away and wiped her face.

"Get over yourself, Anders, and introduce me to your friend. Hi, I'm Courtney."

Alex rolled her eyes as Courtney turned to Quinn and flashed her the smile that had melted more than one heart in Manhattan.

"I'm Quinn. It's nice to meet you."

"I heard you'd be joining us. It's all little Alex here has been able to talk about. Welcome to the Horizon family."

Alex shot her a death stare she hoped Quinn didn't catch. Courtney would pay for that one later.

Thankfully, Quinn didn't seem to notice. "I'm really excited to be here. Are you in the fall show?"

"Yep. Because nothing says exciting live theater like the ever progressive and modern Arthur Miller," Courtney replied.

Alex smirked at the sarcastic comment she had heard come out of Courtney's mouth more than once. Courtney knew exactly who had decided to do *Death of a Salesman* as their fall show: Rick Weston, their soon-to-be retired executive director.

"You're saying I should drink before seeing this one?" Quinn asked.

Courtney sighed. "If only we actors got to partake as well."

"Like you don't have a flask backstage with you at all times," Alex teased.

Ignoring her, Courtney turned to Quinn. "Speaking of which, we're all heading to a bar tonight to celebrate the end of rehearsals before tech week. You should come. You'll love the cast. I promise, we're more fun than this sourpuss." She nodded toward Alex.

"She is awfully serious," Quinn replied with a smile.

Courtney laughed and swung her arm around Alex's shoulder. She pointed to Quinn. "I like this one. You can keep her."

"Court," Alex replied in a tone meant as a warning. She had to get Quinn away from the train wreck that was Courtney before anything else flew out of her unwieldy mouth or any more invitations were given out.

"Let me guess…" Quinn looked at her with a challenging quirk of her eyebrow. "You won't be coming. You don't seem like the mix and mingle type."

Alex shot Courtney another warning glance when she broke out into a laugh. "Oh, she mingles," Courtney said. "Just not with anyone within these walls."

Alex was regretting not running the moment she had heard Courtney call her name. She wasn't going to rise to the bait, though, and wanted to wipe the smug, knowing look off both their faces. She turned to Quinn. "Actually, I was planning on being there tonight."

"Really? You seem more of the *go home and relax alone with a glass of wine* type. Maybe play some chess. Not the *party with your cast* type."

"Well, Quinn, I'd argue you don't know me enough to make those assumptions. I hate wine." Alex could feel the same thickness seep into the air as it had in the rehearsal room. What should have been friendly banter felt like foreplay. For a moment, they maintained eye contact, and Alex almost forgot Courtney was there. When she finally tore her eyes away from Quinn's, she saw Courtney smiling and looking between them like she was watching a movie.

"That's settled, then. You'll both be there. Tonight. At eight. Phone?" Courtney opened her hand to Quinn, palm up.

Quinn reached into her back pocket and handed Courtney her phone. Nobody spoke as Courtney added herself as a contact, but Alex's stomach was doing loops at the recent development. Seeing

Quinn later, especially in a bar, was not how she thought this day would end.

"Now you have my number in case anything changes. Oh, and I added Alex's in there too." Courtney winked as she handed Quinn her phone.

"It was nice meeting you. I guess I'll see you tonight," Quinn responded, though she was looking at Alex.

Courtney kissed Alex's cheek again as she sauntered past them down the hall. Without turning, she shouted back, "And by the way, Quinn. You were right. She does play chess. See you tonight!"

"Let's go to theater before we go find Mikey," Alex said without looking at Quinn.

As they walked, she couldn't see Quinn's face, but somehow knew she was smiling.

She really was going to kill Courtney.

CHAPTER EIGHT

S he's hot. I'll give you that. If you weren't so smitten, and I
didn't have my eyes on a certain stage manager, I'd try my
hand there." Courtney took a sip of her staple red wine, her already
glassy eyes dancing behind her drink.

"I'm not smitten. Please stop. You've already done enough."
Alex took a sip of her own drink as she looked around the bar. She
was on edge thinking about Quinn arriving. "How are rehearsals
coming?" Changing the subject seemed like the best route for her
increasing nerves.

"Good, good. Rick is easy enough to work with," Courtney
replied, waving to some people who just walked in.

Alex recognized the man leading the group over as Mark Kemp.
He was in the fall show with Courtney but had also done a handful
of shows at Horizon in past seasons. "Alex, hey!" He leaned over
the table and placed a quick kiss on her cheek. "Courtney didn't tell
me you'd be here. I would have worn my tie."

"Like you need to dress up for me. With that face, you could
wear a trash bag and still break hearts."

"If I didn't know which way you swung, I'd kiss you over a
comment like that. But alas." She smiled as she turned to the rest of
the group so Mark could make some introductions.

"Alex, this is Jennifer, Max, and Spencer. Jennifer and Max are
in the show with us, so you've probably seen them around. Spencer
is doing a show up at the Republic." Alex gave a slight nod of hello.

"I probably don't need to tell you who this is," he said to the group, pointing to Alex. "She runs the theater, after all."

As everyone settled into their seats, they began chitchatting as Alex observed. Quinn wasn't wrong that she wasn't the *going out with the cast* type. It was hard to get close to people whose contracts you signed.

Too many times in her past, she had gotten close to someone in the company, only to have to tell them that her father wouldn't be casting them again. Despite being in the same industry, she felt as if she had less and less in common with actors.

She looked around the room that was much busier than the last time they were there. As her eyes grazed over the bar, she noticed a familiar face coming out of the back room carrying clean glasses.

"Shit. I'm going to have to stop coming here," she said so only Courtney could hear. She turned away from the bar in the hope that Gabby wouldn't notice her. "Since when does she have every shift?"

"You still haven't broken it off with the poor girl?"

Alex looked away with a slight heat creeping up her neck. She did feel a bit guilty for leading Gabby on. She should have ended things with her earlier in the week instead of letting her come over.

"I knew you were going to fuck her again," Courtney said with a smile.

"Please go get us refills so she doesn't come over here. *Please.*" Alex did her best to muster puppy dog eyes.

"Ugh, fine. But stop doing whatever it is you're doing to your face. It's creepy."

"I was going for cute."

"You can't do cute. You can do sexy and domineering. And don't talk back to me when I'm saving you by distracting your last fuck so *you* can get distracted by your new one."

Courtney nodded to the door and stood. She gave Alex an exaggerated wink and headed to the bar for their drinks. Alex didn't need to turn. Lately, nothing gave Courtney that same mischievous look of glee like the subject of Quinn.

She tried to ignore the somersaults in her stomach at the prospect of seeing her gorgeous face, which she knew was utterly ridiculous.

She was not the kind of person to feel giddy about a woman. But she finally turned to see Courtney give Quinn a quick hug. After a moment talking, Courtney pointed at the Horizon group, and Quinn locked eyes with Alex. The professional resolve she had maintained started to feel incredibly feeble with the smoldering stare Quinn was sending her way.

It wasn't just that Quinn looked sexy in her dark blue jeans, simple white T-shirt, and leather jacket. It was her expression. It felt as if everyone else faded from the bar, and they had a mutual understanding that they had some magnetic pull. She couldn't help returning her growing smile as Quinn made her way toward the table.

"Quinn, I'm glad you could make it," Alex said as she stood awkwardly. Luckily, Quinn seemed more relaxed than she did.

"You too, Alex." She put her hand on Alex's arm, leaned in, and gave her a quick peck on the cheek.

Alex tried her best not to blush, even though her cheek felt like it had a fever. *From a peck.* Courtney needed to hurry up with those drinks. She was losing it fast, and Quinn had just walked in. "Here, you can take Courtney's seat."

"I've noticed that you're a little bossy," Quinn said teasingly as she moved past Alex to slide into the chair across from hers.

Alex felt steadier the second there was a table between them. "I've heard that before."

Courtney shuffled over, struggling to hold three drinks. Quinn stood to help her, putting a glass of dark liquid in front of herself. Alex couldn't take her eyes off the way Quinn's lips pressed against the glass as she took her first sip. She pictured herself kissing that soft throat as she swallowed.

A soft jab from Courtney in her ribs brought her back to reality, and she grabbed her own drink, taking a long sip to hide the blush she could clearly feel. Thankfully, Courtney didn't do anything other than smile as if she'd won a contest.

One of the women Mark had introduced her to leaned across the table toward Quinn. "I saw you in a Fashion Week show a couple years back. And I read your book. I'm Spencer." She reached to shake Quinn's hand but held on longer than Alex thought necessary.

As Quinn pulled back, she gave a polite smile. "Thank you. It's nice to meet you."

Mark chimed in next and reached out to shake her hand. "I'm Mark. We're all doing the fall show at Horizon, so you'll see us around the dungeon."

Alex rolled her eyes. "Can we please not call it the dungeon to new artists?"

"Dungeon?" Quinn asked.

"It's what we call the rehearsal space," Courtney responded. "No windows, black floor, scary blond master coming downstairs and cracking a whip at us all the time."

"Yes, you poor fair maiden," Alex replied.

Spencer hadn't taken her eyes off Quinn and now moved down a chair so she was right next to her. Alex ignored the tightening in her stomach at the blatantly flirtatious move. She did her best to remind herself that Quinn was just an artist in her theater, and she had no say in who hit on her. "I'm a big fan of Jenna Matthews. I've seen her in *everything*. Do you still talk?"

"No. We don't," Quinn replied, and Alex couldn't help but notice the way she tensed, moving her chair back slightly. "Have you been in New York long?"

Alex could appreciate deflection when it worked. And for someone like Spencer, who probably needed constant validation, it worked beautifully. Spencer was more than willing to tell her whole life story, which Alex tuned out in lieu of subtly stealing glances at Quinn. She wondered what that soft skin would feel like under her fingers.

She had no idea how long she had been daydreaming, but when she finally came back to the conversation, Courtney was scrolling through her phone, and Spencer was still rambling on.

"Then, I decided NYU was the right route, and I've been here ever since. You'll have to come check out the Republic sometime. We're doing a new musical this fall."

"That sounds great." Quinn's response was polite, but Alex could see she wasn't overly enthusiastic about the invite. Spencer, however, remained clueless.

❖

The night had been so much more fun than Quinn could have predicted. The Horizon actors were warm and welcoming and so different to many of the people she had met in the modeling industry, who always seemed like they were looking over their shoulder, trying to spot the knife.

Perhaps these people were simply better at hiding it, but so far, she couldn't help but have a good time. Except for the presence of Spencer, who was so obvious in her interest in Quinn that it was slightly uncomfortable.

Maybe she should have sent Mikey a thank-you text for the outfit because Alex was giving her many of the same obvious looks that Spencer was. She had noticed Alex's eyes graze her tight T-shirt more than once, and she had *definitely* checked out her ass when she'd gone to the bathroom a bit ago.

The subtle attention was certainly welcome. Especially since Quinn wasn't doing a good job keeping her eyes off Alex, either.

Alex must have come straight from work because she still had on the tight pencil skirt paired with the simple black blouse. Her hair was down, falling elegantly past her shoulders. Her heels accentuated her long, tan legs, and it wasn't until now that Quinn realized how much she appreciated the hot, professional look.

"Quinn?"

Spencer was talking again, but Quinn had been so lost in Alex that hadn't heard the question. "Sorry, what did you say?"

Spencer leaned forward slightly. "I asked if you had someone you needed to get home to or if you wanted to come with us uptown to a different bar. Some of our other friends are congregating there."

Quinn considered for a moment. Spencer hadn't tried to hide her interest, and Quinn couldn't deny that she was pretty. But Alex's bright blue eyes were boring into the side of her face, and that alone got her heart rate up to an unnatural speed.

Before she could answer, Mark saved her. "Damn, Spence. Easy on the new girl."

"Plus, she could live alone and still be seeing someone. Your line of questioning was faulty," Courtney added playfully.

To her credit, Spencer rolled with their teasing. "Just because I invited her with us doesn't mean I'm trying to get into her pants. I invited *you*, didn't I?"

"Ooo, burn," Courtney said with a laugh and turned to Quinn. "But really, are you single?"

"*Court*." Alex gave Courtney a pointed look, and her tone didn't leave much room for argument. Quinn tried to ignore the shiver that ran up her spine upon hearing Alex's authoritative voice.

Courtney held up her hands. "Don't worry, Al. Just finding out for when the masses start asking me."

"It's fine," Quinn said, looking at Alex. "I am single." She turned to Spencer and the others. "But I'm not really looking right now. Trying to focus on the show."

"You'll love this bar," Mark said excitedly. "It has drag queen karaoke."

"Count me in." She looked over at Alex, who returned her gaze. She couldn't really picture her at a karaoke bar, but she still hoped she'd be joining them. Before she could ask, a pretty bartender came up to their table and stood close to Alex.

"Hey, you. Can I get you guys anything else?" she asked.

Alex looked slightly uncomfortable as she looked up. "No, just the check, please." The dynamic screamed of something more than customer to bartender. There was an energy between them that Quinn could probably have guessed at if she had to.

"Are you sure?" the bartender asked again, resting her hand on Alex's shoulder.

Alex tensed, and Courtney laughed quietly. "Yes, I'm sure," Alex said, and this time, she looked the bartender in the eye, leaving no question that the conversation was over.

The bartender nodded before walking away. Or *storming* away would have been a more accurate description.

"Friend of yours?" Quinn tried to keep her tone light, even though she had a burning sensation in her stomach. Was it jealousy? No, she's just met Alex. She couldn't be jealous of some random woman in a bar. But the familiar way she'd touched Alex's shoulder and the sultry, expectant look she'd given her rubbed Quinn the wrong way.

"Not a close one," Alex replied as she reached into her purse. "Court, be a dear?" she asked as she slid her credit card over the table.

Courtney rolled her eyes but took the card anyway. "Be right back. But I'm paying for all the drinks. Every round. As my fee."

"Like you wouldn't have made me pay anyway," Alex shot back, but the look on her face was one of gratitude.

Courtney walked to the bar while the group watched her go, having seen the awkward exchange with the bartender. Spencer looked like she was ready to burst with a million questions, but her loose lips didn't seem to apply to Alex.

"Shall we?" Mark asked the others when it was clear Courtney was finishing up.

As the group began putting on their jackets, Quinn stole a glance at the bar. The bartender was wiping down the counter with a scowl, and Quinn wasn't surprised by the revelation that Alex was a heartbreaker.

The group waited on the street outside while Courtney finished up inside, but Alex stood slightly away, scrolling through her phone. As the group rehashed their rehearsal, Quinn moved over to Alex. "Are you coming to the next bar?" she asked, causing Alex to glance up.

"No, you guys go on. I think I'll head home." She paused and smiled. "Maybe play some chess."

"Do you live alone?"

"Yes."

"Then how do you play chess? Are you flitting from one side of a table to the other? I'm picturing brandy, a cigar in hand, maybe a fireplace next to some lush pillows."

Alex stared before a slow smile crept onto her face. "You do know that I live in the same era as you, right?"

Quinn laughed. "No cigar, then?"

"No. And I don't flit from pillow to pillow." Alex looked at her phone again. "I play against a computer."

Quinn's smile only grew. "Computer chess?"

Alex narrowed her eyes. "I'll have you know that chess sharpens the mind and keeps your strategic thinking fresh. It can also be highly athletic."

Quinn held up her hands. "No judgment. You just didn't seem like a video game nerd." As she said it, a blush crept up Alex's neck. "Oh my God, you play video games too, don't you?" Quinn loved teasing her. It felt as if with each playful jab, she could feel the heat emanating off Alex increase, but it didn't feel like anger. The slight twinkle in her eyes now indicated that Alex was enjoying their banter just as much as she was.

"It helps my dexterity," Alex replied in a voice so low and sexy that Quinn could feel her smile drop.

Alex's heated expression melted her to the spot, and there was no question that she meant it as an innuendo. Quinn's mouth went dry. "I'm sure that's helpful at times," she whispered.

"You have no idea."

She could almost feel Alex's breath, and she had no idea when they had gotten so close to each other.

"Not to interrupt whatever this little moment is, but we're heading uptown now if you're coming, Quinn." Courtney draped her arm around Alex's shoulder and gave Quinn a wide smile. "Unless you two were making other plans," she added as she looked between them, the smile never leaving her face.

Alex looked like she was considering something, and Quinn was convinced she might even ask her to hang out, but just as quickly, she schooled her features into a polite smile. "No. I was just saying good-bye. Card?" She held out her hand for her credit card and grabbed Courtney's hand tenderly. "Thank you."

"We still on for coffee tomorrow?" Courtney asked as she pulled Alex into a hug.

"Sounds good," Alex replied before turning to Quinn and putting her hand out.

Quinn thought it was a little ridiculous to shake someone's hand after she'd just spent two hours drinking with them, but she wasn't about to say no. As she took Alex's hand, she noticed how long her fingers were. The contact shot warmth straight to her center, and neither of them seemed to want to let go.

"Alex, it was lovely to see you." Mark's presence at their side broke the moment, and Alex swiftly dropped her hand.

"You too, Mark."

As the group made their way up the street, Quinn reluctantly followed. When she looked back, Alex was still standing on the street, scrolling through her phone again, and Quinn couldn't help but wonder where she would go now. Something told her Alex wasn't the subway type, so she was probably within walking distance of her home or had a private driver.

Though, perhaps she was going back into the bar to see the eager bartender. As her stomach tightened, Quinn pushed that thought from her brain as best she could. The last thing she needed while meeting new friends was to feel a wave of unjustified jealousy coursing through her.

CHAPTER NINE

Courtney set her phone in front of Alex at their favorite midtown coffee shop. "Look, I'm famous."

Alex looked down as Courtney ran up to the counter to make her order. Smiling back at her on the screen was the face she hadn't been able to stop thinking about all night. Not even video games had distracted her. It just caused her to lose faster.

But it wasn't just Quinn's face in the photo. Next to her were Mark, Spencer, and some random drag queen. Quinn had tweeted the image last night with a short caption: *I see you NYC <3 #Horizon #NewFriends #NotADrag*

Alex glanced up to see Courtney chatting casually with the barista as she waited for her coffee, so she took the moment to look at the picture. Quinn looked just as sexy as she did at the bar but with a slight flush to her cheeks, as if she had been dancing the night away. It took Alex only a moment to notice that Spencer's arm was wrapped around Quinn, her fingers touching the bare skin on Quinn's waist under where her T-shirt had ridden up. Alex tensed at the sight.

"Why do you look like you're going to murder my phone? Don't murder my phone." Courtney sat with her coffee, pulled her phone back, and cradled it against her chest like it was a child. When she glanced down, she raised her eyebrows. "Is someone jealous? Is that what I detect here?"

Alex scoffed. "I'm not jealous. Though Spencer seems very bold for someone doing a show at a hundred-seat theater."

"Don't be a pretentious snob. I've done three shows there, and you still respect me. Let's talk about what's really going on here. You have a big fatty crush on our little fashionista, and you can't deal." Courtney took a sip of her coffee triumphantly, as if she just figured out the meaning of life.

"Are we going to have to do this every time we see each other until her show closes?" She was already unfocused enough. She knew she had a crush on Quinn, but she couldn't very well tell Courtney she hadn't slept a wink last night thinking about her.

Courtney's face softened. "What's really going on? Like, I get your whole rule, even while I make fun of it. But you seem legitimately attracted to this woman. So why can't you just act like a normal person for once and bend the rules a bit?" She scrunched her nose. "Sorry, that sounded much more emphatic in my head."

"Because my father has mentioned more than once that he hopes there won't be a repeat of past transgressions. If I start sleeping with her, it'll just prove to him that I'm not ready for Rick's job."

"It's that important to you?"

"It's what I've been working toward for almost ten years. It's certainly worth more than a couple rounds in bed with a model who will be off to her next project as soon as the show closes."

"Okay. I get it." Courtney put her hand on Alex's and squeezed gently. "But if you do decide to go there, just know, the world won't end. I got to spend some time with her last night, and she's great. She's not Sloane. She's solid. And just so you know, she seems to be put off by Spencer. That was a no go."

Alex shouldn't have cared, but Courtney's words made her feel instantly lighter. She wanted to ask more, but she had just chastised Courtney for talking about it, so she held her tongue. She decided to bring up a safer topic. "Janet wants to feature me in the piece on Quinn that the *Times* will be doing. Something about how I'm the one to bring her show here."

"And you're feeling very uncomfortable about that."

Alex simply nodded. Courtney knew her. For the world, she put on a careful mask of poise and control. But Courtney had seen her at her lowest. She was the one who'd let Alex cry into her chest for hours after her mom had passed. Courtney knew what Alex had gone through to put her life together again after that.

She squeezed Alex's hand. "Remember the first time I ever met you? I was so nervous for that audition. Just a wee little freshman and I had no idea what kind of shark's mouth a college audition was."

Alex smiled at the memory.

"I was sitting there waiting for my turn when you came out of the room. And instead of leaving the building, you saw a scared girl, new to the school, and you gave me a piece of advice. Do you remember what you said?"

"I'm pretty sure I asked you to come back to my dorm."

"That was after my audition, you egomaniac." Courtney paused as she regarded her. "You asked me how long I've been acting. I told you my whole life, and you told me that I had earned my shot and to take it."

"I don't even remember saying that to you. I vaguely remember you asking me to fuck you harder but not that whole bit."

"Well, you did say it," Courtney said, moving past the obvious deflection. "And I'm telling you the same thing. Which is what Janet is also telling you. *You* are the reason Quinn's show is here. *You* are the reason there has been a surge in original programming at Horizon. You're the reason millennials are trying to buy season subscriptions. *Season subscriptions.* Like, something they have to think about more than a week before. You did that. Not your dad's 'legacy' or whatever the fuck they call it. If Janet wants to feature you, let her. You earned that."

Alex smiled.

Courtney reached into her bag. "Also, I have to show you something,"

"Very cryptic, Court."

"Read this." She slid a piece of paper across the table.

"What is that?"

"It would help if you read it."

"Fine." Alex grabbed the paper and read it, then stared at Courtney indignantly. "This is an audition notice."

"Yes. For which you are perfect."

"I'm not going in for an audition."

"Why not?"

"You know why not."

"I know you miss it."

"Of course I miss it. That doesn't matter." She pushed the paper back across the table. "Can we please get back to the article?"

"Okay. Worth a shot."

"I guess I'm just worried that mentioning me in the article about Quinn's show will seem too self-promotional. My father doesn't react too kindly to that."

"Your dad is surrounded by actors every day, and let's be real, usually into the night. He has no issue with people being self-promotional. He has an issue with you doing it."

"Whatever his issue is, I have to play by his rules. And this could push him over the edge. He's always been paranoid about me taking the spotlight."

Courtney pursed her lips. "The thing is, I think Janet gets that. Putting you front and center may force his hand. He can't really dethrone the woman who saved his company."

Alex felt a weight lift off her. Courtney and Janet were right. What could her father really say to a *Times* piece, a sold out run, and glowing reviews? He'd have to give her Rick's job; otherwise, it would look petulant.

"God, this girl better be good," Alex said before she drained the rest of her coffee.

"Onstage or in bed or—"

"I will kill you."

Alex glared at Courtney for only a second before she felt a smile break out.

Chapter Ten

At the end of the week, Mikey and Quinn once again sat in Alex's office, waiting for the managing director to finish a meeting. It wasn't long after they sat that Alex breezed into the room, and as she passed, Quinn could distinctly smell her perfume. She had noticed it the other night as they'd stood close together outside the bar. The scent was more masculine than she would have expected, but it fit. Alex smelled delicious.

She didn't speak until she sat. "Hello. How are you two settling into the city?" Though she spoke to both, Quinn found her gaze resting solely on her.

She had never seen eyes that were so hard to look away from, even if Mikey was sitting right next to her. At times, like when they were in the bar, they looked crystal clear. Almost like the blue sky after a tropical storm. But right now, they were dark and moody. It was clear Alex kept her feelings guarded, but her eyes gave her away, at least to Quinn, and she couldn't help but wonder what meeting she had just come from.

"I tried George's. Best bagel I've ever had." She mentally smacked herself for resorting to bagels again. That was until she saw Alex smile, her eyes shining a bit brighter than before.

"I'd like to take you over to meet Simon and Rick. They're in my father's office now waiting to meet you," Alex said, ignoring the bagel comment. "Mikey, you'll need to wait here. My father can be a bit rude to people he deems to be purely on the business side of things. Especially ones from LA."

"I understand. I had a call earlier today with Janet Jameson, and she gave me some insight," he replied.

"I imagine she did," Alex replied with a smile.

It was childish, but Quinn felt excluded from some inside joke. She didn't even know who this Janet person was. "But you're on the business side of things," she said to Alex. "Shouldn't that put your dad off too?" The moment the question came out of her mouth, she regretted her clumsiness.

Luckily, Alex's smile didn't diminish. She simply looked amused. "Indeed, it does," she said as she rose and moved toward her door.

Mikey and Quinn followed, and after saying their good-byes to Mikey, Alex led Quinn down the short hallway. As they walked, Quinn couldn't help but admire the formal black slacks Alex wore with a plum, button-up blouse. She wondered if Alex ever dressed casually. Her fingers itched to undo the top button of Alex's shirt so she could see the soft skin underneath.

Alex stopped in front of a door, and Quinn was so distracted that she bumped into her back. If anyone had passed them in the hall, they would have looked like they were wrapped around each other. A small gasp left Alex's mouth, and when she turned, the front of their bodies touched lightly. For an intense moment, they stayed close, allowing Quinn to quietly study the rhythm of Alex's breathing. But soon after, Alex leaned back against the door, and they were no longer touching.

"Rick is easy. Just flatter him," Alex said in a quiet voice. "But with my father, I suggest you follow my lead."

As Quinn nodded slowly, Alex's eyes flicked to her lips. But just as quickly as it happened, she turned and pushed the door open.

The first thing Quinn thought as she entered the large office was that she was looking at Alex's male doppelgänger. He didn't just share Alex's blond hair and piercing eyes, he also carried himself with the same authoritative elegance. But where Alex had a softness to her features, Simon's face was hard and weathered.

Rick was leaning against the windowsill and was everything she'd pictured an executive director to be. He was as handsome as

Simon but with silver hair and a long, slender build. He had a much gentler air about him than his business partner.

"Father, Rick, this is Quinn Collins. Quinn, this is Simon Anders and Rick Weston. Please, sit." She motioned for Quinn to take one of the seats across from Simon's desk.

Rick leaned back farther against the window, gently folding his arms. He had a kind face and gave Quinn a genuine smile.

"Ms. Collins, we are very excited to have you here this season," Simon said. Hearing her last name out of his mouth didn't give her the same thrill it did coming out of Alex's. On the contrary, she felt like she was in trouble somehow. "I take it you've settled in nicely?"

"Yes, thank you. And please, call me Quinn. I'm also excited to be here. Writing a show for New York audiences has always been a dream of mine." Alex shifted slightly next to her.

"Have you settled into an apartment? You've gotten everything you need from HR?" Rick asked. His voice was like velvet, and she was caught off guard by the sincerity in his tone. It was such a stark contrast to Simon's icy demeanor.

She should have asked Alex what the goal of this meeting was because the way Simon was appraising her, it felt like much more than a meet and greet. It felt like she was a calf at an auction. "Yes, I'm not too far from the theater, and my manager is living close by, so it's perfect. I start rehearsing next week."

"Good, good," Rick said clapping his hands. "I'm sure Alex here will make sure you have everything you need, but please don't hesitate to find me anytime. And I assume you'll be at the opening for *Death of a Salesman*? We like to have our company artists attend."

Alex gave her a small nod. She'd need to remember to mention that to Mikey, who was handling her schedule.

"I've heard my daughter secured Diego Ruiz for you. He's very good. You're quite fortunate," Simon said.

Quinn wondered if this was their game: Rick played good cop to Simon's bad. She wasn't sure why the room felt so tense every time Simon looked at her.

Alex finally spoke, though not in the same commanding tone Quinn was used to hearing from her. "I merely made the recommendation. Diego asked to work with Quinn once he read her script."

Simon gave her a smile for a beat too long. "Ms. Collins, as I'm sure you've realized by now, my daughter is a fan of your work. Catching the eye of the unshakable Alexandra Anders, and in a festival no less, is no easy feat. I look forward to seeing more."

Alex was unreadable as she continued to stare forward. What did he mean by Quinn having caught Alex's eye? And why did she feel like some pawn in a familial squabble?

"We all know Alex's taste is impeccable," Rick chimed in, easing some of the obvious tension that had settled over the office. "I, for one, cannot wait to see what you do here." He smiled at Quinn, who didn't know what to say.

Alex stood, silently commanding Quinn to do the same. She seemed to want this meeting over as much as Quinn did. "We can work out some progress check-ins for you both. As long as Diego and Quinn are comfortable with early audiences. But for now, I just wanted to drop by so you could meet her."

"It was a pleasure," Rick said and moved forward to enthusiastically take her hand.

Simon was much slower to rise but also reached out for a quick shake. "Indeed. I'm sure Alex will take care of any needs you have." He sat back down, staring at his daughter as he did. If looks could kill, Quinn hoped the one Alex was directing at her dad never came her way.

Back in Alex's office, Alex closed her eyes and leaned against her desk. Quinn felt like she was intruding on a private moment. She didn't know if she was supposed to just leave after the awkward meet and greet.

Alex kept her eyes closed as she exhaled. "I'm sorry about him."

"Rick seems nice," was all Quinn could think to say.

Alex opened her eyes, a small smile settling on her face. "He is. I meant my father. I should have warned you before we went in there that he might be—"

"A dick?"

For the first time since they'd met, Alex laughed, and it was unlike any sound Quinn had ever heard. It wasn't carefree, and it certainly wasn't a giggle. It was low and sexy. Every bone in Quinn's body vibrated as if a train had rolled past.

"That's one word, I guess," Alex said. "He likes things to be his idea, especially if they're successful. You weren't his idea. But it's not to say he'll be a problem for you, so don't worry about that."

"I'm not. But I am curious about what he said."

Alex continued to lean against the desk, searching Quinn's face.

"Mikey and my agent made it seem like they chose this theater. Not that you saw my show and handpicked it."

Alex shrugged. "I put in a call to your agent when I was putting our winter series together. It just so happened she was shopping it around at the time. I guess it was just right place, right time."

"You could have told me this whole thing was your idea before we went in there," she replied, feeling defensive.

"It doesn't matter how it happened. I didn't do it as a favor. I don't even know you. Your show deserves a stage, and mine is the best. It's that simple."

Quinn almost missed the compliment. Alex was so calm, as if she was discussing the weather, and if it might rain that day. Quinn didn't know why it bothered her to feel so out of the loop on her own show. "It matters to me," she said quietly. "This work is personal. I know I let Mikey handle a lot. But I'm not an idiot who can't be told things related to my own career."

Alex regarded her quietly. "I know that."

The softness in her tone caused Quinn to regret her sudden outburst. This was probably why Mikey didn't let her go to meetings on her own. Though she wasn't used to having meetings with women she was this attracted to. "It does mean something to me that you liked it," she added.

"You inspired me. When I saw your show, something woke up in me. So I did what I do best. I'm giving you a stage. But you'll do the rest."

Quinn wasn't expecting such an emotional response from someone so stoic. How could *she* inspire Alex?

Alex looked down and smoothed her top, signaling that the moment was over. When she glanced back up, her face was one of detached professionalism. "I'm sending Mikey a schedule of events that we'd like you to attend. Nothing is contractually obligated except the winter gala. But we have Rick's opening night soon."

The abrupt shift in mood happened a lot with Alex anytime things got too personal. Without much else to say Quinn simply nodded. "Well, I'll leave you to it. Thanks for the *super* fun meet and greet." As she turned to leave, something stopped her from opening the door. She pointed to the poster behind the desk that she had noticed during their first meeting. "An all-women version of *A Streetcar Named Desire*. Very bold." Alex's brows pulled together. "Before our first meeting, I was doing some light research on the theater and stumbled upon a video of your play." When Alex continued to stare, she barreled on. "I watched it. All of it. I wasn't going to, but it was just so good. *You* were just so good."

She moved back into the office and closer to the desk. "You took my breath away. I've never seen anyone take over a stage that way. With such elegance and power. It wasn't until I met you that I saw that was more you than the character. You're inspiring too, Alex." Quinn was surprised by her own words. She hadn't been this forward, not even with Jenna.

A war of emotions swirled behind Alex's eyes. When she remained silent, Quinn felt a wave of embarrassment, so she turned to the door. But as soon as she reached for the knob, she felt a hand on her shoulder. Alex gently turned her around.

Before she could even react, Alex took another step, causing Quinn to gently bump against the door. Alex's lips were close, but she didn't press in, almost as if waiting for Quinn to make the final move.

Not able to wait, Quinn lifted her mouth to close the distance between them, and as soon as their lips touched, Alex seemed to lose all hesitancy. Quinn's brain short-circuited as she opened her mouth for Alex's probing tongue. A low moan left her, only to be swallowed by Alex's greedy lips. She provided Quinn no time to breathe or think. Only time to inhale Alex's scent and allow her to have her way with her mouth.

One of Alex's hands moved into her hair and gripped it gently, pulling her closer. She easily obliged. In that moment, she would have done anything Alex and her talented mouth asked.

Quinn placed her hands firmly on Alex's hips and pulled. As Alex's body slid up against her, she let out a low moan that Quinn could feel all the way to her center. She pulled Alex into her again, eliciting another erotic sound.

Alex's free hand lingered on the side of her breast. Quinn gasped and began to slide down the door, no longer able to hold herself up. Alex pushed in harder, lowering her hand so she could support Quinn's weight by cupping her ass. Her entire body felt like it was on fire as Alex sucked her bottom lip into her mouth. She let out a groan, but just as the sound left her, it was joined by laughter sweeping past the office in the hallway outside.

As if she'd been burned, Alex pulled her head away. Her breathing was heavy as she looked at Quinn's wet and swollen lips. "I'm sorry. We can't," she said, dropping her hands and taking a step back.

Quinn took Alex's hand and waited until she looked at her. "Your office probably isn't the best place."

"No, I mean, we can't do this. I can't date artists here. It's just something I can't do." Despite her words, she didn't remove her hand from Quinn's, and her breathing remained heavy.

"Alex, we're both adults. And I think it's obvious we're attracted to each other. I think we can handle the ramifications of dating, don't you?"

"Maybe in most situations. But you met my father. Meetings like that will be even worse if he finds out I like you. I need this show to be successful on merit alone."

Quinn couldn't help a smile. "Oh, so you like me, then?"

Alex smiled in return but didn't answer the question. "Your show doesn't deserve to be cheapened, and that is what will happen if we date," she said, dropping her hand.

Quinn wanted to argue that Alex's fear was a completely ridiculous reason not to date someone. That she didn't care how it would affect her show if she could just kiss Alex *like that* one more time. But she did care. She had spent years running away from a relationship scandal that had humiliated her publicly.

This was clearly different. There was no scandal here as far as she could see. Alex was single, gay, and into her. But as she thought back to Mikey's warning, she felt a pang of guilt. She didn't want to hurt all the people who depended on her. Mikey, Eve, Will: her actions with Jenna had affected all of them. She needed this show to work because *they* needed it to work. If Alex was right, Quinn didn't want to give Simon any reason to pull the show.

"No kissing, then?" Quinn asked innocently. Even if she couldn't date Alex, there were no rules against continuing to flirt with her.

"No kissing," Alex responded in a low voice that didn't sound convincing.

"How about lunch?" Quinn did her best to make the question sound casual. She wanted more time with Alex, even if it didn't involve kissing. She'd prefer it did, but it couldn't be that hard to keep things professional.

"Lunch?"

"It's where you eat in the middle of the day. Usually follows breakfast and precedes dinner?"

"Yes. I'm familiar with the concept."

"Oh good. That makes the whole thing an easier sell. Then you know that at lunchtime, the sun will be out. No dark lighting or hidden corners. Just a sandwich. I'll even dress down so there's no temptation to kiss me again." She paused before saying what she really wanted to say. Alex was the type to scare easily, and she didn't want to do that. "I just want to get to know you better."

Alex's expression was unreadable. As if she was trying to find something hidden in Quinn's meaning. When she spoke, her voice was quiet. "I guarantee, there's nothing you could do to dress down. But lunch sounds lovely."

"When?" she asked in a whisper, not daring to move and have Alex change her mind.

Alex turned abruptly back to her desk. "I'm out of town this weekend," she said, sitting in her chair. "Monday. Meet me at Single Shot at noon."

Quinn took that as her official dismissal. She simply nodded and turned to leave, but before she did, she locked gazes with Alex. She took slow, deliberate steps back to the desk and internally smiled at how nervous Alex looked. She put both hands on the desk and leaned over it. "For the record, if you think bossing me around will keep this thing between us professional, I can assure you, it will backfire. It just makes me want to bend over this desk for you."

Alex's eyes widened, and Quinn felt a rush of satisfaction that she could unnerve her. Part of her couldn't believe she'd just said that. The other part was physically throbbing at her own boldness. She shot Alex one last smile and left her gaping at her back.

CHAPTER ELEVEN

A lex should have canceled. That was what she told herself over and over on the weekend. Going to lunch with Quinn was all but sealing her fate. But Quinn's words were stuck on repeat in her mind no matter what she did. No sense of logic could keep her from this lunch. And that kiss. She had never had a kiss like that. Her whole body felt like it was still on fire.

As she took her seat in the restaurant, she was more nervous than she could remember being in a long time. Quinn was also different than any woman she'd met in a long time.

It just makes me want to bend over this desk for you.

She let Quinn's words roll around in her head for maybe the hundredth time. Quinn wasn't even there yet, and Alex was already vibrating with anticipation. Perhaps Courtney was right, and she should give in to her desire. What harm could really come of it? But she pictured her father's sneering face and knew exactly what would happen. He was bad enough during the meet and greet last week, acting as if Alex was the only reason Quinn even had a shot in New York. As if Quinn wasn't a best-selling author in her own right.

He would use any whiff of a theater romance as reason not to promote her. It was almost as if he was challenging her to sleep with Quinn. She wouldn't give him that satisfaction. So what was she doing here? She didn't get lunch with random artists at the theater. And yet, deep down, she knew the answer to that question. She might have been playing with fire, but she wanted to get to know

Quinn better. She wanted to hear more deliciously dirty things come out of her mouth.

Before she could school her thoughts into the platonic ones she should have been having, the door to the restaurant opened, and her mouth went dry at the sight of Quinn coming in. She was wearing a simple white dress that flowed over her curves. The top was cut low and tighter than the rest, which gave Alex a healthy view of her cleavage. Her hair was down, cascading over the thin straps and her pale shoulders. She looked stunning, but the only thing Alex could focus on was her lips, which were painted bright red. Set against her white dress and shoes, that was the only color Quinn was wearing.

She smiled slowly as she walked over to the table. "You look like you've never seen a woman in red before."

Alex had yet to stand, say anything, or perhaps even blink. She shook her head slightly as she watched Quinn sit. "You did that on purpose," she whispered, not able to find her voice yet.

"Mad about it?"

"On the contrary. You look lovely."

Quinn's eyes, which a moment before had danced with humor and a challenge, now gazed softly. "Thank you. You always look good."

Alex loved how pale Quinn's complexion was, illuminating even the softest of blushes. She took a sip of water so she had a reason to not get lost in those beautiful eyes. Quinn was a near-perfect specimen, but it was her eyes that haunted Alex's every thought. "I didn't ask if you were a vegetarian, but they should have some options if you are," she said as she put down her water and nervously picked up her menu.

"I've noticed that you generally don't ask. You tell. But, no, I'm not a vegetarian. Though I don't eat fish."

Alex studied Quinn as she browsed the menu. Each time she saw something that looked good, Quinn let out a small hum. Normally, that kind of thing would annoy Alex, but with Quinn, it was charming. Her intense focus on Quinn was interrupted when a server approached the table to take their orders.

After he left, Alex turned her attention back to Quinn. "No fish?"

"I love fish. I even own some. It's too mean to eat them."

It was official. Quinn was the cutest person Alex had ever met. She couldn't help but laugh at the proclamation. "I have so many questions."

"Oh please, ask away."

"You have fish? Like Nemo? In a tank?"

"First of all, I'm honestly shocked you know who Nemo is."

"I don't live under a rock, you know. I also know who Buzz and Woody are."

An easy laugh bubbled out of Quinn. "Okay, then. Yes, I have fish. Leo, Don, Raf, and Mike. I named them after the Teenage Mutant Ninja Turtles."

"What if you got another one? You're out of reptile siblings."

"Already prepared. Splinter. Or April. Or Shredder. There are a lot of options."

"Of course. Next question. Why is it mean to eat a fish but not the chicken you just ordered in your sandwich?"

"It's not. I've just always loved fish. I can't eat them." Quinn stuck her bottom lip out, and Alex had the urge to grab it. "Now you know about my fish. Which to be fair, is highly personal. Tell me something about you."

"No fish."

"What about parents or siblings? I met your dad, so I kind of know how that one is, but are you close with your mom?"

"She passed away." Alex looked at the table and played with her fork. "But we were very close."

"I'm so sorry. How old were you?"

Alex didn't want to talk about this, but she'd known it would come up. Once she'd lost a parent, she'd realized just how often that topic came up. It was easier to simply get it over with. "My junior year of college. It was breast cancer. She was diagnosed right after that production of *Streetcar* you watched. I moved back in to take care of her."

"That must have been hard."

"For both of us. I think the hardest thing for my mom was walking away from acting."

"She was an actress?"

"The best you've ever seen. She actually started Horizon with my father. It was their other child." The mood was notably heavier now, and Alex regretted not ordering a real drink.

"Did you ever finish school?" Quinn asked.

"Not at NYU for theater like I was. But I did get a degree in business while I was her caretaker."

"Were you doing that alone? No brothers or sisters?" Quinn's eyes showed a compassion that normally would have made Alex defensive. The line of questioning was making her fidget and uncomfortable, but there was something in the back of her head that urged her on. Quinn felt safe.

"No siblings. I'm pretty sure the first thing my dad did after I was born was go to a different floor of the hospital for a vasectomy. One child was enough for Simon Anders, I can assure you. But my mom hated other people in her house, so I took care of her."

"That must have been really hard on your own."

"I wanted to be there. I used the credits I was able to transfer and did online classes and night classes until I got a degree." Alex took a sip of water and was reminded why she tended to keep conversations centered on other people. Luckily, the server returned with their dishes, and for a moment, they were both quiet as they dug into their food.

Quinn hummed as she ate, lightly rocking her head back and forth as if listening to a song. She only stopped when she noticed Alex watching her. "Sorry, I just really love food. Bread was my kryptonite as a model."

"I think I remember a chapter in your book called 'Bread.'" Alex realized after she said it that she'd just admitted to having read her book. The expression on Quinn's face indicated she was just as surprised, but she graciously let it slide. "Did you go to college?" Alex asked next, hoping they wouldn't go back to the topic of her parents.

"No. My parents thought it better to take advantage of the modeling offers I was getting at the time."

"Did you want to go?"

"At the time, I agreed with them. It was just so easy, and the money was good. I got caught up in the whole fashion machine." She gazed off at another table for a minute, lost in thought. "Everything in modeling is very fleeting. One wrong move or a pound too many, and it all comes crashing down. I wish I had thought about what else I'd do if people valued me over how I look." She turned her attention back to Alex and grinned. "I sound like such a brat. Like, life is so hard for me." She laughed again, but her usual lightheartedness didn't reach her eyes.

"And what did mini-Quinn want to be when she grew up?"

"A writer. I know, kind of stupid," she said, looking at her napkin.

"How is that stupid? You're a best-selling author and now have an Off-Broadway show. Seems pretty fitting."

"Most people don't see it that way. Plus, people are interested in me for a lot of reasons that have nothing to do with my writing. Even Mikey thinks this show is an opportunity to move me into the acting side of things."

"But that's not what you want?"

"No. I don't know. Maybe. I like performing. But I liked writing my show even more. And I'm just being myself in it. That's not the same as acting." She shrugged as she looked at the napkin her anxious hands had torn apart as she spoke. "Sorry, I don't usually talk about this."

"We can stop if you're uncomfortable. You can tell me what your favorite fish is instead."

"It's okay." Quinn smiled before she went on. "I can't really complain. I've had a good career and luckily still have offers coming in." She waved in a way that said she was ready to move on to a new topic.

After more conversation, they both stopped pretending they were at all interested in their food and let the server remove their plates. Without the dishes in the way, Alex noticed them both leaning in. "While you were creepily stalking me on the internet, did you happen to notice that Courtney was in that NYU show with me?" Alex asked.

Quinn let out an exaggerated scoff and reached across the table to pinch her arm. Alex tried to not to focus on how warm her fingers felt. "I was not stalking. I was doing my due diligence as an artist at *your* theater."

Alex was legitimately laughing, and she couldn't remember the last time she'd felt so carefree in a conversation.

"But, no, I had no idea. I didn't recognize her at all. Who was she?"

"*Stella,*" Alex said as she raised her fist in the air.

"I can't believe I didn't recognize her," Quinn said as she shook her head gently. "You guys went to school together?" Alex nodded. "And there were never any sparks there?" She flicked her eyes to Alex's lips.

"No," Alex replied, transfixed on Quinn's mouth. "We tried when we first met, but it never clicked that way for us."

Bringing her out of her trance was the server asking if they needed anything else. Sensing danger, Alex handed her card over without even glancing at the bill.

Quinn simply watched. "Why didn't it click with Courtney?"

"I like to be in control."

"Clearly," Quinn said as the server returned and handed Alex the card folder. "And why was that an issue?"

"Courtney seems to think she does as well."

Quinn waited for the server to leave again before asking her next question. "Don't you ever miss it?"

"Sex with Courtney?"

"No, smartass. I meant performing."

Alex paused for a moment. "At times."

Quinn looked like she wasn't convinced but seemed to know it was better not to push. "You know, sometimes, you ramble."

"Constantly. Did you ever enjoy modeling?"

"I guess it felt nice to finally get attention for something. I had tried to get my parents interested in my writing for years. But the moment I started to book modeling jobs, they began putting up my various photos around the house, telling their friends about me and stuff. I guess it was nice to get some of the validation they usually reserved for Eve."

"What about the show? Do you enjoy doing it?"

"I love it. I love the energy from the audience. I love sharing this unique part of my history. Letting people get a glimpse into the fashion world. And I really love changing it. Writing new scenes and new concepts to make it fresh."

Alex smiled at the dreamy expression on Quinn's face. "A writer at heart."

Quinn looked like nobody had ever called her a writer before. "We keep going back to me," she said after a moment. "You're good at not talking about yourself."

Alex checked the time. She didn't want to leave, but she was also going to be late for a meeting with Janet. "I think any further interrogations will have to wait. I have a meeting with your publicist."

They had only ever agreed on lunch, but based on the look on Quinn's face, she seemed as disappointed for their time to end as Alex was. As they left the restaurant and stood just outside the door, Quinn scrunched up her nose. "I hate media stuff. Please tell my publicist that I'm on vocal rest and can't speak to anyone."

"First week here and already making diva demands? I'm pretty sure only singers get to claim vocal rest."

"Didn't I tell you?" Quinn gave her a playful smile as she twirled. "My show is now a one-woman musical. Jazz hands and all." She waved her fingers.

"Please don't stop on my account. You're very cute."

As Quinn dropped her hands, she turned serious and took a step closer. "If you keep saying things like that, it's going to make it hard not to kiss you." She took another step into Alex's space.

"*Quinn.*" She said her name in a warning tone but stared at her lips.

"*Alex.*" She leaned in slowly but moved her mouth until she was next to Alex's ear. "Can I text you?" she asked in a whisper as she lightly touched Alex's lobe.

Alex couldn't hide a small gasp. She longed to feel Quinn's lips on her ear again. "Yes," she said, mirroring Quinn's whisper.

Quinn lifted her head. "Thank you for lunch," she said before she placed a small kiss on her cheek.

Alex meant to respond, but she felt dizzy and couldn't seem to form words. Quinn gave her one last smile before she walked down the street. Alex knew she was late to her meeting, but she felt frozen to the spot. She didn't trust her legs to move properly, so she gave herself a moment to close her eyes and breathe.

As she started the short walk to Janet's office, she did her best to tame the throbbing between her legs. This meeting was going to be long and painful.

CHAPTER TWELVE

Quinn sat distracted at her laptop, contemplating the surprising turn of events of the past two weeks. She never would have guessed that she'd still be in a near-constant text conversation with Alex. It wasn't that she couldn't feel the intensity of their connection. But she was surprised Alex was giving in to whatever was growing between them. She just wished it extended past their text messages.

Since their lunch two weeks ago, whenever Quinn ran into her at the theater, Alex was her overly professional self, often not even making eye contact. But so far, their run-ins at the theater were disappointingly rare. She hadn't felt like pushing things by asking for another lunch, not with the fall show opening this week. Alex had mentioned that it was stressful and busy in the offices around an opening, especially one with Rick's name attached to it.

She also didn't have a great excuse to be at the theater yet, and she figured being there to stalk Alex wasn't a good enough one. At least not until her official rehearsals began. She needed to focus on rewrites and prep for her first rehearsal with Diego next week. She had plenty of time before her opening night at the end of November, but she was still anxious to get started with him.

Her show was the first of the three winter series productions. Mikey had theorized that Alex wanted to start off with a bang. At least, Quinn hoped that was why she was first and not that if she failed, they'd still have two shows to help cover up her mess. Deep down, she knew that wasn't the case, and Alex would never put something on that stage that she didn't believe in, especially with the pressure she seemed to feel from her dad.

Quinn wished she knew more about their dynamic, but Alex became closed off any time the topic of family came up, and Quinn didn't know if that was because of her dad or her mom, but either way, it was better not to push things over a communication format as impersonal as texting. And yet, their texts didn't feel impersonal. Alex was inquisitive, and her texts held the same intensity. She was the opposite of Jenna.

With Jenna, it had been impossible to know where Quinn stood. Alex was honest and direct. Jenna entered a room like a whirlwind of energy. Alex was controlled and precise in everything she did. She was stoic at times, but the passion brimming underneath was no less noticeable. Jenna was loud and forthcoming with past stories and experiences. Alex was measured in what she told and how much of it she was even willing to tell. Jenna had wanted Quinn because she was a model and the perfect arm candy. Quinn had been young enough to believe that someone as beautiful and famous as Jenna Matthews would want her as anything more than a headline.

Jenna had gotten her desired effect. A jealous husband, a very public reconciliation between them, and a forgotten model left in the messy media storm. But Quinn had never seen desire in Jenna's eyes that she had seen it so potently in Alex's.

Quinn couldn't help but be completely and utterly fascinated by her. Something about her seemed sad: losing her mom and everything else she'd given up. Each layer that Quinn pulled back made her want to know more. And she was becoming increasingly frustrated with the limitations that came with a short conversation here and there.

As Quinn continued to stare at her script without taking anything in, she contemplated asking Alex out again, but this time making it clear that she wanted it to be a date. Alex had already said they couldn't, but she was also flirty and responsive. As much as she seemed to crave control, in this instance, Quinn had a feeling she would need to be the one to push Alex's hand.

She had never been kissed the way Alex had kissed her. She had never had her mouth so thoroughly controlled and devoured. She wanted to feel the strong push of Alex's body against hers again as she took what she wanted.

Quinn's less-than-innocent thoughts were interrupted by the ring of her phone, and like every time she'd heard it this week, she felt a pang of disappointment when she saw it was not Alex. "Hey, Mikey."

"How are the rewrites coming along?" he asked, not even bothering with a pleasant hello. Sometimes, she couldn't tell where Manager Mikey ended, and Friend Mikey began.

"I'm good, thanks for asking. The apartment is looking great. You should come over tonight and see it."

"Can't tonight, I've been invited to an event."

"Aren't I the semi-but-not-really-famous one here? Why are *you* getting invites to parties?"

"Believe me, this is one you'd rather miss. It's at Janet Jameson's office. She runs PR for Horizon." His voice sounded muffled for a moment.

"Yeah, no thanks." Quinn pushed back from her desk since she wasn't likely to get much else done tonight in terms of work. "Did you call for fashion advice?"

He laughed quietly. "No, I think I'm good on lesbian chic. I called to make sure you know that you need to be at the fall opening this Friday. It's an eight o'clock show."

"Did you really just call me to tell me about a show I already knew I needed to attend?" Quinn moved to her bedroom and plopped on her bed.

"Because you're just so responsible and all?"

"No. But it's not like I have that many events to remember."

"I'm also calling to tell you that you've been invited to dinner after the show. Before the cast party." He sounded muffled again.

"What are you doing over there?"

"Trying on shirts. *Anyway,*" he said, emphasizing the word like he wasn't the one distracted. "Janet has invited you to join her table for dinner. Apparently, it's something she does on opening nights, and it's an honor to be invited."

"And she's the PR lady?"

"Correct."

"I'm confused. Are we considering new representation?"

"No. She owns an agency that handles PR for the theater. But she's hosting a dinner on opening night, and she asked me to invite you. Alex Anders and some of the board will also be there."

Quinn's stomach did a flip. "Why me?"

"You're the next big thing coming up in their season. Why not?" He always treated her as if she had the same A-list status as her ex, but she held a bit of notoriety at best and not fame. Some people didn't understand, or didn't care, about the difference, and perhaps Janet was one of those people.

Lost in thought, Quinn said something out loud that she meant to keep to herself: "Wonder why she didn't mention it."

"Who?"

"Oh, just Alex. We spoke earlier, and she didn't mention it." She tried to keep her voice casual, but this was Mikey, and he knew her better than anyone. Maybe even better than Eve.

"Why would she? It's an invite from Janet."

"Yeah, yeah, right," she said and decided to change the topic before he could ask anything else. "You sure you don't need outfit advice? I can literally hear you throwing discarded options on the floor."

He scoffed. "I would never throw Gucci on the floor. I'm dressed. And I have to go. But on Friday, just head to Napoli's across the street from Horizon and ask for Janet Jameson's table. Or you know, let your girlfriend escort you."

"Hey, wait wha—"

"Call you tomorrow, Q, love ya."

The call went dead. Quinn leaned back on her pillow and huffed. Apparently, she wasn't as subtle about Alex as she thought she had been. She probably shouldn't have smiled at his use of the word girlfriend, but she did.

CHAPTER THIRTEEN

If there was one thing Alex would never tire of, it was the energy spilling into every facet of the theater on an opening night. Nights like these made her forget that so many of her days in the office blended into the mundane.

The week before opening night was always a nightmare, with fire drill after fire drill. There was always some kind of disaster she had to deal with. But by opening, most of those details had been ironed out.

She was in the lobby schmoozing with a board member she could actually tolerate when she saw Quinn sweep in, and she lost ability to focus on anything else. Quinn was wearing a silver dress that tightened around her middle and flowed out toward the bottom. Up the side of the dress was a slit that came to her thigh and showed off her long legs and smooth skin.

Alex was vaguely aware of the board member talking, but at that point, the only thing she could process was how beautiful Quinn looked. Before she could get sucked into another topic, she gracefully excused herself and made her way over. She felt a rush of satisfaction at the way Quinn's eyes raked over her body, as if Alex was a glass of water she desperately needed. She silently applauded her choice to forgo the dress she had picked out in lieu of a custom-made tux she rarely wore.

"Good evening, Nemo," Alex said. As she leaned into Quinn, she reminded herself that she couldn't rip the dress off her right there in the lobby and to keep the kiss G-rated and firmly on the cheek. But somehow, her lips seemed to hit the side of Quinn's mouth despite what she'd just told herself.

Quinn gently squeezed her arm as she leaned back from the peck. "Hey, Alex. You look amazing." Her eyes roamed her body again. Apparently, Quinn's inner voice was not telling her to be subtle.

Alex motioned for them to move over to the side of the lobby that wasn't as crowded. She should have been talking to the donors and board members, but she found herself drawn to only Quinn. "You really look beautiful," she said as they stood in a corner.

Quinn smiled slowly. "Thank you. It was for you." They were both quiet for a moment before Quinn spoke again. "You'll have to point Janet out before we head to dinner. I have no idea what she looks like."

Alex furrowed her brow at the mention of "we" and "dinner" and "Janet."

"She invited me to dinner at her table tonight. I thought you knew."

"Oh. No. I didn't. She doesn't usually invite the artists to her opening night table."

"Is it weird?"

Alex had never seen Quinn seem so self-conscious, but Mikey usually handled the business side of things for her. She couldn't remember Janet ever inviting an artist to the table. But Janet was also a social butterfly and often gravitated toward fame, so it wasn't that surprising. "Janet likes to make new connections, so not that weird," Alex replied as the lights started flashing. "Meet me here after the show, and we'll head to the restaurant together."

"Always bossing me around," Quinn said as she smiled.

Alex leaned in close to Quinn's ear and put her hand on her lower back. "You haven't seen anything yet, Nemo." She flashed her a mischievous smile and turned into the crowd of people making their way to the theater doors. She could feel Quinn's lingering gaze on her.

❖

Ever since her first field trip to see a community theater production of *Anything Goes*, Quinn had loved the theater. But this show really made her question that. By the final curtain, she thought she deserved an award for staying awake. It wasn't that the performers weren't amazing; they were, all of them. But the source material was beyond dry. Quinn couldn't help worrying that if this was the kind of show Horizon was used to producing, her show was going to be a very different detour.

Alex already stood where they'd agreed to meet, scrolling through her phone. Quinn walked slowly so she could take her in. There was something so feminine and delicate about her features that offset her confident, almost domineering personality. Her hair was pulled back into a low side bun tonight, which just helped to showcase her smooth skin and a full, entirely too kissable mouth. Standing there in her tuxedo with an air of such serious confidence, she looked untouchable.

As if Alex could hear Quinn's thoughts, she looked up and directed a smile her way that seemed reserved just for her. "Hello, again. Ready? We should get there soon so we can head to the party." Alex put out her elbow for Quinn to grab, and she did, feeling like she had the sexiest date to a post-opening dinner that had ever existed in the world of theater.

CHAPTER FOURTEEN

T ell me more about Janet," Quinn said as they crossed the street. The moment they were alone, Alex pulled her closer. "I feel like her name keeps coming up, and now she's invited me to dinner. I don't even know who she is."

Alex let out a low chuckle that made Quinn's knees feel a little less stable than they should have been. "Janet was my mom's best friend. So I've known her for, well, forever, I guess. She owns the PR agency that we use for all Horizon shows."

Quinn scrunched her nose up, and that seemed to make Alex smile before she continued.

"I know, a publicist, right? I feel the same way in general. But Janet is all right. She was always there for my mom, and she seems to have a distaste for my father. Basically, her husband died when she was in her early twenties, and she never remarried. She's a big patron of the arts and one of our main donors. Every opening I go to, Janet is usually there."

"I didn't see your dad tonight," Quinn said. "I thought he'd be there."

"I haven't known him to sit through an opening night. He says its bad luck. The *worst* luck. He sits in his office and starts drinking once the opening curtain rises."

"He had to have seen one before, right? What about when you were in shows?"

Alex slowed as they arrived at the restaurant. It was a small Italian place conveniently next to the venue that would host the opening night cast party. "He's never seen me perform."

All Quinn could do was stop her mouth from hanging open, but before she could respond, she heard a high-pitched squeal from across the street. A woman who looked like she was in her sixties was striding toward them, the wealth of jewelry on her arm and neck making almost as much noise as she was. Quinn couldn't tell what was dress, what was shawl, and what was some other weird fabric contributing to her outfit, but she knew at once that this must be Janet. "Darlings! I'm so glad you're here. Now, I know that was a bore, but no long faces at my dinner," she rang out as she came within feet of them.

Alex leaned in to kiss her on both cheeks. "Janet, always a pleasure." She already seemed more at ease with her than she did with anyone other than Courtney.

Janet made a show of dramatically pushing Alex aside so she could turn her attention on Quinn. "And here she is. Our beautiful fashion victim. The one who's going to steal all our hearts soon. Hello, Quinn. You look positively stunning." She leaned in, kissing both Quinn's cheeks, and then held her arms so she could make a show of getting a closer look. "And you *are* stunning," she added before she glanced at Alex with a small smile.

"Thank you. I've heard many things about you, but I'm going to make you guess whether they were good," Quinn responded with an easy smile.

"Cheeky, cheeky," Janet replied, wagging her finger. "Let's eat, shall we? That play made me hungrier than Oliver Twist." With that, she left them in a wake of overpriced perfume and walked into the restaurant.

Alex smiled when Quinn raised her eyebrows. "Yep," Alex said. "That's Janet." She motioned for Quinn to enter, and Quinn felt very naked not having Mikey there as a buffer.

❖

Dinner was more casual than Quinn expected it to be, based on her first impression of Janet. She also didn't mind that she was sitting next to Alex, and their thighs were firmly pressing against each other, sending bolts of warmth straight down south.

She was thrilled to know Alex wanted to maintain as much physical contact as she did tonight. If Janet hadn't been watching them like a hawk, she might have even tried to hold Alex's hand under the table.

It was nice to see Alex relax more than she ever seemed to do in the theater. She and Janet had an easy rapport that could only come with years of history. She was also slightly surprised by how few people there were at the dinner. She had expected a long table with board members and influential theater patrons, but this was far more intimate.

At the table sat Janet, Quinn, Alex, and a board member she was introduced to as Tim Delvin. She recognized him as the person talking to Alex when she'd arrived at the theater earlier. Alex introduced them and described Tim as her "favorite" board member. She didn't know Alex well enough to know if that was schmoozing or if it was actually how she felt. It didn't take long to realize she must have been sincere. Tim was funny, charming, passionate about theater, and while not a good friend of Alex's, it was obvious he was someone she respected.

Janet, on the other hand, was everything Quinn pictured when she thought of a loud, brash New York publicist. She made every question into a production, and even the most mundane statement came out as if she was telling the biggest secret in the world.

She peppered Quinn with question after question, as if she was the most interesting person Janet had ever met. After a while, Quinn was completely sick of talking about herself, so she attempted to steer the conversation. "Alex tells me you're a longtime family friend. Are you from New York?"

"God, no," Janet replied. "I'm from a very small town in Ohio you've never heard of. I met Alex's mom Peggy when I moved to the city for an internship. Back in the ancient times, when the printing press was invented."

"My mom was the one who hired Janet to represent Horizon," Alex told Quinn. "They were quite the duo back in the day."

"Quite." Janet smiled softly. "I even got Alex working for me for a time before she decided that PR was the devil."

"You worked for a PR company?" Quinn asked Alex.

Janet looked amused. "Don't look so judgmental, dear. It's not as if I said she interned for the Mafia."

"Oh, no, sorry, I didn't mean—"

Alex held up her hand. "Don't worry. Janet knows *exactly* how I feel about working for a PR company."

Janet scoffed. "My dear, it was hardly slave labor."

"There will always be a tense relationship between the press and those who court them," Tim said as he pointed at Janet. "The artists," he continued as he pointed to Alex and Quinn. "And the money," he finished, pointing to himself. "And here we are, all having dinner together."

"World peace is imminent," Quinn joked.

Tim laughed, and soon, they fell into easy conversation about the show, in which Quinn tried her best to be polite. Their conversation was interrupted when Janet's voice boomed over the table.

"How can you claim it's not, Alex? When is the last time you were in a sold out house outside of Times Square?" Janet threw her napkin on the table as if to exemplify her point.

"What I'm saying is that theater as a whole is not dead." Alex smiled when she noticed Quinn focusing on their debate. "I'm saying that the model for success has changed. Music didn't die with the introduction of records, but the format in which people consumed it changed. For the better, in most ways."

"And what is our modern advancement for keeping the arts alive? My nieces and nephews knew the word 'TikTok' before they knew 'Broadway.' Much to my dismay." Tim placed his hand over his heart as if wounded.

"It's not one thing," Alex argued. "It's thinking about audiences differently and the ways to reach them. It's hard to convince people to buy a whole season of something when they don't know where their next paycheck is coming from. Theater needs to become less elitist and more accessible. It needs to get its head out of the nineteenth century and incorporate the modern technologies humans see in their everyday lives. It needs people like Quinn, who write truly original shows. Shows that allow us to understand the human experience in a personal way we can't get from TV and film."

"Amen," Janet cheered from her seat.

"Indeed. If only more theater directors were like you," Tim added.

Alex laughed. "Most theater directors are dinosaurs and have never even heard of multimedia theater."

"Maybe not. But you've already created a model for others to follow. You're very lucky to have ended up with Horizon. Alex is changing the whole theater scene citywide," Janet said.

It took Quinn a moment to realize the comment had been directed at her. She was still lost in the passion behind Alex's words. It was in these moments, when Alex expressed herself freely, that Quinn's desire for her went beyond just the physical. "I am. Alex and the team over there have already impressed me so much."

Alex kept her eyes on her plate.

The conversation continued while Quinn simply sat back and listened to the merits of the way different theaters operated. She was happy to watch Alex as she spoke about something she clearly cared so much about.

After their dishes were cleared and they were gathering their coats, Janet pulled Quinn into a hug. "I won't be at the party," she said. "I loathe those. But please call me if you need anything. Though something tells me you'll be fine." Janet looked over at Alex, who was putting on her jacket before she turned to Quinn and gave her a knowing smile.

Quinn returned her smile and gave a short nod. She didn't know what was happening with Alex, so it seemed presumptuous that Janet thought she did.

Tim placed a kiss on her cheek. "I look forward to seeing your show. Front row, opening night." He held up his hands in a Boy Scout salute.

"Thank you, Tim. Maybe we can get coffee sometime." There was something she liked about him, and in the back of her head, she felt like maybe Mikey would feel the same.

"I haven't been asked out by a woman in years. And I accept wholeheartedly."

"As long as you know I won't put out."

He threw his head back and laughed, causing Quinn's smile to grow. "And thank God for that."

Finally, Janet put her arm through Tim's and whisked him out of the restaurant, shouting back to Alex that they needed to talk next week about "things."

Without answering, Alex turned to Quinn, a smile resting on her lips. "Look at you. Making friends everywhere you go."

"Well, I *am* incredibly charming," Quinn replied, looping her arm into Alex's, who guided them to the exit.

"Ms. Collins, your modesty is astounding."

As they exited, they were met with the cool, crisp air of fall. Alex pulled Quinn into her as the cold crept into the spaces between them. Quinn considered asking Alex to forgo the party so they could be alone. But Alex needed to put in an appearance, so Quinn steeled herself for an hour or two of more of pointless banter with people she didn't want to see naked.

For now, she'd remain patient. She knew Alex was well worth the wait, and every fiber of her throbbing body knew it too. "Let's go to this damn party. So we can leave the damn party," Quinn said in a low voice that she hoped clued Alex in to where she'd like this night to go.

Alex didn't look at her, but out of the corner of her eye, Quinn could see a smirk on her face.

As they got closer to the party, Quinn noticed a large group of people lingering outside. Alex stopped when they were a block away and gently pulled Quinn behind a bus stop. "I need to go in alone," she said tentatively. "It's just that—"

Quinn put her hand up. "I get it," she said and squeezed Alex's upper arm. She pointed to herself. "Artist." She pointed to Alex.

"Theater boss." She took Alex's hand and smiled shyly. "Two households, both alike in dignity and all that?"

Alex laughed at the reference. "I hope this isn't quite as tragic as that. But, yes." She pulled Quinn farther in so they were fully shielded from the group around the corner. "It's not that I'm ashamed to be seen with you. The thing with my father is complicated. But I like you. And I can't fight that feeling anymore. I'd like to see you tonight. If you want to." She was a hair from Quinn's lips as she spoke. Her hands had somehow made their way to Quinn's waist without her even noticing. She was far too distracted by the words she had waited weeks to hear. "If we do this, we can't be open about it," Alex continued in a low voice. "At least, not right now. Not until after your opening. For you *and* for me. I have things riding on this, just like you do."

It was hard to think with Alex so close, let alone say anything. Quinn tried to sift through her thoughts. "Alex, my show is the most important thing in my life right now. I would never do anything to sabotage that. Not for any woman."

Alex pulled back. "I didn't mean to assume you would. I just know my father. And I want to protect this for as long as I can. Selfishly."

Quinn smiled at that and leaned in slowly to give her a small kiss on the lips. It wasn't as heated or passionate as their last kiss, but it was the most intimate one they had shared. Full of promise and hope for what might come.

CHAPTER FIFTEEN

The only good thing about choosing a play as dull as their fall production was that the party was tame. When they had celebrities onstage or anything that drew a younger crowd, the parties tended to be much larger affairs, with more press to deal with and an overall bigger headache for Alex.

By the time she arrived at the *Death of a Salesman* party, the cast was already inside dancing, and the crew from the theater wouldn't be far behind. As she entered, she looked around and spotted her father and Rick speaking to one of the cast members at the bar. She knew she should at least say a hello and pay Rick her respects, but she was on a high from her last interaction with Quinn, and her father would only ruin her mood.

When she spotted an unmistakable mane of red hair at a distant cocktail table talking to a pretty blonde, she slid past her father without a word and made her way over to someone who wouldn't have that same effect on her. She walked up behind Courtney and slid an arm around her waist. "Ms. Powers, would you sign my program?"

Courtney made a loud squealing noise as she turned to pull Alex into a tight hug. Alex remembered the old high after a show, especially an opening, and smiled at the joyful laugh.

"But really, babe," Alex said as she returned the hug. "You were amazing."

"Even though the show was a bore?" Courtney joked, pulling back from their embrace.

"Even so. You light up every stage and always have." Alex's eyes turned to the blonde waiting patiently.

"Oh! Alex, this is Paige. Paige, Alex." Courtney put her arm around Paige's shoulders as she introduced them, and Alex could already see the tenderness in Courtney's eyes as she looked at her.

"You must be the stage manager," Alex said as she extended her hand. "I've heard great things."

Paige gave her a firm handshake. "And you're the best friend. I've heard some good and some interesting things about you."

Alex could see why Courtney was attracted to her. Paige's big brown eyes were warm and expressive, crinkling at the corners when she smiled. She looked at Courtney like she could do no wrong, and Alex's heart swelled for them. "Anything bad was all a lie. Courtney is just jealous."

"Like she's going to believe you. You look like an evil Bond character in that tux," Courtney replied.

"On the contrary, honey. I think she looks rather dashing." Paige smiled at them before giving Alex an exaggerated wink.

"See, I know you're just trying to make me jealous. But I'm sorry to break it to you darling, the apple of her eye just walked through the door." Courtney nodded to the front door of the restaurant.

Alex's heart began to beat so fast, she could hear the blood rush to her ears. How was it that someone she'd just seen, had just pressed up against a bus stop, could make her heart thud on the spot like that? As Quinn's eyes met hers across the room, she got lost in them once again.

"Earth to Alex," Courtney said loud enough that it jarred Alex's attention. "I was just saying to Paige that you have a little bit of a crush. But that seems rather obvious now that she can see the drool coming out of your mouth."

Alex almost put her hand up to her mouth to check before narrowing her eyes. She needed this part of the conversation to be over before Quinn made it over to them, and she was even more embarrassed. "Shut up, Court. She's coming over."

Courtney merely laughed before turning to Paige. "She's usually a total stoic statue. Not this melting puppy dog you see before you."

Paige put her hand gently on Alex's arm. "Don't worry, Alex. I'm a better wingman than my tactless girlfriend here."

Alex smiled at the blush creeping up Courtney's face. "Girlfriend, is it?" she asked, gladly taking the opportunity to change the subject away from Quinn, who was now cornered near the bar by Rick. "Well, Paige, if you ever need dirt on your *girlfriend*, I'm happy to help."

Courtney returned her smile with a glare. "Don't you have someone to boss around somewhere?"

"In fact, I do." Alex took Paige's hand. She gave Courtney a sly smile before bending down to kiss it gently. "It was a pleasure, Paige. Keep this one out of trouble for me."

Paige gave her a bright smile before putting her arm around Courtney's waist. "I'm a stage manager. Actors don't worry me. And you should go ask that girl for a dance before she's snatched up."

Alex smiled at them again before leaving the table. She wasn't used to feeling as if she was in competition with an entire room, but she shouldn't have been surprised to find Quinn surrounded by an army of admirers. Quinn might not have been a movie star, but she had been a high-end model with one of the biggest agencies in the world. For an Off-Broadway theater company that had just made its audience sit through a play from 1949, Quinn was beyond glamorous.

But to her delight, as soon as Quinn saw her getting closer, she said something to the group and started moving toward her.

"Groupies already?" Alex asked. She felt like there was an elastic band of sexual tension forming between their bodies.

"Just bored actors. Are you enjoying yourself?"

"Not as much as I'd like to be. And I'm not feeling very patient tonight."

"Hmm, that's too bad. Anything I can do to help that?"

"Meet me at my place? I'll leave first."

Quinn's intake of breath was answer enough. She didn't seem to try to mask the huskiness in her voice. "Text me your address."

Alex gave her a small smile before moving toward the door. Once outside, she took out her phone and sent Quinn a quick text: *66 west 38th street, apt 1701. See you soon.* Before she hit send, she quickly added a fish emoji. She should have stayed at the party, but she didn't know how much longer she'd have been able to keep her hands off Quinn, and a Horizon event was not the place to do that.

Maybe Courtney was right, and she was turning in to a "melting puppy dog." She could deal with that pesky problem later. For now, all she could think about was that silver dress on her floor.

CHAPTER SIXTEEN

After making the rounds and congratulating the few people in the theater she knew, Quinn made her exit. Beyond wanting to get to Alex, she wasn't sure how much longer she could be in public with her ruined underwear rubbing against her swollen center.

Putting her head down, she quickly hailed a cab, her body trembling from either nerves or excitement or most likely both. She looked up at the expansive building as she arrived. Alex's building was opulent. One of those high-rise luxury apartments that no normal New Yorker could ever inhabit.

Though, given what she knew about Alex's family, she guessed this *was* normal for Alex. After making her way up to the fiftieth floor, she stood outside Alex's gold door and simply stared at it. She wanted Alex like she had never wanted anyone. But images of Jenna were flashing across her mind. She had wanted her once too. She had trusted her. Should she really be risking her show for someone who wouldn't even go into a party with her? Where could this lead when Alex wouldn't even be seen with her?

But even with her mind racing with every argument she could muster, Quinn knew she wasn't walking away.

The front desk must have given Alex a heads-up, or maybe she had seen Quinn through the peephole. Really, it didn't matter because Alex had opened the door and was standing there looking as debonair as ever. She was still wearing the tuxedo pants, but the jacket and tie were gone, and the crisp white shirt was completely unbuttoned, revealing a simple white tank top underneath. She was holding the door open with one hand, had a dark drink in the other, and exuded such an air of confidence that Quinn couldn't form words.

Thankfully, Alex simply held the door open wider, allowing Quinn to enter the apartment. They walked down a short hallway and into a large, open room that had windows all along the far wall. In fact, there was no wall. It was only windows. Quinn couldn't help but look out at the dark city glittering with lights. She could faintly see the outline of Bryant Park.

She jumped slightly as Alex offered her a glass of champagne. Alex had traded in whatever dark liquor she was drinking for her own glass. "It's my favorite part of the apartment. I love these windows."

Quinn tore her eyes away so she could clink her glass against Alex's. "Are we celebrating something"?

"Opening night. You being here with me. That dress," Alex replied as she took her first sip. Quinn followed suit and savored the pop of flavor on her tongue. "And what did you think of the show?" She moved to the couch and motioned for Quinn to join her.

"How honest can I be without offending your loyalties?" Quinn sat, making sure their legs were close enough to touch.

Alex laughed lightly. "I hope you'll always be very honest with me."

Quinn laced her fingers through Alex's, and the last thing she wanted to talk about was theater. "The cast was phenomenal. Everything about the production was well done, and I really liked some of Rick's decisions."

"But?"

"It was a little dull. I may have pinched myself a few times to keep awake." Quinn took a large sip as she peered over her glass nervously. She knew Alex hadn't directed the show, but she did help with programming.

She didn't look upset, though. "I agree. It was dull." She took a sip. "I didn't have a say in the fall show. It's always Rick's. I don't even think my father cared much for that choice."

"But he doesn't push back on Rick like he does on you?"

"No. Technically, they're equals in hierarchy. But they're also best friends. And very much part of the old boys' club."

Quinn desperately wanted to see the fun, seductive side of Alex again, so she decided to change the subject away from the one topic that would sour the mood: Simon Anders. "What you said earlier tonight…" She paused as she tried to articulate her thoughts. "I like you too. But I'm nervous."

Alex put her arm around Quinn, resting it on the back of the couch. "We don't have to do anything tonight. We can just talk."

Quinn turned so their faces were close. Alex didn't make any moves to get closer, but she also looked like the last thing she wanted to do was just talk. "I don't want to talk anymore."

After a beat of silence, Alex moved off the couch and extended her hand, smiling gently. "Come. I'll show you the rest of the apartment."

Alex guided her through a different hallway. The last room at the end was the master bedroom, and Quinn's heart rate picked up as Alex opened the door and lightly pulled her in. Alex continued to take charge by grabbing the champagne flute out of Quinn's hand and setting both glasses on the large dresser to the right of the door.

Quinn let Alex take the lead, knowing that was what she preferred. She was also trembling from so much anticipation that she couldn't think clearly enough to do anything but follow directions.

Alex seemed free of nerves and was staring at her with pure, lustful determination. "You look so beautiful tonight. I could see everyone's eyes on you," she whispered into Quinn's ear as she slowly pushed her against the door.

"I only cared about your eyes."

Alex began slowly kissing down Quinn's neck before bringing her tongue back up the length of it. She placed her lips right against Quinn's earlobe, causing her to shut her eyes and suppress a moan that wanted to escape far earlier than seemed normal. "I want to make you feel good tonight. I can go as fast or as slow as you want. Just tell me, okay?"

Quinn nodded slowly, unable to do anything else while Alex's mouth was close to her ear. She wanted to feel that tongue run down her neck again. She wanted to feel it everywhere.

When she didn't respond, Alex pulled her head back, gently placing Quinn's hair behind her ear like she had earlier in the night. "I'm going to need a verbal answer before I touch you," she whispered.

Consent had never been so sexy, and Quinn's nerves spiked again as she realized she was about to let Alex do anything she wanted. Because in this moment, she was willing to give Alex whatever she needed. "You don't need to go slow. I want this. I want you so bad, Alex," she managed to pant out.

Alex didn't waste any time pushing her harder against the wall as she took her mouth. The second their lips touched, all hesitation was gone. The slow, painfully tense energy of their previous encounters was replaced by a tornado of touching, teeth, and moans. This time, they didn't need to stop.

There was nothing graceful about this kiss, but the sloppiness, the wetness from their tongues wrestling was the most erotic thing Quinn had ever experienced. She felt physically hungry as Alex's lips took ownership of hers, her tongue forcing Quinn's mouth into quick submission. She turned them around without breaking the kiss, slowing their rhythm as she walked Quinn backward.

Quinn's legs hit the foot of the expansive bed, causing her to fall into a sitting position. She couldn't stop the whimper that came out of her at the sudden loss of contact. Kissing Alex was like a drug she couldn't resist.

Alex kneeled and slid the silver dress slowly up Quinn's legs. She lightly kissed the inside of her thighs, causing Quinn to shake slightly. No longer the image of complete control, Alex's hair was disheveled, her pupils blown, and her lips were red and swollen. She looked up at Quinn as her hands slid up her legs, slowly sliding her panties down and over her heels.

"These are very wet, sweetheart. Is that for me?" Alex's voice sounded low and husky and unbelievably sexy.

Quinn didn't dare tear her eyes away, even though she knew how exposed she was sitting there without any panties. Not trusting her voice but knowing Alex had all the consent she'd need, she took Alex's hand and moved it into the folds of her wet pussy.

Alex leaned her face into the side of Quinn's bare thigh, groaning at the contact. Feeling emboldened, Quinn moved the same hand Alex just had on her pussy to her mouth. She sucked and swirled her tongue around Alex's fingers, savoring the taste of herself on fingers she'd had more than one fantasy about.

Alex's mouth was slightly open as she watched. "You are by far the sexiest woman I have ever seen," she said as she pulled her fingers slowly out of Quinn's mouth.

Quinn's breathing was heavy, and she wasn't sure how long she would be able to hold on to her orgasm once Alex touched her. She gripped the sheets. "Please, Alex."

"Please what, Quinn?" The smile on Alex's face made it obvious she knew she had just regained control of the situation.

"Please, fuck me. Please. *Please*." Quinn didn't even care that she was begging. She couldn't remember a time she had been this turned on.

Alex pulled her forward with surprising strength until her ass was on the edge of the bed. She moved Quinn's legs farther apart before pushing the dress more forcibly up, exposing her wet center.

Quinn sucked in a breath as Alex's hot mouth latched on to her pussy. No longer teasing, Alex sank her tongue deep into Quinn's folds and moaned as she got her first taste, causing even more vibrations to roll though Quinn.

She groaned loudly as Alex set an unrelenting rhythm with her tongue. Too soon, Quinn could feel her legs begin to shake in the familiar lead-up to her orgasm. When Alex moved her skillful tongue higher and began to lick small, tight circles around her clit, Quinn was shouting, "Yes, fuck. Don't stop. That feels so good."

Alex's moans reverberated through her pussy as she devoured Quinn. An earth-shattering orgasm ripped through her, lifting her off the bed as Alex continued to lap at her, pulling out every last strand of her orgasm.

When Quinn couldn't handle any more, she put her hand on the back of Alex's head to still it. Alex gave her one last kiss and gently pressed soft kisses all along Quinn's inner thighs and down her legs. "You taste delicious, Quinn," she said softly as she allowed Quinn to catch her breath.

After what seemed like only a minute, Alex pulled her into a standing position and into her arms, supporting her wobbly, just-climaxed body. With one smooth hand, she unzipped the back of Quinn's dress and let it fall to the ground. She then sat her back down so she could kneel in front of her again and gently, slowly, removed her heels.

As Quinn sat there naked, she realized Alex still had on every single piece of clothing. She ached to see the skin beneath that sexy suit. "I want to see you too."

Alex didn't argue, but she also didn't let Quinn do the honors. Instead, she stood before her, the same intense expression on her face, and began to slowly take off her clothes. Her panties were the last piece to go. Alex took her time moving them down her long body before gingerly picking them up from the ground and letting them dangle from one finger. "Better?"

Quinn took a moment to drink in the sight before her. Alexandra Anders was nothing short of a goddess, with her long sleek hair falling over her back and the light freckles coating her bare shoulders just like they faintly sprinkled her nose. Quinn ached to kiss them. She ached to kiss everywhere.

She couldn't believe she was going to get to touch something so perfect. Alex's nipples, seemed to be hardening in real time, and Quinn could feel herself getting wet again. "You are so beautiful, Alex."

"Thank you." Alex smiled softly, but the expression quickly faded. She slowly moved back to the bed as if she was stalking her prey. "Move up the bed, sweetheart."

It was clear that talking was one of her forms of foreplay, and Quinn couldn't get enough of it. As she moved up, Alex did as well until she was hovering over Quinn so the only thing touching were their breasts. Quinn's nipples grazed the perfect chest above her, and she had to marvel at where they were. Marvel at the fact that Alex had given in to this. But when she looked into the eyes above her, there was no hesitation. No regret, fear, or indecision. There was simply desire.

Alex slowly lowered her body and pulled Quinn's mouth into a passionate kiss. Quinn moaned into her when she could taste herself lingering there. They kissed for so long that Quinn lost track of time. It could have been an hour. Or maybe it was already the next morning. She had never craved lips liked these.

Finally, Alex tore her mouth away and straddled her. She gently took Quinn's hands and raised them so they were resting against the lush pillows. "You can move these hands," Alex said, pushing her wet pussy against Quinn's stomach. "But it would make me very happy if you left them there until I make you come again."

This non-rule became such a sexy thing, Quinn wondered what she even really knew about control. In that moment, she would have gladly done anything Alex asked without complaint. Her body vibrated, aching for another release.

Alex smiled, clearly enjoying the way Quinn was squirming. "I didn't get to appreciate you fully before," she said as she raked her eyes down to Quinn's breasts. She teasingly grazed her fingers over Quinn's nipples and pulled on them gently. "What would you like me to do?" She moved her face down and captured a hard nipple in her mouth.

Quinn moaned loudly, pushing up for more contact. Alex sucked on one, then moved to the other, sloppily kissing and licking until Quinn was a writhing mess.

"Tell me." Alex roughly pulled on her nipple. Quinn gasped as Alex pulled her other even harder. "Tell me," she demanded more forcefully.

"I want you inside me," Quinn managed to cry out between gasps. "Please, Alex. Please." Her chest was heaving now, and sweat started to trickle down the back of her scalp. She wasn't going to last very long with the way Alex was pulling on her nipples and grinding on her.

Alex brought a hand to Quinn's mouth, and she didn't have to ask to know what Alex wanted. They were in sync like years-old lovers. Without any hesitation, she wrapped her lips around Alex's two fingers and swirled her tongue erotically, eliciting a low growl from Alex as she watched with hooded eyes. "God, you are so sexy," Alex breathed out as her fingers left Quinn's mouth.

The truth was, Quinn had never felt sexier than she did in that moment. With Alex looking at her as if she was hungry, she felt more confident than she ever had walking down a runway. Alex made her feel like something precious.

She didn't have time to dwell on what all that meant before Alex was pushing two fingers inside her, and she again lost the ability to think. The louder her cries became, the harder Alex thrust. Quinn's body opened in a way her heart wasn't ready for, and they rocked together in a fast rhythm that filled her but not nearly enough.

"More, please." She gasped as she dug her fingernails roughly into the soft flesh of Alex's back, causing Alex to let out her own moan. "I need more of you." She opened her legs farther, hoping Alex would understand.

Without missing a beat, Alex slid another finger into her pussy. She slowed her thrusts, making sure to hit Quinn's clit with her knuckles each time her fingers slid in and out.

Quinn let out a slew of expletives and deep moans as she continued to dig into Alex's back. She felt wild, but in this moment, she didn't care.

"Come for me, sweetheart. I want to hear how good I'm making you feel."

After two more deep thrusts, Quinn cried out as a second, even stronger orgasm ripped through her body. She clung to Alex's back until she felt her vision blur, and her limbs were too weak to hold her up.

The next thing she knew, Alex's soft body curled around hers, holding her gently as her breathing returned to a semblance of normalcy. She was pretty sure she hadn't passed out, but she also didn't know how they'd come to a spooning position.

"That was…" Quinn put her hand on her forehead, trying to gather her thoughts as every inch of her body continued to pulse under Alex's hands. "I mean, that was…" She giggled at her own ineloquence. "You're amazing," she finally breathed out.

Alex was looking at her lazily, her head resting on one hand, and her standard cocky smirk in place.

Quinn stared for a minute as she let her breathing settle. "But we're not done." She hadn't quite recovered from her own release, but she was desperate to hear Alex moan from her touch. She wanted to hear what pleasure sounded like from those lips.

Alex ran her finger lightly up the side of Quinn's naked body and back down. "No, we're not."

"What do you like?" Quinn asked in barely a whisper as she pushed up and mirrored her position.

"Can I show you?"

Quinn swallowed hard and nodded, knowing she would do just about anything to make Alex come.

"Lie back for me, sweetheart," Alex said in a quiet voice that, despite her use of the pet name, still reverberated with authority.

Quinn had never been in a relationship where there were strict bedroom roles, and she'd never really thought about being a top or a bottom. She just knew she felt a rush of arousal every time Alex gently ordered her around. She found the domineering words, the bruising kisses, and the unrelenting attention sexier than anything she'd experienced.

Alex straddled her again, and Quinn could feel the same wetness from before sliding across her stomach. But instead of staying there, Alex crawled up her body so her thighs were on either side of Quinn's head. She grabbed the bedpost and looked down. "May I?"

Quinn grabbed Alex's hips and pulled her body down to her mouth. Their moans wrapped around each other's as Quinn lost herself in the wet folds above. She licked, sucked, and flicked her tongue against any spot Alex would give her, but Alex was clearly the one driving her own orgasm. Quinn felt gloriously used as Alex moved her body to the rhythm she needed for release.

Quinn could tell she was close by her short breaths as she squeezed her thighs. Quinn urged her on by gripping her ass and increasing the flicks of her tongue. Alex finally stopped moving her hips and allowed Quinn to finish her off the way she wanted to. She sank two fingers deep inside her as she continued to make small circles against her clit.

"Fuck, I'm coming. I'm coming," Alex cried. Her body tensed as she let out a long sigh. A moment later, she relaxed and lifted herself off Quinn's mouth but leaned against the headboard.

Quinn simply stayed where she was, her hands resting on the hips above her. Finally, Alex gently sank down beside her, casually reaching her arm across Quinn's middle.

The room was silent, comfortably so, as they returned to earth. Alex gave her a shy smile, as if she hadn't just ridden her face. "Where did you come from?"

Quinn laughed softly, bringing one finger to lazily trace Alex's profile and down her arm. Her arm felt like deadweight, and she dropped it as she sighed into her pillow. "Sleepy town."

"You came from sleepy town?" Alex's confused face was so adorable, Quinn laughed again.

"No. I'm going to sleepy town right now."

"Oh, you're one of those."

Quinn yawned. "One of what?"

"One of those people who passes out after mind-blowing sex."

"As long as you agree it was mind-blowing." Quinn smiled and pulled Alex's hand down to kiss her knuckles lightly.

"I do agree. Now go to sleep." Alex kissed her temple softly as she pulled the sheets up to her chin. Quinn's heavy eyelids closed, the effort of keeping them open too much now. But the feeling of Alex wrapping her arms around her caused her to smile just as sleep took over.

CHAPTER SEVENTEEN

The sun filtering into her room was not the sun Alex was accustomed to in the morning. This sun was much brighter and peppier, which could only mean it was much later than she was used to sleeping.

She tried her best to get out of bed without waking Quinn. She looked at the clock on her bedside table as she put on her sweats and wasn't surprised to see it was early afternoon. They'd seemed to have released some dangerous sex monster that was never satiated and was always looking for its next orgasmic victim.

She would have gladly stayed in bed to feed said monster, but her stomach had started growling so loudly, she thought it might wake Quinn as she slept beside her. The last thing they had eaten was dinner the previous night, and they could have both done with sustenance, so she decided to venture out. No way could she feed Quinn anything she had in her sorry fridge.

Bagels from her favorite coffee shop downstairs would have to do. She quickly scribbled a note for Quinn in case she woke. Though, considering she appeared to be more log than human right now, Alex didn't think she'd be stirring before she got back.

Twenty minutes later, she brought a tray of coffee, orange juice, and bagels into the bedroom just as Quinn was stirring. "I bring food. Drink. Schmear." She wobbled as she set the tray down and told herself it had nothing to do with the sheet falling down Quinn's chest as she stretched.

"Ah. My favorite food." Quinn flashed her a smile and picked up one of the cups. She dumped almost the whole cup of cream in and more sugar than Alex had ever seen someone add.

"I gather you like some coffee with your cream and sugar?" she asked in a teasing tone as she grabbed her own cup and took a small sip.

Quinn bunched the sheet under her breasts and took a gulp before she answered. "I like it to taste like coffee ice cream. I'm sensitive to bitter stuff."

"It's like coffee for a child." She laughed at the offended look on Quinn's scrunched face. "Don't be mad. I just brought you the best bagels in New York, aka, the world."

"Wait! You told me George's was the best bagel place when I first met you." Quinn grabbed a bagel and began to apply cream cheese while staring pointedly. "Explain yourself."

"George's is second best. You think I was just going to give up my favorite place to a woman I just met? My favorite place that's *in* my apartment building, I might add." Alex grabbed her own bagel and stretched out as she waited for Quinn to be done with the knife. Quinn passed it to her, and as she took a bite, she hummed and closed her eyes.

"You're right," she said, sighing. "I would have stalked this place had I known." She opened her eyes and directed a slow, sexy smile at Alex.

"See? I have to be careful of the stage five bagel clingers."

Quinn continued to eat her bagel, a blissful smile crossing her face with every bite. Alex wasn't used to doing sleepovers. Usually, the women she had over knew that staying the night wasn't something she was comfortable with. But she had an unusual urge to keep Quinn in her bed for as long as she could.

Her phone vibrating on her nightstand brought her out of the moment. She reached to grab it, and when she came back into sitting position, Quinn was staring at where her T-shirt had ridden up with her bagel hanging loosely from her hand.

"You have a really nice body," Quinn whispered as she put the bagel down and moved her fingers into the top of Alex's pants.

"So do you." Alex had always had a healthy libido, but every touch from Quinn set her on fire in a way she had never experienced. Before she could do anything, her phone vibrated two more times. She groaned as she saw the name on it. "Hold that thought. Janet tends to just keep texting if I don't respond."

Quinn laughed and pulled away, immediately making Alex regret the decision to look at her phone. "I understand. My mom is the same way."

Reluctantly, Alex looked down.

No surprise, the review isn't up. Likely waiting for tmw's pub.

We'll send over the clips once it's up.

Stop by Monday at noon, and we'll go over pull quotes. And the details of your feature article with Quinn Collins. The winky face Janet included at the end of her text wasn't necessary, but Alex had been expecting a snide remark from her ever since the dinner last night.

Janet was way too perceptive for her own good. Or at least for Alex's own good. She would need to figure out how to maintain a poker face when Quinn was around. She might not have been able to pull one over Janet, but she needed to do so for whoever the *Times* sent to interview them.

"Everything okay?"

"All good. We're still waiting for the *Times* review to come out for the show last night."

"Are you nervous?"

"Not really. I hope for Courtney's sake that it's favorable. But the show is almost sold out already, so it's more of a prestige and ego thing. Positive reviews help the reputation of the theater. Janet takes them very personally, though. Even though she has no hand in the artistic process. She's just always been like that."

"She's an interesting woman. I'm still surprised to hear you worked for her. You don't seem too keen on the whole PR part of things."

Alex shrugged. "It wasn't my first choice. I wanted to be in my parents' theater, but he wanted me to get some work experience outside of acting. Because of the hours I needed to be with my mom, it was kind of the perfect situation. Since Janet knew everything that was going on, I could come to work when I could. She was really supportive and only sometimes a pain in my ass."

"She does seem rather intense."

"Understatement. One time in the middle of winter, she made me go to Times Square at four in the morning—during a blizzard, I might add—when the papers first got delivered just so she could have the hard copy of a review that was already up online. I've never seen so few people in midtown. I could barely walk there was so much snow. But Janet *needed* her paper."

Quinn smiled and put her hand on her heart. "How brave of you. You've really worked the hard jobs."

"Okay, Ms. LA. How many snowstorms have you weathered for work?" Alex took a small pillow and playfully flung it at Quinn, who managed to grab it in the air before it hit her.

"Terrible throw. And I will have you know that I once had to do a Winter Wonderland photo shoot for a power drink brand. On a mountain."

"That does sound horrible. Craft services in a parka. You win."

"As long as I win." Quinn picked up her bagel again. "But I never got to be by the craft services table. Or if I was, I was just staring at it wistfully. Which is why now, I eat what I want, when I want." She took an exaggerated bite and closed her eyes again, humming loudly.

"I imagine it's hard watching what you eat all the time," Alex mused.

"Now I don't think about food that much. Because I don't have to diet for my job like I used to. But back then, it was always on my mind. There was this little European bakery next to my apartment in LA. I could smell the bread baking from my balcony every morning. That place drove me crazy. I had an ongoing fantasy of breaking into it and eating anything I looked at but could never actually have. I'd literally create a list in my head of the exact order of pastries and cookies I'd eat. Now, it seems pathetic. But when you have to be as careful as I was, food becomes an obsession."

"We always want what we can't have."

"I suppose that's true."

Alex pushed the breakfast tray closer to Quinn's side of the bed. "Well, I, for one, am happy you made the transition to the stage. You can eat two bagels if your heart so desires."

Quinn set her half-eaten bagel on the tray and looked up with a thoughtful expression. "You know, I'm surprised we ended up here so fast. I figured it would take at least two more innocent lunch dates before you caved. What changed?"

Alex raised a questioning eyebrow. "That lunch was anything but innocent. Need I remind you of your red lipstick?"

Quinn swatted her arm playfully. "That wasn't a trick. I happen to like red. But you didn't answer my question."

"I'm not sure. You are pretty hard to resist." She pushed a lock of hair over Quinn's shoulder.

Quinn didn't respond for a moment, and Alex grew uncomfortable under her searching gaze. "When's the last time you had breakfast with a woman? Or is the bagel delivery kind of your thing?"

"How can bagels be my thing?"

"Bring a woman back, have incredible sex, and then show her something even better. Holy heaven." She held up one of the uneaten bagels.

"Holy heaven?" Alex couldn't help but roll her eyes while Quinn giggled to herself. "But let's get back to the moment you said the bagel is better than the sex."

"Not better but equally as satisfying."

"I may need to up my game in bed. This information is upsetting."

Quinn pressed her fingertips against Alex's furrowed brow. "So serious. Last night was amazing. You were amazing. Better than the bagel."

Alex gently took Quinn's hand and lightly kissed it. "So were you. And, no, I don't usually do breakfast."

"Not even with cute bartenders?"

"Not even with her."

"I figured there would be more than one bartender. You have quite the reputation around town, after all."

Alex couldn't tell if this was more sexy banter or if the slight edge to Quinn's voice pointed at something else. She set Quinn's hand down so she could sit up. "What do you mean?"

Quinn glanced at her now empty hand before looking back up with a question in her eyes. "I didn't mean it in a bad way. It's stupid, actually. Mikey had mentioned something before I met you. About how many women you've dated. Forget I said anything."

Quinn wasn't wrong. Alex was aware of her reputation in certain circles. But knowing Quinn had thought she was promiscuous before they had even met made her self-conscious. "But you wanted to go out with me anyway? Despite that reputation?" She tried to keep her tone neutral but could hear an edge to her words.

"Of course. It was just gossip. I'm sorry I even brought it up." Quinn attempted to link their fingers again, but Alex pushed out of reach.

She could feel an irrational response bubbling up, but she could do little to stop it at that point. "What about you? From what I've heard, you have quite the scandalous reputation in LA."

"Excuse me?"

"As I understand it, I'm not the only one about town." She regretted saying it the moment the words left her lips. She regretted it even more when she saw the flash of hurt cross Quinn's face. Intimacy might have been hard for her, but making Quinn feel bad was the last thing she wanted to do, especially after the night they'd shared.

Quinn moved off the bed and began gathering her discarded formal wear. "I should go."

"Quinn. You don't need to go."

"I do. I have a meeting with Mikey."

"But it's Saturday."

Quinn sighed as she grabbed her dress and got on her knees, apparently looking for her underwear. "You're not the only one who takes her job seriously. I have rewrites to do. I start rehearsals this week."

Alex moved toward her dresser and removed a fresh pair of underwear, leggings, and a T-shirt. "Here, wear these. You don't need to put your dress back on."

Quinn gave her a tight smile. "Thanks," she said flatly as she moved to the bathroom to change.

Alex mentally rehearsed the things she could say to get a smile back on Quinn's face. And possibly even get her back in the bed. But when Quinn remerged looking fresh and gorgeous, Alex lost her resolve. She wasn't even sure where things had gone wrong in the first place. "I'll see you this week at the theater?" she asked instead.

"Are we allowed to acknowledge each other at the theater?" Quinn moved quickly toward the front door. When she got there, she turned.

Alex closed her eyes and took a breath before facing that direct stare. She couldn't really blame Quinn's biting tone. She was the one who had set boundaries in the first place. But she hated hearing Quinn's voice like that, and she wanted nothing more than to see the usual spark in her eyes again. "Yes, Quinn. I never said we couldn't talk there."

"As long as it's not in front of your dad."

Alex narrowed her eyes. She'd obviously upset Quinn more than she'd even realized. Or maybe this had been on Quinn's mind since Alex had first said they couldn't see each other.

When she didn't respond, Quinn continued: "Alex, you seem to have a lot of baggage. Which I can understand. But I don't want to do this if I can't even ask you basic questions about your life. You're so concerned about him and what he thinks. Wouldn't it be freeing not to be under his thumb? Why does everything have to feel so dire?"

Alex's head was spinning. Ten minutes ago, they'd been engaging in verbal foreplay, and now she felt as if she was answering for much more than the defensive way she'd responded to Quinn's comment. It felt as if Quinn had been holding that last statement in and only let it out in her frustration.

She was used to people thinking she only had her position in the theater because of her father. But she had worked so hard to turn that theater into what it was now. Worked so hard to honor her mother's legacy. And she knew it was only because of her that it was thriving. Horizon wasn't just a theater. It was the one remaining piece of her mother she had left in this world. And she wasn't ready to let that go.

"That theater is as much mine as it is his now. I wouldn't expect you to understand. You hardly know me." Her words again came out much harsher than she meant, but it also felt like nothing she said was going to fall on receptive ears.

Quinn gave her one final look before she opened the door. "You're right, I don't. See you around," she said without turning back.

All Alex could do was stand there and attempt to process what had just happened. And the only conclusion she could come to was that she'd messed up. And she had no idea how to fix it.

She needed Courtney.

CHAPTER EIGHTEEN

"Y ou're an idiot."

"Thank you, Court." Alex picked up her bourbon from the coffee table.

"Sorry, but it's true," Courtney responded, taking a sip of red wine.

Alex threw her head back onto the couch dramatically and sighed. "I don't know what to do."

"For starters, I think you need to apologize for being an asshole."

"I texted her."

"Texted her what?"

"That I was sorry things ended like that and I hoped her meeting was going well."

"Her fake meeting, you mean. Did she text you back?"

"No."

Courtney was quiet for a moment. "Let's review the main points again. You asked her to date. You brought her back here and had sex. And then, the next morning, when she made a throwaway comment about you being a player, you snapped back in the usual Alex Anders way. Did I cover everything?"

"That sums it up."

"She wasn't wrong. You *are* a player."

"You know why," Alex replied but not in a biting tone. She didn't have the energy to be that offended.

"But *she* doesn't know why. Part of dating people is intimacy. You have to open up. It's not fair to ask her to date just to push her away when she tries to get close."

Alex looked over at her helplessly. Courtney was right. But she hadn't tried dating in years. She was used to being more of an acquaintance than a friend. More of a fuck buddy than a lover. Quinn had changed all that. Alex *did* want to date Quinn, even with the complications it brought. "I don't know what to do."

"I have an idea."

"No."

"You haven't even heard it."

"Nothing good has ever come from you saying, I have an idea."

"Except that day that you were so hungover, you wanted to die, and I convinced you that a little trip to a festival show would help cure your misery. Good thing I had *that* idea, or you never would have seen Quinn's show."

"And I'd be just hungover today. Not worried about what some model thinks of me."

Courtney sat up and put her glass down. "Is this really fun, Al? Playing video games alone with a glass of bourbon in your overly expensive apartment? Having a casual fling every now and then that you usually regret? Because I don't really get it."

"Damn. Don't hold back on how you feel."

"I don't hold back. Not with you. And you don't with me. But I don't think you can honestly tell me that you're happy. And I know you think this promotion will be the thing to change that, but what if it doesn't? And what if Quinn can?"

Alex set her own glass down and put her arms on her knees so she could rest her head in her hands. "I hardly know her." She said the words, but in her heart, she knew that wasn't true.

"So get to know her without being an ass. And while you're at it, listen to my idea without being an ass."

Alex couldn't help but smile. She'd known when she'd called Courtney that she wouldn't hold back on her opinions. She never did. But that was also what she appreciated in their friendship. They were always honest with each other and held each other accountable.

"Okay, Stella. What is your damn idea?"

❖

Quinn arrived at the rehearsal room way earlier than she needed to, but she was too excited to get started with Diego to just sit alone in her apartment. She had done enough of that over the weekend. She hated lying to Mikey, but he'd have been able to tell something was bothering her if they'd talked, and she just couldn't bring herself to tell him about what had happened with Alex.

Maybe if everything hadn't gone to complete shit by the end of breakfast, she would have spent the entire weekend in Alex's bed and not alone in her apartment avoiding calls from Mikey and Eve. Maybe then, she'd have told Mikey what had happened.

But now that seemed pointless. It was clear that Alex had some things to work out. Over the weekend, Quinn had more than one moment where she wondered if walking out had been a mistake. But Alex's snapping tone had reminded her too much of Jenna, and she wasn't going to do that to herself again.

Being with Alex felt like whiplash. In one moment, she couldn't keep her hands off Quinn, and in the next, she was explaining all the reasons it was impossible to be together.

They needed to talk. No matter what, they were going to be in this theater together for the next two months, and Quinn didn't want it to be awkward every time they bumped into each other. But she was resolved not to sleep with Alex again until she'd figured out her baggage. The beginning of a relationship should have been fun and light and sexy. Not filled with fear that Alex's dad would throw a hissy fit over his daughter's relationship.

She knew it might be hard to maintain that resolve now that she'd experienced what Alex was like in bed. But she didn't want to be another random woman to her. She'd fallen for her too much. If Alex couldn't open up and trust her, Quinn couldn't be with her, even just physically.

As she sat in the rehearsal space, distractedly going through her script while really thinking about Alex, her phone rang. Mikey's number. She couldn't keep ignoring him. "Domino's. We're out of thin crust. What can I get you?" she asked as she answered the call.

"Like I would ever call Domino's. Do people even call for pizza anymore?"

"I don't know, but way to ruin the bit," Quinn replied as she closed her laptop.

"So sorry about that. I've been trying to reach you all weekend. Where have you been?"

Her thoughts raced to come up with a viable excuse. "I was nursing a hangover. Opening night party and all."

"For *Death of a Salesman*? I didn't realize it would get so wild. You didn't do anything I'm going to hear about, did you?"

Quinn stretched out on the bench. She wasn't going to tell him what she'd really gotten up to after the party. She wasn't in the mood for a lecture. But she also didn't like lying to him. "You mean besides the keg stand I did in front of Simon Anders? He did one too, so I really don't think it was a big deal."

Mikey sighed. "I hate you sometimes."

"No, you don't. Especially when I tell you that I met your future husband."

"I'm absolutely positive that you didn't. But please, elaborate."

Quinn smiled, and it was the first time since she'd left Alex's apartment that she felt somewhat uplifted. She probably should have called Mikey immediately. Messing with him always made her feel better. "At Janet's post-show dinner thing, I met a guy who's on the board for Horizon. He's rich, beautiful, established, and he loved me. So kind of the perfect fit for you."

"You mean Tim Delvin?"

"You know him?"

"No, but I know *of* him. He's a big-time investor in the theater scene. And he's completely out of my league."

"Nobody is out of your league. I mean, you may be a little uptight, but you're a catch."

"Thanks. I think?"

"I'm going to set it up."

"Please don't."

"I'm going to."

"Quinn. I can get my own dates. Worry about your own lack of a sex life."

Guilt settled in her stomach. Mikey might have been her manager, but he was also her best friend. She should have told him. Maybe he'd even be able to talk some sense into her and strengthen the resolve she'd been working on all weekend.

But before she could say anything, there was a knock on her rehearsal room door, and it was opening. Standing in the doorway was the exact person who had been monopolizing all of her thoughts.

"Alex," Quinn said, staring.

"Alex? What does she have to do with your sex life?" Mikey asked.

Quinn sat up, flustered by the phone in her ear and Alex standing only feet away. "No. I mean, yes. I mean, nothing. Alex just came into the rehearsal room. I need to go."

"And it sounds like we need to talk," he replied. "I'm coming over when you get home from rehearsal."

Quinn sighed. "Fine. I'll see you then." She set the phone on the bench and looked up at Alex, who was still standing in the doorway like she was slightly lost. Only half her body was even in the room. "Hey," Quinn said, not knowing what else to say. She'd figured she would need to find Alex at some point. She didn't think Alex would be the one to come see her. Her mind was also racing with the fact that she'd accidentally revealed the truth to Mikey. She'd have to deal with that later.

"Can I come in, or are you busy?" Alex asked. Her voice was soft and tentative, nervous.

"You own the room. You don't need to ask," she replied, opening her laptop again. "Diego will be here soon, so we should make this quick."

Alex stepped in and gently shut the door behind her. Quinn couldn't help the flip her stomach gave at the sight. Alex was dressed down today in a pair of blue skinny jeans and a fitted white T-shirt. It was the most causal Quinn had ever seen her. And now she really knew that it didn't matter what Alex wore. She always looked hot, and that insight was not exactly convenient when Quinn was trying to hold on to her anger from the weekend.

Alex stood there awkwardly, and Quinn didn't know if she should stand or stay seated. She opted to stay on the bench. "Did you need something, or are you just checking on the room?"

"I brought you these," Alex said, holding something out. When Quinn didn't move, Alex walked over to her and sat. "They don't bite."

Quinn raised an eyebrow. "You came here to bring me Swedish Fish?"

"Well, not only that. But I thought this might be a way for you to eat fish without actually eating fish." Alex put her hand on her forehead and let out a shaky laugh. "And this is really starting to feel like a bad idea now."

They sat there in silence for what felt like a full minute before Quinn opened the bag and popped a fish into her mouth. "Luckily for you, I didn't bring snacks today. And I love snacks."

Alex let out a small nervous laugh. It was clear she didn't really know how to proceed with the conversation, so Quinn decided to take pity on her, even if she didn't really deserve it.

"I'm guessing you didn't just want to bring me fish."

"No," Alex replied quickly and put her hands on her thighs, moving them up and down like she was trying to dry off sweaty palms. "I wanted to talk. And apologize again for Saturday."

"Look, Alex—"

"No, please. Let me." Alex stood and walked toward the other side of the room where there was a mirror covering the whole wall. She paced back toward the bench, anxious and agitated, and if Quinn wasn't annoyed, she probably would have found it endearing. "I'm so bad at this," she said as she stopped a few feet away, a look of pure defeat crossing her features.

"Bad at what?"

Alex looked as if she had swallowed something bitter. "Intimacy," she said quietly, and if she hadn't been standing so close, Quinn probably wouldn't have even heard.

Quinn could tell that this was hard for her, and she wished she knew why. But she also wasn't going to put herself out there again just to be shot down when it got too personal. "You got overly defensive when I brought up a fairly benign topic. I don't want to be with someone who snaps at me like that."

"I know. And I'm so sorry. And about how I let you leave." Alex took a deep breath and sat, closer than before. "I meant what I said at the party. I like you. More than I've liked anyone in a long time. And sometimes, I can be an idiot. Just ask Courtney."

Quinn couldn't help a small smile. But she wasn't ready to let things go. Alex Anders was one big walking red flag. "I need to know why that comment set you off so much."

Alex gazed at her hands before she brought her eyes back up. "Because it's true. And I was embarrassed that you already thought that of me."

"Why is that so embarrassing?"

"You're right. I have baggage. And I'd like to open up to you about it. I guess I overanalyze things, especially when it comes to this place." Alex waved around the room. "I knew I liked you before you came over that night, but I had no idea what it felt like to *be* with you. And I panicked."

"You don't need to tell me everything at once. I just want to know that we're moving toward some kind of intimacy. Otherwise, I don't really know what this is."

"I want to date you. And I'm sorry if I haven't made that clear. That's why I'm here."

Quinn glanced around with a small smile. "Alex, sharing candy on a bench in a rehearsal room doesn't really count as a date."

Alex's low, sexy laugh rolled out of her, and Quinn couldn't deny the way that sound made her feel. "I'm not *that* clueless," she said, moving her hand closer.

Quinn picked up her hand. "It's honestly hard to tell. So far, you've really bombed."

"I have. But maybe I can make it up to you."

"Hmm. And how do you think you can do that? You've already ruined New York bagels for me."

Alex let out a small gasp. "No! I promise, I'll make you enjoy those again too. In fact, I'll just stay silent as you eat."

"That feels like food porn. You can speak if you behave."

"I promise, I will," Alex replied, crossing her fingers over her heart. "Will you go out with me? On a real date? So I can show you I'm not the worst?"

Quinn felt butterflies in her stomach. She paused to look at their hands. She knew what she was going to say, but it couldn't hurt to make Alex sweat it out for a moment. "You brought me candy, and now you're asking me out. Will I get to wear your letterman jacket?"

"No, but I do have a cape from when I was Little Red Riding Hood in *Into the Woods* from, like, eighteen years ago. You could wear that if you want."

Quinn couldn't help a laugh. "That may be the nerdiest thing I've ever heard. Please keep the cape at home with your chess set."

"I already told you, it's on the computer."

Quinn continued to laugh at the offended expression on Alex's face. "But really, why do you still have the cape?"

"You have rehearsal soon. Will you please answer my question?"

"I see it doesn't take much for you to get bossy again. But, yes, I will go on a date with you. When?"

"Tomorrow?"

Quinn smiled at the adorably hopeful expression on Alex's face. "You don't waste any time, do you?"

"I just wasted a whole weekend."

"Smooth," Quinn replied as she narrowed her eyes. "But fine, tomorrow it is. What are we doing?"

"It's a surprise. I can pick you up at your apartment after your rehearsal. Would 5:00 work?"

"I'll text you my address."

"I could just look it up in your artist profile."

"Nerdy and creepy? You're really winning today."

"Hey, I brought you candy," Alex said in a pout that Quinn didn't buy. That was one expression she clearly couldn't pull off.

"That was your only redeeming quality today."

"I'll have to tell Courtney. She said to bring something sweet."

Quinn pulled Alex's hand into her lap and scooted so their legs were pushed together. Their heads were close enough that they didn't need to speak above a whisper, and it wouldn't take much to be kissing. Even the memory of what those lips felt like made her yearn to do just that. "You told Courtney?" Quinn whispered.

"I called her two minutes after you left." Alex brought her fingers gently down Quinn's face and grazed her mouth. Quinn parted her lips and closed her eyes for a moment. "I feel like I should be honest and tell you that she helped me plan the date because if I didn't, then Courtney would. She says the plan will help you think that I'm 'less of a monkey's ass.' Her words. I would never say that."

"I knew I liked Courtney," Quinn said, leaning even closer. "I'll have to send her a text and thank her. Depending on how you do on the date, of course."

"I have a feeling the two of you texting could be very dangerous for me."

"Scared?" Quinn asked. They were so close that she could almost feel Alex's breath.

"A little," Alex replied right before she closed the small distance between their lips.

Quinn cupped her face as they kissed. Alex didn't waste any time slipping her tongue into Quinn's mouth, and their lips moved together seamlessly. But their mouths didn't get the chance to become fully reacquainted. At the sound of a new knock on the rehearsal room door, Alex jumped off the bench at lightning speed.

"Where is my star?" a voice boomed into the room.

A sigh of relief came out of Alex's mouth "Diego," she said with a warm smile before moving over to him.

Quinn was still trying to calm her heart from their kiss, and it took her a moment before she also stood.

"I was just checking on Quinn before you got here. How was your trip in?" Alex's words helped remind her of the reality of their situation. They could banter and kiss all they wanted when they were alone, but inside the theater walls, Alex Anders was still clearly off-limits.

"Fine, fine," he said with a dismissive wave, leaning in to give Alex a quick kiss on the cheek. "But I want to know how she is," he said, looking at Quinn. "This gorgeous specimen." He skipped over to her, lifted her off the ground, and spun her around. She couldn't help but let out a squeal as they twirled, and when he set her back down, Alex was looking at them with a small smile.

"Well, I see you don't need the likes of me lurking around," Alex said as she moved to the door.

"You are always welcome, darling," Diego called.

Before leaving, Alex made eye contact with Quinn. "Speak soon, Ms. Collins." She turned to leave, closing the door behind her.

"Now, it's you and me," Diego said as he moved to a desk and set down his bag.

Quinn felt an onslaught of emotions. She wanted more time with Alex, but she was also more than anxious to start rehearsals. She steeled herself to focus on what was important and waited for him to settle in.

He took what looked like a script out of his bag, and Quinn's stomach dropped when she realized it was *her* script. Diego turned back to her with a wide smile. "*Model Behavior* by Quinn Collins. Are you ready to bring this to life?"

Quinn responded with her own smile. "Fuck, yes."

CHAPTER NINETEEN

After rehearsal with Diego, Quinn was more inspired about her show than she had been since she'd first written it. But she was also hungry, and the gross, healthy concoction Mikey was calling dinner was not going to cut it.

All she had eaten all day were the Swedish Fish Alex had given her, and she could feel her stomach grumble as she reached into her cupboard for some bread and peanut butter. It might not have been a proper dinner, but it was better than Mikey's.

She walked back into the living room with her sandwich and took an exaggerated bite when Mikey looked up from the takeout he'd brought over. "You are so dramatic. It wouldn't kill you to eat something healthy for once. You are getting older."

"If you can tell me what it is that you're eating, then I'll try it."

"Fine," he said putting his fork down and sliding it over to her. "It's an acai bowl."

"Nope. That sounds fake."

He pushed the bowl closer. "Do you need me to pull up Google? It's a thing. A popular thing, actually. It's mainly fruit. Try it."

Quinn scrunched her nose up before shoving the last of her sandwich into her mouth. She put up her finger to indicate she couldn't talk. Mikey rolled his eyes and waited for her to swallow. "Sorry, can't," she said with her mouth still half-full of sandwich. "I'm full now. Want to watch a movie or something?"

"No, I have a date. I just came to bring you food, which I guess was a waste of time and money."

"One, you knew I wouldn't eat that. You literally brought me fruit for dinner. Two, I know you just wanted to see my beautiful face. And three, who is the date with?"

"You don't know him. We met at Janet's event last week."

Quinn stretched out on the couch and hugged a pillow. "I bet he's not as cute as Tim Delvin."

Mikey put the rest of his bowl, plus Quinn's uneaten one, back into the bag they came in and walked to the kitchen so he could throw them away. When he came back, Quinn could see him smiling despite the effort he was putting into not reacting to her. "I told you, he's out of my league," he said as he sat.

"I see that smirk, Michael Rubio. You can't hide from me. I will find you *and* that smirk anywhere in the world."

"Okay, calm down, Carmen Sandiego. And tell me why Alex Anders stopped by your rehearsal today."

"She's the manager of the theater. I assume that's a common occurrence."

"I heard your voice when she came into the room. Are we lying to each other now?"

His words cut deeper than he probably meant. But she had felt bad about lying to him. Alex might have needed to keep this quiet, but she wasn't ready to continue to lie to her best friend. "No, I don't want to lie to you. We slept together."

He let out a sigh, but he didn't look as annoyed as she'd expected. "I guess I figured that would happen. You haven't looked at anyone like that since Jenna. Just…I don't know, Q. Just be careful. I know how much this show means to you. And I also know what hell Simon will make if he finds out you're sleeping with his daughter."

She threw her head back onto the cushion and let out a groan. "I'm so *fucking* sick of hearing that man's name in association with my sex life."

"I'd get used to it if you're determined to go down any road with Alex." There was a beat of silence, and his eyes shifted from stern to tender. "Is it just sex?"

"No," she responded quietly. "I like her. And when she's not being a self-sabotaging ass, I think she likes me too."

"Just be careful for me?"

"She's not Jenna."

"I can see that already. But I don't trust her dad. From what Janet told me, Simon is only loyal to Simon." Mikey looked at his phone and stood. "I have to go. The banker awaits."

Quinn walked him to the door. "Ew, a banker?"

"What do you think Tim is?"

"Tim's a banker?"

"He's in wealth management. Same thing."

"Then I already know he's your type."

Before he could leave, Quinn pulled him in for a tight hug, and she was thankful he returned it just as fiercely. "Have a good night. Be good," he said as he pulled back and gave her a warm smile.

"I'm not the one with the date. *You* have a good night. Be safe. Sexually, I mean. Be safe sexually."

"And that's my exit," he said, rolling his eyes dramatically at her before leaving the apartment.

CHAPTER TWENTY

As Alex arrived at Quinn's apartment, she started to worry about the plan she had made for them. Quinn didn't seem like the type to want to be in a stuffy restaurant on their first date, but maybe Alex had read her wrong.

She wanted to do something personal. Something that could show Quinn that she wasn't an emotional statue. And the plan she had would do that. In fact, the night's plan was partly what was scaring her. Revisiting memories from her past wasn't something she was used to doing.

Her desire to be in Quinn's presence was enough to override any other nerves she was feeling, and as she walked up to the apartment door, she took a deep breath and knocked.

Quinn appeared a moment later, and Alex felt an instant rush at seeing her beautiful face. She had on a pair of black jeans, a gray cashmere sweater, and a black beanie. She looked so cute that all Alex seemed able to do was stand there and smile.

She didn't judge women who wore makeup, but she also loved how natural Quinn kept her face. She didn't need anything to enhance her features and looked like an elegant ballerina. As if Alex had opened a music box and there Quinn was.

"You look really cute in that shirt. I love the plaid," Quinn said.

Alex managed to tear her eyes away from Quinn's face so she could urge her body into the apartment, but the entryway was small, and she was standing closer to Quinn than she was expecting. "Courtney thinks I look like a lumberjack in this."

"But a hot lumberjack."

Alex smiled as she reached up to pull on the end of Quinn's beanie. "I like you in a hat."

"Noted."

"I'd kiss you hello, but then, I don't think we would leave." She wasn't sure why she was whispering, but the small dark hallway carried her voice regardless, and Quinn's close body seemed to be drawing the air out of her lungs.

Quinn let out a dramatic gasp. "You promised me a date, Ms. Anders. I will not be deterred by your insane sexual magnetism."

Alex laughed and moved so they were almost flush against each other. "I'm sorry. My what now?"

"Just kiss me," Quinn breathed, pulling on Alex's collar so she could bring their mouths together.

Alex gently held Quinn's face and took control of the kiss. Their tongues lightly touched, but she didn't deepen it past that. While her body was vibrating with the need to feel Quinn under her again, she also wanted to show her a different side. She didn't want this to become just about sex, as much as she wanted that sex again. "I did promise you a date. And I'm going to deliver on that promise. So this…" Alex leaned in for another kiss. This time, their tongues slid against each other's, and Alex moved her hands around Quinn's back so she could anchor herself as they swayed. She broke them apart but didn't let go of Quinn's waist. "Will have to wait."

"You think I'm going to sleep with you on the first date?" Quinn asked, lightly pulling on the bottom of Alex's shirt.

"Who said anything about sleeping?"

"Are you going to tell me where we're going?"

"Nope. Are you ready?"

Quinn pulled away, opened a closet, and grabbed a coat, and the loss of her body heat made Alex regret saying that they should go.

After riding the elevator back down to the ground floor, Alex moved toward the car she had waiting for them. When she sensed that Quinn had stopped walking, she turned.

"You said casual," Quinn said, pointing to the vehicle. "Is it even legal to park there?"

"There's a driver." Alex could feel a slight blush creeping up her neck. "I don't drive. But I promise, this is the fanciest part of our date."

"I've had trouble picturing you on the subway. Now I know I'm right. You don't take public transportation." She didn't pose it as a question, and Alex could do little to correct her.

She scrunched her nose. "Not often. But we can forgo the car if you'd rather take the subway." She thought about where they were going. "A very long subway ride, that is."

"I want to go on the date you planned. Please, whisk me away in your sexy luxury car."

Alex smiled as she held out her hand. "In that case, sweetheart, your chariot awaits."

Chapter Twenty-One

O cean Parkway?" Quinn asked as the driver turned off the freeway. The drive so far had been quiet but not uncomfortable. She could sense Alex's mood shift the closer they seemed to get to wherever they were going. Their flirty teasing from the apartment didn't continue, but as Alex gently held her hand as she looked out the window, Quinn didn't mind the change. She had a feeling their destination was somehow important.

Alex simply looked over with a soft smile. She squeezed Quinn's hand, and even that small gesture made her stomach flip. "Here is fine, thanks," Alex said to the driver after a few more minutes, and he pulled the car over at a busy intersection. Alex put her hand on Quinn's arm. "Wait."

A moment later, she was on Quinn's side of the car, opening the door for her. Quinn was so distracted by the lights and noise that she couldn't even focus on how sweet Alex was being. "Are we on Coney Island?" she asked, looking around. There were more people than she would have expected to be out and about in October, but the weather was mild, and she saw a wide array of families, couples, and others milling about.

"Have you been?" Alex asked as she took Quinn's hand.

"No, I've always wanted to, but I never have. I almost forgot about it. You don't hear about Coney Island much these days."

Alex looked around the street and smiled before she nodded to the right and gently pulled Quinn to begin walking. "It feels a little forgotten. But it was my mom's favorite place. She loved New York. Everything about it. But this place was her favorite."

Quinn moved in closer to avoid bumping into the people passing them. Her eyes darted around to as many things as they could while she let all the noises and smells sink in. Colorful murals peppered the walls around them, and in the distance, there were some shutdown rides. "Did you come here a lot with her when you were younger?"

"All the time. It was our secret getaway. It always felt so different from the rest of the city. I think part of why I loved it so much was that it was ours. My father never came with us. Having a hot dog on a boardwalk isn't really his style. So it was just my mom and me."

"I love hot dogs."

Alex stopped walking and pointed ahead. "I'm glad to hear that. Because that's what we're getting. Nathan's. Have you heard of it?"

"Isn't that where they do the hot dog eating contest?"

"Why am I not surprised you know that random fact? But, yes, they do. There are other Nathan's around the country now, but this one is the original."

"Only the best for Alexandra Anders."

"It's still just a hot dog. Sorry if you were hoping for a Michelin Star."

"This is perfect. And I'm starving. I may eat two."

"I would expect nothing less, Nemo."

And she wasn't kidding. As they left Nathan's with their food, Quinn did her best to balance two hot dogs plus her lemonade, eliciting a chuckle from Alex.

"I won't be able to handle your sad face when you drop that, so please, let me help," Alex said as she reached over and took one of the hot dogs.

"I'd be careful. A girl could get used to this kind of treatment. First a car door, now you're carrying things for me? What's next, pulling out my chair before we eat?"

Alex began leading them down a quieter street. "We're going to the boardwalk, and there's only benches there. But I could try."

"I don't know what I was expecting, but hot dogs on the beach wasn't it." When she saw Alex's brow furrow, she spoke again quickly. "I love it. Thank you for showing me something important to you." She wanted to be holding hands again, but it was too hard with a drink in one hand and hot dog in the other. She simply followed Alex onto the boardwalk and to a bench next to a closed arcade.

They sat, and Alex handed Quinn her second hot dog. She put her own on her lap, another shy expression on her beautiful face. The Alex Anders Quinn was experiencing tonight was so much more tentative and softer than she was accustomed to seeing.

"I hope you weren't planning to challenge me to a game of pinball." She pointed to the closed arcade.

"I wouldn't do that to your ego on the first date," Alex replied as she took a bite.

Quinn stared as Alex closed her eyes, completely forgetting about her own hot dogs in lieu of watching the blissful expression on Alex's face.

"Oh God. That takes me back." Alex glanced at Quinn's hot dogs. "You have a lot of hot dog to get through. I'd start."

Quinn smiled as she took her first bite. She could feel Alex's attention on her but couldn't stop the loud hum that came out of her mouth with the first mouthful. "That really is good."

They both ate in silence. At least, Alex ate in silence. Quinn could never help the sounds that came out of her when she ate. And by the way Alex was gazing at her, she didn't seem to mind one bit.

Quinn had only gotten through three bites of her second hot dog when she put it on the bench next to her. "Okay, I admit defeat."

Alex laughed as she scrunched up the foil. "I'm in awe of your effort. You would have done my mom proud." She added Quinn's wrapper to her own pile. "I used to sit right here with her. She'd order two hot dogs too. And after we ate, we'd play Skee-Ball in this arcade." She shrugged. "It was a lot bigger and more glamorous when I was a kid."

Quinn interlaced their fingers. "Will you tell me about her?"

Alex glanced at their hands. When she looked up, her face didn't feel guarded in the way it had the other night, and Quinn felt like she could truly see her. "Walk with me?" As Alex stood and held out her hand, Quinn couldn't miss the difference between the sweet way Alex was asking versus the commanding tone she usually used.

They were quiet as they walked down the boardwalk, and it gave Quinn a chance to absorb the stores and closed stands scattered all along the way.

"I haven't really talked about this much outside of Courtney," Alex said as they walked slowly. "I don't really like thinking about the end much. She was so much more to me than the frail woman I said good-bye to."

Quinn squeezed Alex's hand. "Then tell me what she was like before she got sick."

"She was vibrant. When she walked into a room, she pulled the energy toward her and not only when she was on the stage. And not in the way Janet demands attention. My mom had a way of naturally drawing people into her orbit. It was effortless. And wonderful. She was also very social. She loved having parties, lunches, things like that. She loved hosting. But she didn't do it politically like my father does. She just loved people. She had this laugh that boomed out of her. She could just be sitting there, and it would come bubbling out. I always knew when she was in the theater watching one of my shows because of that laugh." Alex stopped talking for a moment, seemingly lost in thought.

"I'm glad you had one parent who supported your passion for acting."

Alex moved over to a rail and look out at the long beach and ocean that was becoming harder to see with the setting sun. She dropped Quinn's hand but moved so their bodies were pressing against each other. "She said her favorite thing was to see me onstage. The only times I ever saw her really fight with my father was when they were arguing about my desire to become an actor."

"Why didn't he want you to be onstage if you loved it?"

"Maybe because he didn't want me living in her shadow?" She paused. "He always claimed that he was doing me a kindness. Because he knows what it takes to make it in this business."

"Implying you don't have the talent?"

Alex continued to stare at the ocean, a pained expression across her face. "He didn't just imply it. He told me. He said I was smart enough to be successful in something else. Which I think he thought was a compliment. It's hard to argue against a man the entire city bows down to. And I knew my talent could never touch my mom's."

"Well, I never saw your mother onstage. But I have seen you. And I've seen firsthand from a YouTube video that you have more talent than ninety percent of the actors in this town."

"I think that's a little hyperbolic."

"Doesn't make it not true." She gave Alex a playful nudge. "And stop using big words just to sound smart."

Alex let out a small laugh.

"Did your mom love him?" Quinn asked.

Alex didn't respond for a full minute, and Quinn started to think that maybe she'd gone too far with her questions. When Alex responded, it was in a low, quiet voice. "I know she did. She loved me too, fiercely. But sometimes, I think she didn't know how to do both. She was an amazing mom, but she wasn't perfect. I was alone a lot. Don't get me wrong, she gave me time, certainly far more than my father did, but Horizon was her life too. And I gave up everything to be there with her at the end. And I guess I convinced myself that she let me do that because she believed him and knew NYU was a waste of time. That I just wasn't good enough." Alex's eyes were the clearest Quinn had ever seen them. There was the hint of wetness in the corners but not enough for tears to fall. "I've never told anyone that."

Quinn caressed her face. She moved some hair behind Alex's ear before holding her hand. "Is that why you've given up acting? You don't think you're good enough?"

"I don't know. Maybe. But not anymore. Now it's just too painful. I don't know how to separate what I feel onstage with the loss of my mom. They've always been linked."

"That must have been heartbreaking to let go of."

"But I also love what I do. I get a rush watching the curtain rise on a show that I produced or discovered. Just as much as I did when I was walking out onstage. But one hurts less. Does that make any sense?"

Quinn couldn't imagine a talent like hers going to waste, but she wasn't going to push her on something that caused her so much pain. She knew as well as anyone that having a talent for something didn't mean you had to do it. She could have extended her modeling career into different areas of the fashion world, but it hadn't made her happy. "I do understand that. And I may be biased, but I happen to think you're also very talented off the stage." When Alex quirked her eyebrow in a suggestive way, Quinn lightly smacked her arm. "I meant *in the theater*. Get your mind out of the gutter."

She was happy to hear a small laugh escape Alex's lips. But as she continued looking at Quinn, her face grew serious again, and she seemed like she wanted to say something. She turned out to the water that now looked like a black wall before returning her gaze.

"My mom used to call things that she thought were perfect—you know, things that could never be replicated—*lightning in a bottle*. It was her favorite phrase. She called Coney Island that. The last show she ever saw of mine was *Streetcar,* and she said it about that too. And when I was a kid, she would always say that about me when she kissed me good night." Alex put her arms around Quinn and grazed them up her back. Their faces were close, but Alex didn't seem to be done talking, so Quinn just waited, even though all she wanted to do was kiss her.

Her heart rate was faster with their proximity, and she couldn't help but hold her breath at the intense look Alex was directing her way. "Her words were the first thing I thought of when I saw your show. The first thing I thought of the second the stage light came on, and you were sitting on that stool. Before you even said a word, I knew you were special." Alex brought their lips together, and Quinn was glad because she had no response. Alex's words were the most romantic thing anyone had ever said to her.

There were so many things in her life she could look back on, and how she'd gotten there was clear. But standing on a boardwalk next to the ocean as Alex held her in her arms and kissed her *like that* was something she could never have predicted. And more than any other moment they had shared, when she looked back on tonight, she would be able to identify this as the moment she really began to fall in love.

When their lips parted and Quinn was able to stare into Alex's eyes, she could tell that she was also affected by the moment. Alex brushed her thumb across Quinn's lips as she smiled. "This was an amazing first date," Quinn said. "Thank you for sharing this with me."

"You think I'm just going to take you to get a hot dog and tell you a sad story? I have more game than that, you know."

Quinn let out a quick laugh. "The date's not over?"

"Not even close. But we should go, or we'll be late." Alex guided them along the boardwalk. After only a few more minutes, they stopped in front of a large structure.

Quinn let out a small gasp. "We're going to the aquarium?"

"Is that okay with you?"

Quinn let go of her hand so she could jump up and down like a child. She pulled Alex into a hug.

"I guess that's a yes," Alex said with a laugh.

Quinn knew her face was red, and her hair was probably a mess, but she didn't care. Alex kept outdoing herself, and the anger Quinn had felt all weekend was good as gone. As they walked through the aquarium entrance, she tried to keep pace with Alex and not walk too quickly. The ticket lines were empty, and the place seemed deserted. "Is it closed?" she asked with a frown.

"Not for us."

She had never seen such a young, gleeful expression from Alex, and she knew her own smile matched. "What do you mean? We have the aquarium to ourselves?"

"Not the whole thing, but we'll be able to wander the inside exhibits alone."

Quinn felt speechless. She knew the Anders family was well-connected, but being treated to a night alone in an aquarium seemed like a stretch, even for them. "How did you do this?"

Alex shrugged casually like it wasn't a big deal. "It really wasn't as hard as it seems. My family knows someone on the board of directors."

"This is incredible."

"Unfortunately, I could only get us ninety minutes before the security team needs to do a final sweep and close things up. Someone is waiting for us in the lobby."

"That's more than enough time," Quinn replied, doing her best to control the glee in her voice.

"Ready to see Nemo, Nemo?" Alex said with a wide smile that was so opposite to how she looked only moments ago when she was talking about her mom.

As Quinn nodded and they began walking toward the entrance, she truly couldn't remember ever being on a better date than this one.

CHAPTER TWENTY-TWO

Alex felt lighter than she had in years, and it wasn't hard to figure out why. Visiting Coney Island again and retracing steps she had taken with her mom didn't feel as emotionally taxing as she would have predicted. In fact, talking to Quinn about her mom was probably the first time she didn't feel as if her heart was being torn out at the same time. It felt good.

Courtney had urged Alex to let Quinn see more of her. And the biggest influence on her life had been her mom. She was glad she'd listened to her advice. But while Courtney might have helped with the first part of the date, calling in an incredibly last-minute favor to get access to the aquarium was all Alex. And as she watched Quinn's eyes light up, she was happy that she had.

"What exhibits can we see?" Quinn asked after a security guard let them into the main room. Her focus was solely on the large tank near the right wall of the room.

Alex read the map and pointed. "We'll go through the Conservation Hall to see the Reef Room. Then, we'll go through the exit there to the shark and spineless exhibits."

"Did you just say spineless?"

"Where things like jellyfish and octopuses are. Apparently, there will be a guard there who can show us out once we're done." They didn't have much time, but she also didn't want to rush. Quinn looked like a child seeing wildlife for the first time. The blue from the tank was lightly reflecting onto her face, and Alex had to take a deep breath as Quinn smiled widely.

"Sorry. I know I'm excited, but this is amazing. It's so quiet in here."

"Don't apologize. I love seeing you like this," Alex said, and her stomach gave a flip at her use of the L word. Even if she wasn't saying it directly, she was starting to feel it.

Luckily, Quinn didn't bat an eye, grabbed her hand, and led her through the Conservation Hall. As they made their way into the Reef Room, Quinn dropped her hand in lieu of running to the closest window. "Alex, come see how beautiful they are."

"What kind of fish do you have in LA?"

"They're all angelfish. I had another small species in there, but there was a rumble, and it wasn't pretty."

"A fish rumble? Did they have to agree on weapons?"

"I don't think the Ninja Turtles made it all that fair, to be honest. They came out of it unscathed."

"That's brutal," Alex replied in a serious tone as they continued to gaze at the fish. "Do you have a favorite?"

"I guess I just love them all. I love the quiet way they glide through the water. So regal and sure of their place in the ocean. There are tens of thousands of different species, but they coexist in this ecosystem so much more seamlessly than humans do."

Alex was no longer looking at the fish but at Quinn's perfect profile. "Did you spend a lot of time by the ocean as a kid?"

"A lot. My parents are really into boating. We spent vacations boating through the San Juan Islands. My sister and I tried to identify as many species of sea life that we could. We had this diary that we journaled our discoveries in. I think my love for fish comes from that. That was before modeling, when it was just Eve and me against the world, also known as my parents."

"It must have been nice to have a sister you're so close to growing up. I was always envious of people with siblings."

"It was," Quinn said softly, looking at a particularly colorful fish. "I wouldn't have survived my parents and their extremely high expectations without Eve."

"And does she share your love for fish?"

"No. In fact, when I was younger, I asked her to feed my fish when I was away for a week at camp. And when I got home, two of them had died. She only fed them once that whole week."

"Suddenly, siblings don't sound as great."

Quinn laughed lightly. "That was one of her only transgressions."

"And how do you feel about sharks?"

"Let's go see them and find out," Quinn replied as she slipped her arm through Alex's and led them out the exit that would take them to the building next door.

Even Alex had to admit that the coral reef tunnel in this part of the aquarium was cool to see with no people around rushing them. Quinn simply walked back and forth from one end of the tunnel to the other with her head pointed at the ceiling.

"Did you have any pets growing up?" Quinn asked. "Somehow, that doesn't seem like a thing your dad would allow."

Alex leaned against a wall and watched her skip down the tunnel. "And you're right. No pets. My house was a bit like a museum. One that didn't go with dog hair on the furniture."

Quinn leaned against the wall with her. "That sounds stuffy. And lonely. Not just because of the lack of a dog."

"It was at times. My friends at the private schools didn't really understand why I preferred getting in costume and pretending to be Hamlet over talking about boys. I guess I never really felt as if I connected with anyone until I met Courtney."

"I understand. I felt very similar before I started modeling and met some more like-minded people. And queer ones," she added with a small laugh. "Mikey was my Courtney."

"You two are really close," Alex said. She had seen the easy comfort they shared.

"He's my best friend. And the person I tell everything to, outside of Eve." Quinn opened her mouth to say something only to close it again.

"What's up?"

"I told Mikey about us. Actually, he guessed it. But I feel like you should know." She looked fearful, and Alex felt an instant rush of guilt.

She had been the one to set so many boundaries. She could understand why Quinn feared crossing them. But she also didn't want Quinn to think she was ashamed of their relationship or connection or whatever it was. "That's fine. I don't want you to have to lie to someone you love. I wouldn't ask that. Not now. We just need to be careful at the theater."

"We can trust Mikey," Quinn said, but the worried expression remained.

Alex pushed her fingers lightly into Quinn's brow so she could smooth out the lines. "I know. Thank you for telling me. Now, are you ready for whatever this spineless exhibit is?"

"That's the one I've been most excited to see." Her brow was no longer furrowed, but Alex could tell her mood had shifted slightly.

As they entered the next exhibit, Quinn put her arm back into Alex's and led them to a bench by one of the tanks. Alex could tell something was on her mind, but she didn't want to push, so they both sat in silence as they watched the floating creatures.

When Quinn finally spoke, her voice was quiet. "The other night, you mentioned a scandal of mine from LA."

"I'm sorry. But just so you know, I don't really know anything about what happened, and you don't need to tell me until you're ready. I should never have said that in the first place."

"Maybe you shouldn't have said it *how* you said it. But you weren't wrong. I did have a situation in LA. Mikey was the first to know about that too. And he was also the one who helped clean up my mess. I guess I'm just thinking about it now because I want you to trust him."

"Quinn," Alex said, sliding closer. "I trust you, so I trust him. And I hope that soon, the theater situation won't even matter."

"I want to tell you about Jenna."

Alex placed a small kiss on Quinn's hand. "Only if you want to. And it doesn't have to be tonight among the jellyfish."

Quinn smiled. "I think the jellyfish might help. I'm over her and what happened. I just feel like you should know since it comes out with a simple Google search. Which, by the way, I can't believe you haven't done yet."

Alex shrugged and smiled. "I'm old-fashioned."

"You're a classic," Quinn replied with her own smile before turning to look at the tank again. "Jenna is pretty connected to the fashion industry. She started out as a model when she was younger and had a lot of ties to brands and designers. She ended up doing a collaboration with a designer, and I was in his show at LA Fashion Week a few years ago."

"And that's where you met?"

"Yep. We met at a party after the show. I was fairly established in the industry by then, and she approached me as if she knew who I was. And she was persistent. At first, I resisted. I didn't even go home with her that night when she asked. As far as I knew, she was married. But she got my number from a friend and just didn't let up."

"That doesn't sound very attractive."

"I guess with most people, it wouldn't be. But Jenna wasn't really like anyone I had ever met. And I guess it felt good to get attention from someone like that. You know, someone everyone fawned over. Does that sound terrible?"

"Not to me."

"We hung out a few times, but nothing romantic happened. I wasn't interested in falling for a married woman. Once she convinced me it was over with him, I was just scared about being a rebound. Turns out, both fears were valid."

"So what made you go for it?"

"She was charming and beautiful and incredibly persuasive. And we had a chemistry I couldn't deny. One day, I was over at her house, and there was an envelope on the counter. She *told* me it was her divorce papers."

"It wasn't?"

"I don't know. I assume now that it was a script or something. All I know is that they never officially got a divorce, though they were separated for a time while we were together, since I spent almost every night at her place." Quinn stopped talking for a moment as something large floated slowly by them in the tank. "Slowly, our dynamic changed. We were together, but we couldn't go anywhere. She said she would eventually come out, but I think part of me knew she never would. She was hyper-concerned about her image. And after months of that, you'd think I'd have been the one to pull away, but I had gotten in so deep, and I was so in love with her that I just clung on harder. She may have been the one to pursue me, but slowly, I became the one texting her and asking her where she'd been all night."

"And she was with him?"

"Yes. One night while we were at a private party, we were photographed kissing, and the photos were leaked to the media. The next day, Max came back crawling to her, and she left me in a heap of media attention."

"I'm so sorry. You deserved better," Alex said quietly. Quinn didn't seem sad, though. She'd told the story almost as if it was about someone else. Her voice was the most detached Alex had ever heard. "She sounds like an even bigger asshole than I am."

Quinn laughed, and Alex loved being able to make her smile after such an emotional story. "She would never have done something like this." Quinn waved around the room. "Or taken me to get a simple hot dog because that was what she did with her mom." Quinn put her fingers under Alex's chin so she could lift her face. "You're not an asshole. You're pretty sweet."

"Don't tell anyone. It will ruin the reputation I've taken years to build."

"You should let people see the real you."

Alex could only take so much vulnerability in one night, so she attempted to move the conversation back to Quinn. She was also invested in the story by now. "What happened after she went back to him?"

"There was a messy media storm for a couple of months. She ended up doing an interview where she was asked about me and the photos. She said she's never been queer and only dabbled because she was so heartbroken. I was basically painted as a lesbian predator."

"Did you try to put the truth out there?"

Quinn's jaw clenched, and Alex knew she had hit a nerve. "No. My team thought it would just make me look like 'the other woman.'

Some disgruntled model trying to ride the coattails of Hollywood's elite. I had already made the decision to quit modeling, but that only made it easier. I quit the two agencies I was with. I felt like people were whispering everywhere I went, even if they weren't. After a while of watching me mope around my apartment and drink myself to sleep, Mikey called Eve and her husband, Will. And they had the idea that I go spend some time with them in Seattle. That's when I wrote the show."

"Have you heard from her again?"

"Only to tell me that she'd sic her lawyers on me if I included anything about our past in my show. But that was through her team, and they reached out to Mikey. So only indirectly."

"Thank you for telling me," Alex said when Quinn was quiet again, her focus glued to the tank.

"I think there's a first date rule that you're not supposed to talk about exes. I really broke that one."

Alex laughed and put her arm around the back of the bench so she could pull Quinn in closer. "I'm glad you told me. Besides, we slept together before our first date, so I think we already broke a rule. And who made these rules?" Out of the corner of her eye, she saw a security guard come back into the room, and she knew their time was almost up. "I think we need to go," she said, nodding to the guard. "But I can help you break the rules and tell you my own story. If you want to come back to my place. We can just talk."

Quinn glanced at the security guard before moving in. Alex shifted so that her own body was blocking the guard's view. "You don't have to tell me everything in one night. This has been perfect. And frankly, I don't want to talk anymore."

Alex could feel the small space between them heat up. Quinn's lips were close enough to kiss, but she didn't want to give the security guard a show.

"Take me home," Quinn whispered.

"Let's go, Nemo." Alex pulled her up and led her out of the aquarium.

CHAPTER TWENTY-THREE

A lex looked at her watch for the fifth time since she had entered her father's office. She was used to their weekly check-ins being a grueling affair, but with her mind so distracted by thoughts of a certain person, it felt excruciating to be sitting there.

Rick was leaning on his usual perch by the window, and his attention looked to be about as focused as Alex's.

"I think that about covers it for now. We're in good shape on *Death of a Salesman* with the reviews in. On to the winter gala. We're confirmed on the date?" her father asked Alex.

"November thirteenth. It only gives us two weeks in between the gala and Quinn's opening night, but we had to move the entire winter series timeline up to account for the final show. The set is a bit more extensive than we were expecting, and we need more load in time. But the invites are out, and the main players we would expect to attend have confirmed."

"Young artists think they need so much pizzazz. Good directors need the stage and the actors," Rick said from the window.

Alex was used to comments like that from him. He often spoke in platitudes, and he couldn't seem to understand the value of anything that pushed the traditional envelope. She was the one who pushed for shows that were more experimental.

But she didn't feel the need to debate him or her father on program decisions. They'd made it clear that the winter series was hers. She'd worked for months to painstakingly choose the best productions. And while she might have been a bit biased toward Quinn's show, she was also incredibly proud of the two other artist groups she'd picked. The last one that Rick had just mentioned were a rising group from Berlin, and it was a coup for Horizon to even secure the contract.

"Two weeks isn't much time to drive buzz about her show. How are you planning to sell tickets?" her father asked.

"Quinn's show won't have any trouble selling out. She's one of the biggest names we've had in this theater in years," Alex replied in what she hoped was a bored tone and not a defensive one.

He stared at her for a moment, his typical fake smile plastered on his face. It never seemed to reach his eyes. "A model is not a name, Alexandra. I hope you're not putting too much faith in this experiment."

"This has nothing to do with my faith. Even Janet said that she's received more interest from the media around Quinn's show than any other." She took a steadying breath before she continued. "Janet has secured a *Times* feature that will be coming out on Quinn's show the day after the *Salesman* closing, which should give her a bump even before the gala."

"We've never announced the winter series programming before the gala. That's highly unorthodox."

"The world is changing. How audiences get their info and the things they want to see is changing. We should take advantage of the buzz Quinn's show will give us. The earlier we announce, the easier it is to do that. There really is no reason to wait just because that's what we've always done. We'll still be announcing the other two shows at the gala."

"I'm not sure I agree with you, but the winter series is yours. We're putting our trust in your hands," he replied, his tone making it obvious that he didn't trust her at all.

"If we expand our marketing into new channels, we won't need to rely on the subscription model as much, which we all know is struggling for Horizon." Alex had been on this merry-go-round before, but Quinn's show was the perfect example of how she was trying to veer the theater into the future.

"She's not wrong, Simon," Rick said, and Alex once again appreciated his presence in these meetings. If it was only Alex in this office, her father would just put his fingers in his ears and refuse to listen. At least he pretended to behave in front of Rick.

"And a feature in the *Times* is a new channel?" her father asked her, ignoring Rick's comment.

"No. That's just the exclusive to kick things off. A feature in the Saturday paper still means something. But once that runs, Janet's marketing team will coordinate with Quinn's team, and they'll leverage her highly influential social media channels to create an online campaign." When he just stared stubbornly, Alex finally let her annoyance show. "That's on the internet."

"I know that, Alexandra." His voice took on a distinctive and familiar tone. As if every word was covered in ice.

She knew when to push him and when not to, and by the look of rage simmering just under the surface, now wasn't the time to keep pushing. "If you don't trust me on this, then trust Janet," she continued in a much less combative tone. "She's never failed us before. Nobody knows the New York audience better than her." She intentionally didn't mention the fact that the *Times* feature would also include a quote or two from her, knowing how that would go over. And not for the first time, the whole interview idea made her stomach tighten with anxiety.

Her father began to shuffle the papers on his desk, one of his signs that the meeting was over.

Alex picked up her laptop and stood. "I'll send you both the timeline for the next thirty days once I get back to my office. I'll also send you the agenda for our meeting tomorrow on the spring show. If we want to tease that at the winter gala, we need to make a final decision." She moved to the door.

"The decision has been made. We don't need to have that meeting," her father said, avoiding her eyes.

She looked back over to him. When he continued staring at something on his desk, she looked at Rick, who seemed to be focused on smoothing down his tie. "What do you mean it's already been decided?"

"Rick and I made the decision already."

For a moment, Alex stared at them both. It wasn't unusual for her father and Rick to choose the programming for the Horizon shows, especially if they were the ones directing it, and her father was directing this one. But given her hand in the winter series, plus the fact that he had asked her for recommendations for the spring show, she'd assumed she would be involved. "What did you decide on?"

"Dave Coe's new work," he replied without elaborating.

Alex had trouble schooling her features and simply narrowed her eyes.

"It just had a sold out run in London. He chose Horizon for his New York debut," Rick added in an obvious attempt to appease her.

Her father smirked. "That's in England."

"I know that, Father," she said, mirroring his words from earlier. "Did you look at the options I sent you?"

"Yes. And we decided that this show was the best for our audience."

"Coe's play doesn't have any female characters. Not to mention, some of its more controversial themes have been called misogynistic by the media."

"The decision has been made. Once you are leading things, you can make all the arguments you want. For now, we made the decision as the heads of this theater. You have the winter series."

Alex's heart skipped a beat. "Are you saying you're considering me for Rick's role?" She glanced over at Rick to see if she could gauge a reaction.

Until now, they had been circling around the topic, and she had never directly asked. But with Rick in the room, she figured it was the best time to see if she could get any indication on her future.

"Of course, I am," her father replied as he stood. "But this meeting has run over, and I have an appointment to make."

Alex gave him a small nod, deciding not to push the topic any further. She glanced at Rick again, and he gave her a small wink. She tried not to read too much into that, but there was a small kernel of hope growing in her mind that her father's statement and Rick's warm demeanor might mean something significant. "I'll see you both tonight at the restaurant," she said, leaving the office to go back to her own.

Before she was even back, she pulled out her phone to text Quinn. With back-to-back meetings yesterday and Quinn in rehearsal, she hadn't been able to see her since their date, and she was more than eager to lay her eyes on her again. *Are you still here?* Alex was barely inside her office when a quick reply came to her phone.

Quinn: *Yes, Diego just left. I'm taking a call with my team from the rehearsal room. And maybe waiting for a blond bombshell to come kiss me.*

Alex: *I haven't seen any of those around here.*

Quinn: *Then find a mirror.*

Alex: *Very smooth.*

Quinn: *You're not the only one with game, Ms. Anders*

Alex smiled widely as she sat down at her desk. *Noted, sweetheart. When is your call done?*

Quinn: *Ten minutes. Did you get a permission slip to come see me?*

Alex: *No, but I'm going to anyway.*

Quinn: *I've always loved a bad girl.*

Alex: *Shouldn't you be paying attention to your call?*

Quinn: *Why? They're just talking about me and not to me. I doubt they'd notice if I hung up.*

Alex: *Pay attention to your call. I'll be down soon.*

Quinn: *Bossy, bossy.*

Alex: *I think you like it.*

Quinn: *I know I do. Come boss me around in person.*

Alex's insides went from warm to hot in an instant, and she had to squirm to relieve the throb that hit her pussy the moment she read Quinn's text.

The sensation of being perpetually turned on was something Alex was still getting used to. She had never met anyone who she wanted this much, this often. But she now knew it wasn't just about sex. Since their first date, Alex had felt lighter and happier than she had in years, and she was determined to hold on to that. She sent one last text:

On my way.

CHAPTER TWENTY-FOUR

I was too listening. I heard everything. It was riveting."
"What was the last thing we discussed?"
"That you've canceled all my media engagements for forever."
Quinn picked up the phone she had resting on the bench in her rehearsal room and walked to the mirror.

"Not happening," Mikey replied over the line.

"I don't think we were on the same call then," she said as she gave her reflection a quick once-over and tried to brush some of the wisps back into her hair band.

"We discussed the winter gala," he went on. "It'll be on November thirteenth, across the street from the theater, at the same restaurant that hosted the opening party you went to."

"Right, right," Quinn replied distractedly.

"And next week is your interview with the *Times*. Alex will be joining you for that."

Her attention snapped back to the conversation. "Wait, what?"

"I had a feeling that would get your attention. And now I know why you seem so distracted. I'm guessing things are headed in a positive direction on that front?" Only he would ask her "if things were headed in a positive direction" instead of just asking her if she was still fucking Alex. He was always so proper.

"Yes, good sir. They have progressed splendidly and positively, and we are now courting. Alert the kingdom."

"Anyway," he said, sighing. "She'll be at the interview with you. She may answer a few questions about the winter series and bringing your show to Horizon.

Quinn's mind was finally focused on the conversation and not her reflection, and she moved to lean against the wall. "That's interesting."

"I thought so too. She doesn't seem like the type to do interviews."

"Does she know?"

"It's this Monday, so I assume she does. Janet said they have weekly meetings."

Someone knocked softly on the door, and Alex was standing there with a sexy casual smirk.

Quinn pressed a button on her cell to take Mikey off speakerphone. "I have to go," she said and knew he would be able to detect the lower tone of her voice.

"Tell Alex hello from me."

"I don't know what you're talking about."

He laughed. "Sure you don't. Talk later."

She let her phone drop to her side as she continued to stare. Alex had looked so casual the last two times that Quinn had forgotten how hot her "professional" look was. Today, she had on black slacks, a silky black blouse, a fitted black blazer, and a pair of sexy, closed-toe black heels. No color except the gold watch on her wrist. Her hair shone against the darkness like a ray of sunshine, and Quinn's pussy clenched with need.

"Sorry, I thought you'd be done by now," Alex said in a soft tone.

Quinn put her phone into her back pocket as she tried to control her ogling. "I was actually just talking about you."

"To whom?"

"Mikey. He says hello."

"One of these days, I'll need to get to know him better."

Now more than her pussy clenched. Alex always seemed to surprise her lately, and her stomach fluttered at those words. "I'd like that. I can't stop thinking about you."

Alex closed the door and moved to the wall Quinn was leaning against but didn't come close enough to touch. "I can't stop thinking about you either," she said, leaning so she could face her. "When can I see you?"

"Eager, are we?"

"Yes."

"Good. Tonight?"

"It's my father's birthday," Alex said before scooting closer and pushing some hair behind Quinn's ear. "I have to go to his dinner party. Which I promise will be less fun than what I could get up to with you."

Quinn couldn't keep in a groan. Partly from Alex's answer and partly because Alex's touch made her skin feel like it was on fire.

"Tomorrow?" Alex asked, playing with the collar of Quinn's shirt.

"Okay," she replied as she put her arms around Alex's back and pulled her close. "Wait," she said right as Alex leaned in to kiss the corner of her mouth. "Tomorrow is Friday. I'm having dinner with Tim."

Alex leaned back. "Delvin?"

"Yes, he's taking me somewhere fancy, apparently."

"You really do make friends everywhere you go."

"I like Tim. And I think he'd be perfect for Mikey."

"And how does Mikey feel about you being a matchmaker?"

"He doesn't get an opinion on this."

"I see. And what about after you're done planning his future?"

"I was planning on texting this hot blonde for a booty call," Quinn said, lightly grabbing the collar of Alex's blazer. She couldn't seem to stop touching her.

"You don't need to text. Just come over. I'll tell the front desk."

"What if it's late?"

"I don't care what time it is. I just want you as soon as I can get you."

"You'd also make friends easily if you let people see this side of you."

Alex smiled. "You want people to see *this* side of me?"

"No, not this side," Quinn said, leaning in for a quick peck. "I don't want anyone to see this side."

"Nobody will," Alex replied with a quiet intensity. "But it seems we'll never be alone again."

Quinn laughed when Alex attempted to pout simply by pushing her lip out. She reached out and grabbed it. "Now I see the actress. So dramatic."

"God, sometimes you and Courtney sound so much alike. Except, I don't want to do this to her." She leaned in and took Quinn's mouth in a kiss that was the opposite of a peck.

When Alex's leg slipped between hers and moved upward, Quinn had to break the kiss so she could let out a loud groan and push against the wall. "It's going to be really embarrassing when you keep doing that, and I come still wearing my pants." Despite her warning, she pulled Alex into her so she could feel the pressure again. "You'd be really hot wearing a strap-on," she added, not even thinking about what was coming out of her mouth.

A sharp breath came out of Alex's mouth. Her pupils were blown, making them darker than Quinn had ever seen them. "You'd like that?"

Quinn was so focused on controlling her breathing that all she could manage was a slow nod. "Please," she whispered, causing a flash of something else to cross Alex's eyes.

"That can most definitely be arranged."

Quinn was doing everything she could not to ask Alex to put her hand down her pants. By the way Alex was acting, she would comply. But Quinn was also trying to respect the theater boundaries, and technically, this was her place of work too.

Their trance was broken by the sound of people coming down the hallway outside. The rehearsal rooms never stayed empty for long, and Quinn was used to a constant stream of traffic. "Tomorrow then," she said.

Alex leaned back. "Tomorrow."

Quinn couldn't help but laugh at the sight of Alex attempting to smooth out wrinkles from her blazer that weren't going anywhere. "Well, you look like you were just fucked."

"I think you had something to do with that."

"Better go change before Daddy sees you. I don't want him to come looking for me. That conversation wouldn't be nearly as much fun as this was."

Alex narrowed her eyes before she slowly pushed back up against Quinn. She leaned in until her mouth was just below Quinn's earlobe. "I'm going to change anyway before dinner," she whispered. "I need to take care of the mess you've created." She placed a small kiss on Quinn's cheek and leaned back, smiling. "See you soon."

She was out of the room a moment later, but Quinn could only continue to lean against the wall as she tried to catch her breath. Yesterday, she would have said that she craved seeing more of Alex's softer side. But in this moment, with her pussy screaming for release, she wanted an entirely more primal side of Alex Anders. And she knew that the next twenty-four hours would be excruciating.

CHAPTER TWENTY-FIVE

"A re you going to tell me where you got these now?" Alex asked, grabbing her third doughnut from the box Quinn had brought over, even though she had just complained that she had eaten too many.

"The place always has a line outside. I'm not sure I'm ready to divulge that secret."

"After I shared my favorite bagel place with you, this is the treatment I get?"

"I brought you doughnuts out of the pure kindness of my heart. I don't know why you're complaining about anything."

Alex smiled and set her doughnut on the coffee table, scooting closer to Quinn on the couch. She lightly grazed her fingers against Quinn's free hand. "You're right. You're the perfect woman."

Quinn lowered the doughnut hovering by her mouth. "Just don't tell Mikey. He thinks I need to eat more vegetables." She raised one eyebrow before taking an exaggerated bite. "I disagree," she finished with a full mouth.

"You are so damn cute," Alex replied, wiping something off her lips.

Quinn lowered the hand holding the doughnut. She could tell that the energy between them was changing. But tonight, she didn't want to rush anything. She wanted to savor having an entire night with Alex.

Alex wiped her hands on a napkin and leaned back against the couch, keeping her hand laced in Quinn's. "Speaking of Mikey, does he know about his betrothal to Tim yet?"

Quinn joined her by leaning into the couch. "Not yet. But Tim seems into the idea. He got cute and shy when I mentioned it. He says he doesn't date much. Is that true?"

"I don't know him that well outside of theater events."

"You don't seem to hang out with anyone besides Courtney."

"I've never been someone with a lot of friends. Courtney is all I need."

"Is she?" Quinn asked with a small smile. "All you need?"

Alex pulled Quinn's hand more firmly into her own and returned the smile. "I'm starting to think maybe there's room for one more."

They were quiet for a moment as they stared at each other. Ever since their date, there'd been a different kind of comfort between them. Every quiet moment or intense look tempted Quinn to utter words she wasn't ready to say yet. Words she *knew* Alex wasn't ready to say. "I wish we could just stay here eating doughnuts," she said, moving the conversation to a safer topic.

"Like, forever?"

"I was thinking the weekend but good to know where your head is at."

"Look, doughnuts do things to me."

"I'll have to keep that in mind."

"You're just trying to get out of your *Times* interview on Monday. I know how you feel about media engagements."

Quinn scrunched her nose. "I forgot about that. Way to ruin the mood."

Alex shrugged. "It's what I do best."

"Mikey told me you'd be making a guest appearance."

"Are you okay with that?"

"Of course. I think it's amazing you're getting credit for what you do at Horizon. But I guess when Mikey told me, my first feeling was surprise that you wanted to do it."

Alex seemed to waver between concern and indecision. "I don't know," she mumbled, almost too quiet.

"What don't you know?"

"Janet thinks that if I'm featured in the article as part of Horizon's recent success, my father will have to give me Rick's job. Courtney thinks she's right."

"And do you?"

"My father cares about his image and the image of the theater more than anything." She let out a humorless laugh. "He leans on the romance of a 'father and daughter run theater' when asked. But he never would offer that up as his own narrative."

"And you think it will make him angry?"

"My existence makes him angry."

"It doesn't make me angry," Quinn replied, practically sitting in Alex's lap.

"And you're not mad that I'm intruding on your spotlight?"

Quinn brushed her lips across Alex's jaw, eliciting a small sigh. "Please intrude. I'd be happy if you just did the whole interview," Quinn said, turning Alex's head so she could move her lips down her neck.

"Poor, baby," Alex breathed out as Quinn continued. "A media darling. That's the price you pay for being beautiful, talented, and wanted."

Quinn pulled her head back, her breathing heavy. Alex appeared ready for their conversation to be over. "Do you want me?"

Alex stared at her for only a moment before standing. "Bedroom. Now." She turned down the hallway leading to the bedroom, not even waiting for Quinn to reply or follow.

In a way, it reminded her of the first time they'd met, when Alex had so casually commanded her to follow for the tour of the theater. But this time, she knew exactly what the end of their tour held and followed without question.

When she entered the bedroom, Alex turned on some low lights on the nightstand and grabbed a bag from her bed. She moved toward the bathroom on the other side of the room. "I'll be back, sweetheart. Make yourself comfortable."

Quinn was far too aware of what was to come to relax. So she opted to take her time looking around while she waited for Alex to return and make good on her promise.

Chapter Twenty-six

When Alex stepped out of the bathroom, Quinn was on the other side of the room looking at the one photo on her dresser. Alex didn't want to talk about her mom tonight, so she waited.

When Quinn turned, her eyes seemed to zero in on Alex's bare shoulders and exposed neck. She had changed into a simple white tank top and a pair of loose jeans that rode her hips. She had put her hair up into a messy bun since she knew she wouldn't want it in her way tonight.

She felt a rush of arousal when Quinn's eyes moved down her body, focusing on her braless tits before fixing on the pants that were already unbuttoned. "Take off your clothes," Alex said in a quiet voice.

"Very demanding," Quinn replied, but her tone didn't hold any playfulness. She sounded as turned on as Alex felt.

"I'm waiting."

She knew Quinn liked when she took control, and by the look in Quinn's eyes and her complying hands, Alex could tell that tonight was no exception to that. After removing her shoes, Quinn started to unbutton her pants when Alex stopped her.

"No. Start with your shirt."

Quinn froze before she quickly removed her silk blouse. When the shirt was on the floor, she didn't move to take anything else off, waiting for her next command.

Alex was in awe of how well Quinn seemed to be able to read what she wanted. Ever since their first time together, their bodies and minds seemed to work so seamlessly that it was as if they were made to come together like this. "Bra," she said next.

Quinn didn't move her eyes off Alex as her hands went behind her back to remove her bra. The room was so quiet that the sound of it hitting the floor reverberated across the space.

"Pants now, sweetheart."

Quinn returned to her half-buttoned pants and slid them slowly down her legs. When they were off, she moved her hands to the waistband of her panties but stopped when she heard Alex's voice again.

"Leave them on. But you can take your socks off. I don't think you'll need those." She couldn't hide the hint of amusement in her tone as she looked at Quinn standing there almost naked in a pair of black socks.

"Just following orders," Quinn sassed back.

"Next time, I'll be more explicit." As Quinn straightened, Alex let her eyes roam over every inch of her body. "I'll never get over how gorgeous you are."

"I don't want you to," Quinn replied.

Alex's heart skipped a beat. Even though her body was still vibrating with arousal, she also felt a surge of something else. Something entirely more intimate. She took a deep breath and let it out slowly, hoping Quinn couldn't see how affected she was. "Now come here," she said, holding back any larger declarations brewing inside.

As Quinn walked over, Alex quickly discarded her shirt. She gently placed Quinn's hands on the waistband of her pants. "Take them off," she said.

Quinn only had to undo the last two buttons, which she did at a painfully slow pace. Alex helped her move the jeans down her legs and felt a wave of satisfaction at Quinn's small gasp. She grazed her fingers over the soft leather harness wrapped around Alex's body. Alex had always felt sexy wearing a strap-on, but no woman had ever looked at her the way Quinn was, and it made her entire body heat up with need.

"Fuck, babe," Quinn whispered. "You look so hot. God, I want you so much."

"It doesn't even have my dildo in it yet," Alex said, walking Quinn to the foot of the bed. She gently pushed her down. "But I'm glad you're happy with the harness choice. It's new."

"For me?" Quinn asked with an adorable expression.

"Yes, for you. Put your head on the pillows."

Quinn slid up the mattress until she was lying against the pillows. She put her arms above her head and watched as Alex walked to the nightstand and pulled out a dildo and a bottle of lube.

"This is also new," she said as she lay next to Quinn. "And also for you."

Quinn didn't seem to have much patience and moved on top. Their mouths found each other in a rushed, wet kiss. Alex allowed Quinn to grind on the harness for only a moment before she flipped them over so she was above.

She brought her mouth down on the tits that had been teasing her since Quinn had taken her clothes off. She circled both nipples with her tongue before sucking each into her mouth. Quinn squirmed, and as Alex pushed her body down, Quinn let out a low groan.

"Please, babe. Please, touch me," Quinn begged.

"I am," Alex replied in an innocent tone as she pinched Quinn's nipples.

Quinn let out a quick moan and closed her eyes. Alex did it again, pulling harder than before. "Mmm, fuck. Touch my pussy. Please. *Please.* I may come from just your mouth on my tits."

"Then I don't need to touch your pussy," Alex teased again as she brought her mouth back down.

"*Alex*. Please, fuck me. *Please.*"

Quinn was writhing beneath her, and she couldn't drag this out any longer. She let go of Quinn's nipple with a pop and slid her body down the length of the bed between her legs. She could smell how aroused Quinn was, and that only increased as she slowly brought her soaked underwear down her legs.

"I love seeing how wet you get for me," Alex said before placing a soft kiss on the inside of Quinn's thigh.

Quinn could only seem to moan, her eyes shut and her hands grabbing at her own hair. Alex couldn't help but smile. She decided not to tease her any longer and pushed her legs open wider. She was craving the taste of Quinn's pussy, and she also wanted to make sure she was wet enough for her.

As Alex's tongue hit Quinn's wet folds, the sweet, musky taste overrode any other thoughts, and she became lost in the scent and taste. She licked the length of Quinn's pussy, savoring the flavor. "You taste amazing," she breathed out. She slid her tongue up Quinn's wet folds again and focused tight circles on her clit. It began to harden under her tongue, and Quinn's moans grew louder.

When she pulled away and crawled back up the bed, Quinn let out a soft sound of protest until she saw what Alex was grabbing. "Let me," she said as she took the dildo out of Alex's hands.

Alex got on her knees, and Quinn sat up so she could slide the cock into the harness. She looked so sexy doing it that Alex couldn't help stroking her hair before gently lifting her face. She placed one soft kiss on her lips. "There's lube on the nightstand," she whispered.

"I don't need the lube. Just fuck me."

Alex went in for another kiss, but this time, it wasn't quick or sweet as she slid her tongue into Quinn's mouth and gripped her hair. Quinn broke the kiss as she fell back onto the mattress. She pulled her legs up and grabbed her ankles so her pussy was open and waiting.

Alex could have stayed there staring at her in that position all night, but she made herself look away so she could lean one hand above Quinn and use her other to guide the dildo to her wet opening.

Quinn let out a high-pitched moan the moment Alex entered her, but Alex didn't move in more than an inch until Quinn opened her eyes. Her mouth was hanging slightly open in a silent moan.

"Say it again," Alex commanded.

"Fuck me. *Please*."

The verbal consent was so sexy that Alex didn't want to tease, pushing the dildo inside in one swift motion. She put both hands above Quinn's head and began a slow rhythm as she let Quinn get used to the sensation.

Quinn didn't seem to need it. She grabbed Alex's back with both hands and pushed her body up as she let out a low groan. "More, babe. Don't go slow." She panted, scraping her short fingernails down Alex's back.

Alex extended her arms on the bed, pushing up on her knees. She drove herself in deeper before setting a faster pace. She kept her body steady and could feel Quinn's nipples grazing her own as her hips moved in a fast rhythm. The faster she pushed, the harder Quinn grabbed her back, urging her on.

"Tell me what you want," Alex breathed against Quinn's ear.

"Harder, please. Just fuck me harder," Quinn screamed.

Alex lifted her hands off the bed and leaned back to grab Quinn's hips and pull her forward. She switched from quick pumps to long, deep thrusts that brought her pelvis all the way against Quinn's.

"Yes, yes, yes. Just like that. Fuck, I'm so close. Don't stop!"

Each thrust caused Alex's pussy to clench, bringing her closer to her own orgasm. But she didn't want to come like that. Right now, she wanted to be focused on Quinn's pleasure. "You're so fucking sexy. Come for me, sweetheart," Alex replied in a voice that sounded strangled with arousal.

Her words seemed to send Quinn over the edge because a second later, she shoved her hands into her hair and screamed. "I'm coming. I'm coming. Fuck, Alex!"

Alex drove in a few more times so she could squeeze out the last drop of Quinn's orgasm. As Quinn's screams died, she slowed the pace but didn't remove herself completely.

"Mmm, babe. God, that was amazing." Quinn sighed, relaxing.

Alex bent her head to place a soft kiss on Quinn's lips, guiding herself out with her hand.

Quinn gasped slightly, and Alex could tell by the look on her face that she wasn't done for the night.

Once she pulled out, Alex got up on her knees, her chest rising and falling as she attempted to catch her breath. Without saying anything, she pulled the part of the harness touching her pussy aside and gave Quinn a pointed look.

Quinn seemed to understand what Alex needed and moved so they were both kneeling in front of each other. She cupped the back of Alex's head. The depth of her eyes seemed to go on forever. She slid a finger down Alex's naked body until she was gliding through her folds under the harness.

Alex closed her eyes and let out a long groan that she had been holding in since they'd started fucking. She knew she wouldn't last long, even with Quinn teasing her with small, light strokes. "Put your fingers inside me," Alex commanded, and her voice was steadier than her knees.

Quinn complied easily, sliding two fingers inside. Her knuckles hit the harness as she brought them out and pumped them back in, but she didn't seem to mind.

Alex's breathing became ragged as Quinn increased the pressure of her thrusts. But soon, those thrusts began to slow, and Alex's pussy clenched in protest. "Faster, sweetheart."

But this time, Quinn stopped her hand completely. She gave Alex a small, almost innocent smile. Slowly, she bent so that her mouth was close to the dildo. Alex had a feeling she knew what Quinn was doing, but part of her almost didn't believe she would be so bold.

Quinn began to pump her fingers in and out of Alex's pussy at a slow, deliberate pace as she grabbed the base of the dildo. "I want to taste myself on you," she whispered right before she set her mouth on the head and began licking away her own juices.

"Jesus, Quinn," Alex said, not able to say anything more. She had never seen anything more erotic than Quinn bringing her tongue up the length of her shaft as her fingers continued to pump, getting slightly faster with each stroke.

Alex wanted nothing more than to be able to prolong this moment and sear it into her memory, but her body had other plans as her legs shook uncontrollably. "I'm going to come. Faster," she said, putting her hand on Quinn's head. She couldn't feel Quinn's mouth, but when Quinn let out a low moan, the sound mixed with the vibration sent Alex over the edge. "I'm coming. *Fuck.*"

Alex wasn't quiet in the bedroom. She loved to talk throughout sex. But usually, the woman she was with was always louder when they came. But Quinn had a secret code to make Alex lose control of her vocal cords because she moaned and let out a series of expletives as Quinn lifted her head off the dildo but continued to pump her fingers in and out of Alex's pussy.

When Alex was too sensitive for more, she gently put her hand on Quinn's wrist to indicate that she was done. Quinn removed her fingers and came back up on her knees. "Was that okay?" she whispered.

"That was maybe one of the best moments of my life," Alex replied. When Quinn still looked a bit uncertain, Alex cupped her chin and waited until she met her eyes. "That was amazing. And so sexy. And somehow, it's like you know everything I want and need. Things I've never even told other women I enjoy."

Quinn's eyes softened, clear emotion shining in them.

Alex took off her harness and gently pulled Quinn down onto the bed and into her arms.

Quinn turned so they were facing each other. "I don't even know how to tell you how amazing that was."

"It was for me too."

"And now we get to experience my third favorite activity of all time."

"Sleeping?"

"Mm-hmm," Quinn responded through a yawn.

"And what are numbers one and two?"

"Number one is being fucked by you, and number two is eating."

Alex let out an exaggerated gasp. "You mean, I've surpassed bread?"

"I know. I'm surprised too."

"Sex over carbs?"

"You over carbs."

"Good thing you don't have to choose. I like bread too."

"That's a relief. And me? Do you like me?"

Alex moved closer so that their noses were almost touching, and their heads shared a pillow. "I more than like you, Quinn."

"That's a relief too."

Alex placed a soft kiss on Quinn's lips before pulling back an inch. "Sweet dreams, my beautiful girl."

"Sweet dreams, babe," Quinn said before her eyes closed.

Alex watched her sleep for only a moment before the night's activities caught up with her, and her own eyes closed.

CHAPTER TWENTY-SEVEN

Quinn woke slowly the next morning, allowing her eyes to take their time opening. Before her mind could even process the fact that it was awake, Alex's words from the previous night began rolling around in her head: *I more than like you, Quinn.*

She tried to control her growing smile, but it was of little use. Everything about yesterday felt right. From hanging out with Alex on the couch to their impossibly hot sex after, she felt as if she could feel her heart swelling.

When she turned her head and saw that Alex's space was empty, she wasn't entirely surprised. It seemed that Alex lived off very little sleep, while Quinn could probably take a nap standing up at a rock concert.

She walked into Alex's living room and was blinded by the light coming in the windows. When she didn't see Alex on the couch, she made her way to the large kitchen and saw her at a table looking showered, fresh, and beautiful. If this was how Alex looked right when she woke up, Quinn might start to feel a bit self-conscious. The clock on the oven said it wasn't even eight yet.

Quinn hadn't bothered to look at her reflection before walking barefoot to the kitchen. She had thrown on a pair of sweats and a T-shirt she'd found and assumed she looked more than a little disheveled. Her hair always had a party of its own in the morning.

"Good morning, beautiful. Bagel? Coffee?" Alex asked as Quinn took the seat next to hers. Alex had a cup of coffee in front of her as well as what looked like a script.

"Both, please."

Alex moved around the kitchen until there was a black cup of coffee in front of Quinn as well as jars of sugar and cream. "I'd make your coffee, but the amount of cream and sugar you use scares me."

"I like sweet things," Quinn joked, watching Alex put a bagel plate in front of her. She didn't hesitate to grab one and apply a generous amount of schmear. "What are you reading?"

"My father made his selection for the spring show, so I was just reading the script."

"Do you like it?" The scowl that crossed Alex's face was telling enough. "That bad?"

Alex closed the script and tossed it away. "It's worse than bad. It's a complete sexist mess. It has a sold out run in London right now, and my father is friends with the playwright. Even the theater world has an old boy's club."

"What's it about?"

"It follows a man as he attempts to hide a lifelong affair from his wife."

"That sounds terrible."

"It gets worse. They only talk about the wife and the mistress. You never see them onstage. It's all focused on the lead man and his best friend."

"I assume you didn't have a huge say in Horizon doing that one?"

"No, I only found out this week. I thought maybe the winter series was just the start of my leadership in the company. And that I'd be brought in for that discussion, but he and Rick made the choice on their own."

"Maybe they thought you'd try to veto it."

"No doubt." Alex pointed at the script. "This is exactly the type of content I've been veering Horizon away from. And until this season, my father wasn't fighting it all that hard. Even Simon Anders seemed able to see the writing on the wall as to where theater is headed."

"What do you think changed?"

"The only thing that has changed is that he gave me the winter series to handle on my own. And that Rick is retiring."

"Maybe he knows you're the best one to take over for Rick. And he's just resisting."

Alex stared at the table, seemingly lost in thought. Her brow furrowed in the way Quinn had seen before.

"What are you thinking about, babe? I don't know exactly what that look means yet, but it's never been good."

Alex eyes were unguarded and open. "Just thinking about later today."

"Our interview? What has you worried?" She placed her hand on Alex's.

"Last week, my father alluded to me taking over for Rick. He's never said anything about that before, even though he knows I want the job. And I'm afraid doing this interview is too bold. That it'll tip him in the other direction." She twirled her cup as she spoke, seemingly more anxious about today than she was probably letting on.

Quinn wished she knew more about Alex's dad so she could give some real advice. Alex's fears could be completely justified if Simon Anders was the asshole she had heard he was. "I understand why you're worried. And granted, I don't know your dad very well, but this article isn't about you taking over at Horizon, right? It's just about a show in a series you're producing. It's not unusual to include some statements from someone at the helm. What does Janet think?"

"Exactly what you just said. It'll just be a few quotes from me. The rest will be about you. I won't even be in the photo."

"Aw, but we look so cute together," Quinn said, trying to lighten the mood. "Are we being interviewed together or separately?"

"Doesn't your team go over all that with you?"

"They do, but I rarely listen. Mikey is picking me up from my apartment, and there was something said about hair and makeup at the theater. And something else about a photo shoot on the roof. And something else about you. And then I got lost in sexy fantasies."

Alex laughed, and the sound made Quinn's stomach flutter. Alex's laugh didn't come out easily, but when it did, it was a low, sexy sound that Quinn could feel vibrate through her entire body. "You must be a handful to manage, sweetheart," Alex said.

Quinn laughed. "You have no idea."

"We won't be together for the interview. You'll go first, and then they'll set up the photo shoot. While the photographer takes some shots of you, I'll answer a few questions with the reporter."

"Someone pays attention in class."

"I do run the theater."

"It's so hot when you're all boss-like." She got up and slid onto Alex's lap. But just as their lips were meeting in a soft kiss, her phone vibrated in her pocket. She let out a small groan before she looked. "Shit. I have to go. Mikey is going to be at my place soon, and he hates when I'm late."

Alex pushed some of Quinn's hair behind her ear and smiled. "Which I'm guessing is all the time."

"Like, *all the time*." She leaned in for another kiss.

Alex laughed against her lips. "Quinn, you need to go."

"You and Mikey really would be a match made in heaven," Quinn said as she rested her forehead against Alex's.

"I can see one or two problems with that."

"Good, because I'm not sharing you." She gave Alex one more kiss and reluctantly stood. "I'm wearing these sweats home, just so you know."

"Keep them," Alex said as she also got up. "They look cute on you."

Quinn turned at the entrance of the kitchen. "I'll see you in a bit?" Alex nodded and looked into her eyes with a tenderness Quinn didn't think she could ever tire of. "You know you won't be able to look at me like that once I'm all dolled up and ready for my photo shoot."

"I do have an acting background. I think I can handle it."

A mischievous smile settled on Quinn's lips. "You haven't seen my dress yet."

❖

Quinn's apartment was only twenty blocks uptown from Alex's, but as she made her way out of the high-rise, the morning chill hit her. Instead of walking, she found the first cab she could and hopped in.

She cringed when she felt her phone vibrate again, assuming it was Mikey checking on her timing, but when she looked, her sister was calling. "You're up early," she said as she answered the call, leaning back against the seat of the warm cab.

"I'm a teacher. School starts early. I'm slightly surprised to hear you sound so chipper before nine."

"If you thought I'd be sleeping, why did you wake me up?"

"Because I don't care?"

"Fair enough. Anyway, lucky for you, I am up. I have an interview and photo shoot at the theater soon."

"Oh, I'll let you go then. I just wanted to say hi since I haven't heard from you in two weeks."

"It's not for two hours. I'm on my way home now," she said casually, even though she knew Eve would pick up on her meaning.

"On your way home from where, might I ask?"

"I met someone," Quinn said tentatively. But after a minute of silence, she thought maybe the call had cut out. "Eve?" she asked when all she could hear was some shuffling noise.

"Sorry, I had to get comfortable for this. Now, repeat what you just said."

"I said I met someone."

"Okay, jut making sure. Now tell me more. Who is she?"

The cab slowed in front of Quinn's apartment building, and she cradled the phone on her shoulder as she paid and jumped out. "She works at Horizon," she said as she rushed into the building and made her way to the elevators.

"Interesting. In what capacity?"

"She's the managing director. Her name is Alex Anders."

"Anders," Eve said slowly. "Why do I know that name?"

"I have no idea." When she made it back into her apartment, she looked at the time on her phone and noted that she had fifteen minutes before Mikey would arrive. Not much time to wash the sex off her body.

"I think Mikey may have mentioned it at some point," Eve said.

"How often do you and Mikey talk?" Quinn asked as she went into her bathroom.

Eve laughed. "More often than you'd like to know. Doesn't this Alex own the theater or something? I think that's what Mikey said."

"Her dad does. He's the artistic director. And a complete asshole."

"And how does he feel about you dating his daughter?"

"He doesn't know. Nobody can know until the show opens. It's kind of complicated."

"That must be hard."

"Are you going to tell me to be careful like Mikey?" Quinn took off Alex's sweats and T-shirt.

"No, Quinney. I know you will be."

"She's not Jenna," she said as she leaned against her counter.

"Of course she isn't. And you did nothing wrong with Jenna. She was the witch."

Quinn smiled into her phone. For Eve, calling someone a witch was about as bad as it got.

"Do you like her?" Eve asked next.

"I think I love her," Quinn whispered, even though she was alone. She wasn't expecting that to come out, but there was something about Eve's understanding tone that always caused her to be her most honest.

"Tell me about her."

"She's not like anyone I've ever dated before. She comes across as kind of closed off at first. Maybe a bit reserved and serious. But she's soft and romantic too. She's sweet to me. And funny. And she's so talented and doesn't even realize it."

"I don't think I've ever heard you be so effusive about a woman. You hardly talked to me about Jenna."

"I never trusted Jenna. And I was embarrassed at how I let her treat me. But Alex is different. She's special."

There was a pause before Eve spoke again. "Wow. She's really hot."

"Did you just google her?"

"Of course. And wow. I may leave Will and hop a plane to New York to steal her from you."

"Bring it, sis. But I should tell you that she seems to like me a lot."

"Do you think she's in love with you?"

Quinn's stomach dropped, and she paused. She knew Alex felt something deep, but she struggled to process her own emotions. Whether or not Alex was aware of her feelings, Quinn simply didn't know. "I don't know. But I think she may be close."

"I'm really happy for you. You deserve it."

"It's all really complicated. We're not even an official couple."

"You've got a lot going on with the show. Maybe it's not the worst thing to take it slow until opening."

"Always the voice of logic," Quinn replied with a smile. "Anyway, I'd love to talk longer, but Mikey will be here soon to pick me up, and I'm not showered yet."

"Tell him hi for me. And call me later. I want to know how rehearsals are going."

"I will. Send my love to Will, who I assume is still sleeping."

Eve laughed. "You know him well. Love you. Talk soon."

When the call ended, Quinn turned on her shower and jumped in as fast as she could. Mikey would have to wait, but talking to Eve had been worth it.

CHAPTER TWENTY-EIGHT

The rain has gotten worse, so we're setting-up in the lobby. Ready for you in 10.

Alex read the latest text from Janet and began to shut down her laptop so she could make her way to the lobby. She had been getting updates from her all morning on various changes to the plan, the weather being the latest.

She hadn't heard from Quinn since that morning, but if Janet was ready for her, it must have meant Quinn's interview was done, and she was about to shoot the photos. Alex was hoping she'd get a glimpse of the photo shoot anyway, so she didn't really mind the change in location.

In the lobby, the lights were set up on the far side of the room near the balcony staircase. Alex assumed that was where they would be taking the photo of Quinn, but so far, she didn't see her.

Like always, Alex heard Janet before she saw her. "My dear, hello," Janet called as she came over and leaned in to kiss her cheek. "Perfect timing. Jeremy just ran to take a call but is ready for you."

Jeremy Hart. The latest change in the plan. Janet had informed Alex that morning that the reporter writing the feature would be an entertainment writer and not a theater writer. Janet reasoned that Quinn's involvement made the story transcend theater. Alex didn't know if she agreed, but it was too late to do anything about it. She just hoped Jeremy had at least seen a play before.

"Where are we doing this?" she asked.

"Right here is fine. This is where he sat with Quinn." Janet pointed to the long bench against the wall.

Alex stomach fluttered, and she had to remind herself of what she'd told Quinn earlier. She needed to act unaffected, especially by just the mention of Quinn's name.

"I'm going to go check on our little star. I'll send Jeremy over when he's ready," Janet said and walked off.

Alex pulled out her phone to scroll through emails as she waited. A text from Quinn popped up, causing a smile to cross her face: *You look sexy sitting over there all serious in your blazer.*

Her eyes snapped up to see Quinn standing by the photographer, who was in the middle of a conversation with Janet. She was grateful their focus was elsewhere since all her acting abilities went out the window the moment she saw Quinn.

She was wearing a tight burgundy dress. It could almost pass as conservative with long sleeves and buttons that led up to a high, mock neck. But the sleeves were sheer, as was the bodice. It was also so short that Alex's eyes were drawn to her long, smooth legs.

Alex forced her attention back to her phone. She smiled again when she saw the text waiting for her: *You're staring, Anders.*

I don't know what you're talking about. Focus on your photo shoot.

They're still setting up. Plus, need I remind you that this isn't my first photo shoot?

In that case, let me tell you that you look stunning.

Quinn smiled at her phone. When Alex looked back down, she almost dropped hers:

Will it distract you during your interview if I tell you that I can still feel you?

The text sent an immediate throb to Alex's pussy, and she again wondered at Quinn's effect on her. She fumbled with typos before she was able to respond: *You're making this very difficult, sweetheart.*

Then I won't tell you that I haven't stopped being wet since last night. And every time I think about you fucking me, my pussy clenches in this tiny red thong I'm wearing.

Alex closed her eyes and took a deep breath. When she opened them, Quinn was talking to the photographer, and she exhaled in relief. Not that she didn't enjoy their sexy conversation, but she didn't know how much longer she could maintain a neutral facade.

"Ms. Anders?" a young man asked as he walked up to her, jarring her out of any inappropriate thoughts.

"Yes, hi. You must be Jeremy Hart." She extended her hand.

"It's great to meet you," he replied as he shook her hand. "Big fan of what you guys have going on here." He twirled his finger around the lobby.

It wasn't just that he came off as disingenuous; there was also something smarmy that Alex didn't like. He was younger than most of the theater writers she had met over the years, around her age or maybe younger. And his coifed hair, tight jeans, and fake bowling shirt made him look like a hipster who'd rather go to a local trivia night than see a play.

"Thank you," she replied. "Should we start?"

As they both sat on the bench, Janet made her way over to them and sat next to Alex. "Oh good. You've met," she said. "Don't mind me, Jeremy. I'll just listen in."

Alex had been around the theater scene long enough to know how these media engagements worked, but she had rarely been interviewed. Janet had assured her she would be watching over things on behalf of the theater to make sure the agreed upon story was adhered to. And in that moment, Alex was grateful she was sitting there.

"As I understand it, this is your first year at the helm of the winter series, is that correct?" Jeremy asked, sounding bored.

"I've been involved for many years, but this is my first year leading the program from start to finish."

"And how did you come across Quinn Collins and *Model Behavior*?"

"A friend who works at Horizon told me about her show, and it sounded intriguing. There are a lot of hidden gems in the New York festival circuit. And I'm just lucky enough to have happened upon one as amazing as *Model Behavior*."

"Since becoming managing director, you've also led the charge on other programming, including choosing the rental companies that come into the space. Where do you see the future of Horizon going?"

"Audiences are changing, and with that, the arts need to adapt. I want to produce shows that are inclusive and showcase the modern human experience. It's not to say we can't honor traditional work, but for theater to survive the streaming culture, we need to appeal to younger audiences. And they expect progressive thinking. They expect us to push the envelope. I want Horizon to be at the forefront of that change. One that is accessible and relatable to everyone in New York and not just the elite."

"And do you think that change is the reason the theater has seen an increase in revenue over the past couple of years?"

The question caught Alex off guard. She hadn't expected an entertainment writer to do his research on theater finances. "Yes. I think when theaters can shift focus away from the subscription model and focus on targeting each show to the right audiences, they'll see a change for the positive. But it's also about what kind of programming theaters choose. And making sure they diversify that programming."

The interview went on for a bit, with Jeremy asking one mundane question after another. When they appeared to be wrapping up, Janet interrupted. "I need to go make sure the photographer has what she needs. I'll be back. But you have what you need?" she asked Jeremy.

"Yep. I'll just finish up here with one or two more questions." He seemed to wait for Janet to leave before turning to Alex with an entirely less polite smile. "What is it that intrigues you about lesbian content?"

She was more than a little thrown by the sudden question and the cutting tone behind it. "I don't choose shows based on that, Mr. Hart. I choose the best show," she replied slowly.

"Of course. And have you always been interested in fashion?"

He was baiting her, and she was determined not to fall into his trap. She wished Janet would come back. "The three shows for the winter series all bring a unique voice to our theater. The themes matter to me just as much as the topic itself."

He looked at her for a moment before glancing at the notepad in front of him. "There was an actress who worked here four years ago," he said. "Sloane Dyer. Tell me what happened there."

She felt all the blood drain from her face, and for a moment, she just opened and closed her mouth, not able to get anything out. "What?" she finally whispered back.

"Sloane Dyer. She was an actress here. I'm sure you remember. Is it true she sued you for sexual harassment?"

Alex stood as fast as she could make her legs work, which with the way her whole body was shaking, wasn't very fast. "This interview is done."

"Alex, what's wrong?" Janet was walking back.

"This interview is supposed to be about the winter series. Not my personal life," Alex directed at Janet.

"And you're absolutely right. This interview is over, Jeremy," Janet said to him in a sterner tone than Alex had ever heard from her. She moved in front of her. "Go. I'll take care of this," she said in a quiet voice. "I'll call you later."

Alex didn't even look at Jeremy again and turned to the nearest entrance that would take her into the theater from the lobby. Once she was alone in the dark, she allowed herself to breathe. She slid into a chair halfway to the stage and put her face in her hands.

Her mind was racing, and she couldn't seem to get her heart rate under control. She'd had reservations about doing this interview but not because she thought the past would come up. She thought if anything, her father's ego might be hurt that she'd received some attention from the media instead of him. She had to talk to Janet before Jeremy made this into a story.

Alex had known that eventually, everything could get out. After all, the theater world was a small one. But after years of silence, Alex had started to think it wouldn't. But Sloane must have talked, which Alex still didn't understand. She had walked away from that situation with her reputation intact and money in her pocket.

She assumed the reporter and photographer were still in the building, hopefully already being handled by Janet, so she sank farther into the theater chair, closed her eyes, and waited.

❖

Quinn couldn't hear anything from all the way across the room, but she knew Alex's face well enough to know that she wasn't happy as she walked into the theater. She couldn't follow without making it obvious, so she waited until Janet came back to the photographer, and they decided they had what they needed.

"Thank you, Quinn. You've been wonderful," Janet said, looking up from the shot she was being shown on the camera.

"Thanks. I have rehearsal soon, so I should be going," Quinn said quickly as she grabbed her bag. It wasn't a complete lie. She did have rehearsal with Diego that afternoon, but she had other plans before she went. When Janet was focused on talking to the photographer, she moved to the same theater entrance Alex had gone through. The theater was dark as she walked in, but she could see Alex's hair peeking over a chair. "Hey, you," she said quietly as she slid into a seat in the row behind her. She put her arms on the chair in front of her and leaned in.

Alex didn't respond.

"I can go if you need to be alone." She didn't want to leave, but she also could tell that Alex was in emotional pain.

Alex shifted so she could put a hand on Quinn's arm. "I don't want you to go. We won't be bothered in here," she mumbled, moving her hand so she could rub her face.

"What happened, babe?" When Alex didn't respond, Quinn moved to the same row so she could sit next to her. "Alex. Talk to me. Tell me what happened."

Alex took in a long breath before she started talking in a low voice. "There was a woman. About four years ago. Her name was Sloane."

"Is this the story you were going to tell me in the aquarium?"

Alex nodded. "I guess you could say Sloane was my version of Jenna. She was in a summer workshop here, and that's where we met. Courtney was in the same one. It was a big deal to even get into the workshop, only some of the top theater talent was accepted."

"So she's talented?" Quinn asked and hated how her stomach tightened with jealousy.

"She just graduated college, so she was a handful of years younger than I was. And I guess I found her refreshing. She didn't know me during my mom's sickness, and it was easy to be with her. Courtney was never a fan."

"Why not?"

"Courtney got to know her during the workshop and told me she was bad news. Sloane and I didn't have a healthy relationship. She just isn't a healthy person. There was a lot of drinking and fighting and more drinking. We partied a lot."

"*You* partied?"

"I hadn't dealt with my mom's death. Sometimes, it felt as if Courtney was too close to the situation, and she knew me before my mom died. It was nice being with someone who didn't make me process things like an adult. Because Sloane didn't act like an adult."

"What happened?"

"After the workshop, we became more serious. She was staying at my place almost every night. By the fall, I was tired. I was sick of waking up every day hungover, and I wasn't really in love with her. After a friend told me that she was getting into things harder than alcohol, I decided to take a break from everything." Alex rubbed her face again before she continued. "She was in the process of auditioning for the fall show here. My father was directing. And she made it to the final callback for the lead. It was between her and another woman. I obviously had no say in casting at that point."

"And I'm guessing Simon didn't cast her?"

"By that time, I had broken up with her. When she found out she didn't land the role, she completely spiraled. At first, she accused me of convincing my father not to cast her."

"Why would you do that?"

"I wouldn't. Even though I understood my father's decision. The other actress was better. In one of our final fights, I decided to tell her that. Which was mean, but I didn't really know how far she'd take things." She looked over with devastation in her eyes. Quinn wished she could do something to change it, but she also wanted to know the full story. "She ended up threatening to sue me for sexual harassment. She claimed that I used my position of power unethically."

Quinn didn't know what to say. She knew Alex was reticent to talk about this past relationship, but she'd had no idea why or that it was that bad. "Why would suing an Off-Broadway theater company help anything? It doesn't get her the role, and it's not as if any theater is bleeding money."

"I think at first, she just wanted to make my life hell. Then, she talked to some lawyers. And they saw the real pot of gold."

"Your dad."

"Sloane knew enough from our conversations to know what my relationship was like with him. She knew he would protect his theater at any cost. He paid her off, and it probably wasn't even a dent in his bank account. Janet was brought in just in case anything got out after that ended. But nothing ever did."

"Why would he pay her off? She had no case."

When Alex spoke a few minutes later, her voice was quiet, and she didn't sound like the Alex that Quinn had come to know. "She didn't. But he wouldn't allow the threat to blossom into reality."

"What happened in there earlier?" Quinn asked, nodding in the direction of the lobby.

"He asked about Sloane. I have no idea how he found out and if she's talking about it, but the moment Janet walked away, all his questions were about that. And he implied I brought your show in because you're gay."

"That's not true, though," Quinn said, even though it was a stupid statement since the media never really cared about truth when it came to scandal.

"I know that. And I didn't answer his questions. But that's why my father is so concerned about my dating life. Sloane handed him the perfect excuse not to trust me."

"He has to know she played you."

Alex gave her a soft, sad smile. "But he still uses it against me every chance he can."

"So what are you going to do?"

"I'll talk to Janet and have her ensure the reporter doesn't include whatever it was he was after. That kind of sensational reporting doesn't align with their outlet, and they won't want to mess with Janet. I hope. Did he ask you anything out of the ordinary?"

"No, the questions weren't very inspired, but they were all about the show. Not one question about you."

"That's good," Alex said, but her brow was still furrowed.

"Hey," Quinn said, taking Alex's hand. "I don't really know how to fix any of this. But I'm here. If you need me."

Alex stared at her for a moment. Her brow began to smooth out slightly as her gaze traced Quinn's face. "I know. Thank you," she said as she brought Quinn's hand to her lips.

"Have you seen or heard from her since everything went down?"

"Last I heard, she moved to LA. But she's not doing theater anymore."

"I'm sorry all this happened today. I know you were already nervous about the interview."

"It's not your fault."

"I know that. But I—" Quinn caught herself before she finished what she wanted to say. "I care about you. And I hate seeing that little furrowed brow," she added, tracing her fingers across Alex's forehead.

Alex gave her a long look but didn't say anything. "What does the rest of the day hold for you?"

"Rehearsal. Then, I thought maybe a certain someone might want to come over for dinner. And other things."

"Chess?"

"Only because you had a rough day. But you should know now that I don't cook."

"I don't cook, either."

"I already knew that. I've seen your fridge."

"If we weren't in this theater, I'd kiss that smirk off your face."

"You can kiss me later. For now, I think you should go find Janet."

Alex rubbed her face one more time and nodded. "I'll text you later to figure out timing."

Quinn gave her a kiss on the cheek before moving out of the aisle and toward the back of the theater.

"Quinn," Alex called before she walked out. Alex gave her a slow, shy smile. "I—" She paused and let her smile grow wider. "I care about you too."

It took Quinn a moment before her meaning sunk in. Quinn's smile slowly reached her lips as she stood and stared. One thing was clear, she didn't think she was in love with Alex Anders. She most definitely was.

CHAPTER TWENTY-NINE

Quinn sat in her quiet rehearsal room going through Diego's notes from the day. She knew she had been distracted, and it wasn't her best rehearsal, but she couldn't stop thinking about Alex and their almost declaration in the theater earlier that week.

She had only seen her a couple times since, and it had always been late at night, and they were both too tired to do much talking. She was impatient to have more time with her, which was a feeling that was becoming more and more common.

She could feel tension from Alex since the interview, but she supposed that was to be expected, considering how it all went down and the amount of time Alex had spent at Janet's office since.

"Knock, knock." Courtney was standing in the doorway on the other side of the room.

Quinn's eyes widened as she took in her unusually put together look.

"I just saw Diego leave so figured I'd stop in. Busy?"

"No, come on in," Quinn replied. "But only if you tell me why you look like a hot secretary."

Courtney put her hands on her hip and posed. "Actually, I was going for a smart, confident graduate student who's been pressured into law school by her conservative parents but is about to break out and realize her real talent is in photography."

Quinn pretended to give the outfit a thoughtful look. Courtney had on a black pencil skirt, heels, and a tight white blouse. Her unruly red hair wasn't completely tame, but it was more contained than Quinn had ever seen it. "Now that I'm really looking at it, I can totally see that. It's like *Law & Order* meets *Carol*."

Courtney threw her head back and let out a loud, bubbly laugh. "It's like you're in my head."

"Why exactly are you dressed like that?"

"I need to send in a taped audition for a film. It's a long shot, but I was using one of the rehearsal rooms. Anyway, are you staying here, or do you want to walk out with me?"

"I was just about to pack up and leave," Quinn replied, moving around the room to grab the few items she had with her. "Want a snack? I have extra today."

"I think I'm going to adopt you. What kind of snack?" They made their way down the rehearsal room hallway and toward backstage.

"Goldfish crackers and this thing they call a granola bar but looks more like a block of chocolate."

"I'll take the block of chocolate."

She reached into her bag and handed Courtney one of the fake, sugary bars. Courtney didn't wait a second to rip the wrapper open and take a bite. "Fuck, yes. That tastes like a snack you got in daycare in the nineties. I fear for our health if we hang out too much."

"It's already bad enough with Alex, who only seems to consume bagels, coffee, and bourbon."

"I'm afraid you'll have to learn to cook if you ever want something other than takeout with that one. At least I can make a few dishes. The last time Alex cooked for me, I cut my lip on some sharp plastic in the potatoes."

Quinn laughed as they both made their way down the dark aisle of the theater. "I can't even believe Alex cooked once."

"She lost a bet on when Garfield would appear in the Macy's Day Parade. She called it way too early. So she had to cook one of our Thanksgiving dishes. Just one. And there was plastic in it."

"That's kind of endearing."

"Says the girlfriend. It caused light bleeding."

Quinn slowed as they entered the lobby. She and Alex hadn't used that label yet, but her stomach was erupting in tiny little butterflies, and she had to admit that she liked the sound of it rolling off Courtney's tongue so easily.

Courtney stopped walking. "Oh, hey. Sorry. I didn't mean to make you uncomfortable. I don't know if you're even there yet. See, this is why I need Paige with me at all times." She pointed to her mouth. "No censor."

"No, it's okay. We haven't used the girlfriend word, per se, but I'm there. I think she is too?" She didn't mean for the last part to be a question, but talking about this with Alex's best friend was making her nervous.

"Me too," Courtney replied. "I hear the *Times* interview on Monday didn't go very well."

"Have you seen her?"

"No, but we spoke on the phone. She didn't tell me she's worried because she's Alex, but I could tell."

"She's been with Janet all week trying to fix it."

Courtney stayed quiet for a moment. "Don't let her push you away," she said, and Quinn couldn't hide her surprise. "Because after this media fiasco, I guarantee she will. Besides setting the feminism movement back twenty years, Sloane also did a number on Alex. Maybe I shouldn't be saying this, but ever since her mom died, she's been pretty closed off emotionally, and it just got worse after Sloane. But I also haven't seen her this happy. Ever. So I'm just asking you to be patient."

"Is this the best friend talk?"

"No. I know you won't hurt her. I'm worried about her hurting you. Don't let her go into her Alex cave. I'm sure I don't need to tell you, but she's worth it. Once you get through the stubborn, emotionally constipated part, that is." When Quinn didn't respond, Courtney looped her arm into hers and guided them toward the exit. "She's never taken me to Coney Island, and she knows how much I love hot dogs. Your boobs must be fantastic."

Quinn smiled at the joke. "They are." Once they were outside, she could see Mikey leaning against one of the stone pillars at the base of the theater steps. "Oh, you should come meet Mikey," she said, pulling Courtney along. "Just don't talk about my boobs. He hates that topic."

Mikey slid his phone into his jacket pocket.

"Hey, Mikey. This is Courtney. Courtney, Mikey. My manager and best friend. In that order. Courtney is Alex's best friend," Quinn said.

"Finally, the best friends meet," Courtney said, extending her hand. "They've been keeping us apart for too long. Does Quinn keep you in a cage like Alex does with me?"

"Uh, no?" Mikey responded as he shook her hand. "But it's nice to meet you."

She took a step back and made a show of looking him up and down. She let out a small whistle. "Damn, Mikey. I'd climb up all over you if something wasn't telling me that we're both friends of Dorothy."

He just blinked before he seemed able to form words. He looked between them. "Oh God, there's two of you."

"Mikey only likes to use the muscles in his face a few times a day," Quinn said. "So please excuse his lack of smiling."

"I see why you didn't want me to bring up your boobs," Courtney replied in a dry tone. "Anyway, I need to go. But thanks for the chocolate."

Quinn simply nodded as she laughed at Mikey's expression.

Before leaving, Courtney turned to Mikey and saluted. "And it was nice to meet you, Mr. Mikey."

As soon as she was gone, Mikey turned to Quinn with his eyebrows raised. "I didn't know you were coming by," she said, ignoring his judgmental expression.

"I thought I'd walk you home." He motioned for them to start in the direction of her apartment.

She batted her eyelashes. "Are you going to carry my books too?"

"You don't have any books."

"I have a bag."

"I'm not carrying it."

"You're a terrible manager."

"Yes, poor baby. Anyway, I come bearing gossip, but if you don't want it, I won't tell you."

Quinn let out a gasp. "But you never have gossip. Who does this gossip pertain to?"

"Me."

"And you never tell me anything juicy about yourself. You officially have my attention, Mr. Rubio. Speak."

"Well, I thought since you were the orchestrator, which we still need to talk about, by the way, you should know that I have a date with Tim tonight."

"Delvin?" Quinn shouted and stopped walking.

Mikey grabbed her arm and forced her to keep going. "Yes. Now please stop shouting before everyone in Manhattan knows."

"I think you should be thanking me, not admonishing my volume."

"So it was you who gave him my number?"

"Who else? I told you I was going to. You can call me Yente." When Mikey simply gave her a confused side glance, she let out a sigh. "She's the matchmaker in *Fiddler on the Roof*. You really know nothing about theater."

"But one of the city's biggest theater investors is going out with me tonight, so apparently, it doesn't matter."

"That's just because you have that pretty face."

"Thank you. I think," he replied as they turned down Quinn's street. "Anyway, I have other gossip too. I just came back from Janet Jameson's office, and Alex was there." Quinn's attitude morphed from teasing to concerned. "I assume you heard about what happened at her interview?"

"I was in the lobby when it happened. The asshole completely blindsided her."

"They didn't go into a huge amount of detail, but it sounded like personal questions?"

Quinn simply nodded. She couldn't tell Mikey about Sloane, even if he was her best friend. She wouldn't betray Alex's trust about something so intimate.

"Apparently, earlier this week, Janet offered to have the story squashed, but Alex wouldn't let her," he said.

"What do you mean?" Quinn slowed as they reached her apartment building. "Are you coming up?"

"No, I need to get ready. Anyway, Alex said that it would hurt your show to squash the entire feature, and she didn't want Janet to do that just to spite the paper. And Maggie and I agree."

"So surprised *my publicist* agreed with that," Quinn replied with a roll of her eyes. "What about Alex's interview? What is Janet doing about that?"

"She seems to think she's done enough to scare them. It was an unethical interview, and she seemed confident it won't run."

"Did Alex seem okay?"

Mikey stared for a long moment before he responded. "Are you in love with her? Because I've seen this face before." His expression was soft, and his expression held none of his typical judgment.

"Yes," she said in a quiet voice.

"And have you told her?"

"No."

He gave her another long look before he nodded. "I might wait on that. She was pretty stressed out by the whole situation."

Quinn's stomach tightened. She couldn't remember caring about Jenna's welfare like this, but it was as if she could physically feel Alex's stress, and she wished she could take it away. "She's coming over tonight."

"It sounds like she's been looking out for your interests with Janet. I like her."

Quinn's eyebrows shot up. It wasn't just that he had never said that about Jenna. He had never said that about *any* woman she had ever dated. "You do?"

"She's trying to make it seem like she's looking out for the show and the interest of the theater. But anyone who knows the truth can see through that facade. I have to go, but I'll see you soon." He leaned up to give her a quick kiss on the cheek.

"You too. Tell Tim hello for me," she replied as he stepped back down the stairs and onto the street.

"I certainly will. He's taking me to the symphony. I feel so cultured."

"Look at you, maestro. That should be fun." She let out another exaggerated sigh when he looked confused. "Maestro? The name for the conductor of a symphony? Mikey, do you know anything outside of fashion?"

"I don't hear you complaining when you need help getting dressed."

"Fair enough. Have fun tonight." She turned and ran up the stairs. As she walked into her apartment, she took out her phone so she could text Alex. Based on her conversation with Mikey, she assumed she was out of her meeting with Janet, and Quinn wouldn't be interrupting at this point:

I'm home now. Come over any time. She added a kissing emoji to the end and sent it before moving to the bathroom to take a quick, post-rehearsal shower. Before she stepped into the water, she saw Alex had responded.

Leaving Janet's office in a minute. Can't wait to see you.

Quinn knew she probably looked like a lovesick fool, but she couldn't bring herself to care. She was a lovesick fool. She just hoped she wasn't the only one.

CHAPTER THIRTY

Quinn was so used to waking up to an empty bed when she was with Alex that she was surprised when she could still feel her warm body next to her. That surprise lessened when she looked over at the clock on her bedside table and saw that it wasn't even seven yet. It wasn't until she sat up that she realized the reason she'd woken up was buzzing on her nightstand.

She groaned at whoever it was. Anyone who knew her knew not to call before ten in the morning on the weekend. When she heard the vibration again, she forced her eyes to open so she could grab her phone. But it wasn't just one missed call. It was four missed calls. All from Courtney. Plus three text messages.

Hey, Quinn. Please call me. I've been trying to reach Alex, but she's not answering. Its urgent. She needs to call me.

Wakey, wakey. Have Alex call Janet now, please.

I'm going to try calling you.

Quinn read through the texts with increasing dread. She glanced over at Alex's sleeping body, and her heart clenched at the peaceful look on her face. She didn't know what Courtney needed, but the urgency couldn't be good, nor could her mentioning Janet's name.

Quinn grabbed the shirt she had thrown to the side last night and quickly put it on. She hopped out of the bed as quietly as she could and made her way to her living room so she could call Courtney. She figured that, whatever the news was, it would be better if she told Alex herself instead of her waking up to a handful of urgent and confusing texts. She sat on the couch in just her underwear and called Courtney back.

"Finally," Courtney said the moment she picked up. "You two are really hard to get ahold of."

"It's 6:30 in the morning. I think everyone is hard to get ahold of this early. What's going on?"

"The feature on your show came out. Paige woke me up when she saw it."

There were almost too many questions going through Quinn's head to pick just one. "Wait, what? You mean the *Times* feature?"

"Yes, I guess you could say that one."

"But it's not supposed to come out for another week."

"Well, it's out, and it's not exactly a feature on your show. It reads more like a gossip scoop, and it's in the *Post*. Not the *Times*. I'm sure Janet has been trying to reach Alex. She needs to call her. Now."

Quinn didn't want to ask, but she knew she needed to if she was going to prepare Alex accordingly. "Tell me what it says."

"I'll send you the link. It's online as well," Courtney replied in a tone that was so different than her usual playfulness. "But, Quinn, it's not good. For either of you. I'm sorry. I don't know what Janet can do now that it's out there."

"How bad?" she asked in a whisper.

"It's sensationalized garbage. But Simon won't think of it that way."

"I need to wake Alex," she said, but she couldn't seem to get her legs to work.

"I'm sending you the link now. Read it first. And Quinn?"

She was still too stunned to form many words, so she just made a noise to indicate she was listening.

"Please take care of her. She's going to need you right now."

"I will. Talk later."

It took only a few seconds before her phone was vibrating again, and a text from Courtney came through with the link to the story. When she clicked on it, she was taken to a section of the site called *The City Scoop*.

Quinn cringed when she read the headline on the page. "Sapphic Success: How One Off-Broadway Theater Company Changed Their Fortune." By Jeremy Hart.

The article clearly wasn't going to be a feature about her show. The photo wasn't even of Quinn. It looked like some old photo of Alex in front of the theater. She forced herself to take a breath and read on.

In a time when memes have replaced dialogue and "binging" and "the weekend" go hand in hand, New York's once thriving theater scene has become a relic of our past.

A recent survey from New York Today *found that both Broadway and Off-Broadway ticket sales have dropped dramatically in recent years. Off-Broadway companies have been hit particularly hard without the advantage of tourism dollars and have seen a decrease in attendance by almost thirty percent over the past decade.*

But where others are failing, one New York City theater company is thriving.

Horizon Theater, an Off-Broadway company started in 1995 by Manhattan-based theater investor and director Simon Anders and legendary actress Peggy Anders, has seen a surge of new revenue, sold out shows, and a loyal audience base of millennials. In just five years, the theater has seen an increase of forty percent in ticket sales and a dramatic sixty-five percent increase in attendance from the twenty-four to thirty-five age group.

So what is the secret to their success?

Well, it's not a "what" at all, but a "who." Meet Alexandra Anders: Horizon's managing director and the daughter of Simon Anders.

While Ms. Anders may not have the artistic hand of her father, she certainly has a business one. Beginning with the theater in 2010, she has made multiple changes to Horizon's business model.

While the theater has notably seen a spike in revenue with Ms. Anders at the helm of operations, it's truly the introduction of new, modern programming that can be attributed with Horizon's latest surge in attendance.

Ms. Anders's own role within the theater has been a core influence on their shift in programming. This year has even seen her taking over the theater's historically popular winter series that features three new works from emerging artists.

But perhaps it's more than Ms. Anders's financial savvy or eye for the future that has her theater barreling through the midtown competition. A source close to Horizon granted the Post an interview and gave us insight into some of the darker secrets lurking behind the theater's curtains:

"Alex Anders has an eye for talent. But she has a stronger eye for a pretty face. Her choice of shows and rentals is a direct reflection of her relationship status with the latest actress to come through their doors."

Ms. Anders's latest choice in programming comes in the form of Quinn Collins, a former runway model who has turned her best-selling book, Model Behavior, into a one-woman show. And according to our source, Ms. Anders choice to include that show in Horizon's winter series, may not be completely unbiased.

"Everyone in the theater knows they're dating. Alex saw her show in a festival last year and set her sights on Quinn. We'll see what happens when the show closes, and she moves on to her next actress," said our source.

A relationship within the confines of a business is not the most unusual thing to hear these days. But given what we've learned about Ms. Anders's enduring pattern, it begs to be asked: is something sinister happening at Horizon?

"Considering her leadership role in the company, the ethical nature of these relationships is suspect," our source says. "And you won't hear about the ones that didn't end well. The Anders family does a good job keeping them out of the court and media."

Though Ms. Anders refused to answer our questions on the subject of her workplace affairs and settlements, she did sit down for an interview on where she sees Horizon going in the future.

"I want Horizon to be at the forefront of the new theater. One that is accessible and relatable to everyone in New York and not just the elite."

Take note of Alexandra Anders, Broadway. This theater maven is coming for your dollars—and your leading lady.
Model Behavior opens Nov. 27 at Horizon Theater Group, 240 W 52nd St.

Quinn quickly read through it again and knew there was little she was going to be able to say to Alex to make this okay. Courtney was right. It was bad.

As she walked back to her bedroom, she mentally rehearsed how she would wake Alex and tell her, but when she entered the room, Alex was awake. She was sitting against the headboard and staring at the phone in her lap.

"You read it?" Quinn asked as she slowly moved into the room.

Alex nodded as she continued to stare at her phone in a daze. Quinn crawled back onto the bed. She didn't want to smother Alex, but she also didn't want her to be alone, so she simply put her hand on her leg. "I don't know what to say. I'm just so sorry." When Alex didn't move her leg, she kept her hand there.

"I don't get it," Alex replied in a hollow voice. "What happened?" she asked, bringing her eyes up to Quinn's.

Her face was paler than Quinn had ever seen it, and she couldn't remember ever seeing her freckles stand out so starkly against her skin. Her eyes were still wide, as if stuck in shock.

Alex's phone vibrated. "It's Janet," she said as she picked up the phone and read the text. "She wants me to come to her office."

"What about your dad?"

Alex rubbed her face in the same way she had earlier this week in the theater. Quinn wished there was some way to make this better, but she had no idea how, especially considering she couldn't offer to go with Alex. Not after what the article implied. "He doesn't get up this early on the weekend. Most likely, he hasn't seen it yet. I need to go to Janet and get to the theater." Her voice was small, and the melancholy that settled over the room so thick, Quinn's hands began to shake.

Alex put her phone down and took Quinn's hand. "I'm sorry you got pulled into this. You left one media scandal just to be brought into a new one. I am so, so sorry for that."

"Hey," Quinn said as she gently cupped Alex's chin. "You did nothing wrong. Besides, I'm barely a blip in this story. I'm just worried about the fallout for you."

"This was supposed to be your story. About your show. How did this happen? Why is it in the *Post*?"

"Don't worry about my show. I already have multiple other interviews lined up next week. And we still have the gala announcement."

Alex picked up her phone again and looked at the article for a few moments before tossing it to the end of the bed.

"Who was the source he kept quoting?" Quinn asked tentatively, not wanting to upset Alex further but too curious to hold it in.

"I don't know."

"Do you think it was Sloane?"

Alex shrugged, but the dark expression on her face implied she thought Quinn's guess could be accurate.

"They can't just make things up with some unnamed source and then make it seem like you were being uncooperative." Quinn's voice was raised in her frustration on Alex's behalf. But she knew that even if the story was retracted for false claims or libel, the narrative was now out there.

"Technically, he didn't make anything up," Alex responded.

"He made it sound like some systematic behavior when it so obviously isn't."

"I have to go. I need to get to Janet."

Quinn wished Alex would say more, but she probably hadn't even processed what had happened yet. Nothing would really come to light until she talked to Janet anyway, so Quinn decided not to push her. "I know. I'll grab you some clothes that aren't leggings." But before she could move off the bed, Alex grabbed her hand. She felt as if her heart was being painfully squeezed when she looked up to see such a helpless expression on Alex's face.

"I don't know what will happen when I talk to my father. I'm not sure when I'll be able to see you. But I'll text."

Quinn gently pushed Alex's hair behind her ear before interlacing their fingers again. "I'm honestly just happy you didn't have a total freak-out and kick me out of the apartment already."

"It's your apartment."

"You know what I mean."

Alex placed a soft kiss on Quinn's knuckles. "I won't lie to you. My first reaction was to run out of here. But this article doesn't change the way I feel about you."

"I hope you know it doesn't change the way I feel about you, either. That article is disjointed, homophobic trash masked in investigative reporting."

A small smile crossed Alex's lips before it disappeared again. "I don't know that everyone else will read it that way, but thank you for supporting me. I've never had that."

"Now you do. But I really should try to see what pair of pants I can find for you that don't have holes in them." Quinn hopped off the bed so she could rifle through her overcrowded closet.

"And preferably a shirt that doesn't have a dinosaur on it," Alex said, looking at the tank top Quinn had given her the night before.

A few minutes later, Quinn was coming out of her closet with a simple blouse and a pair of black pants. "The pants may be a little short for you, but they should work." She set them on Alex's lap and then leaned down to eye level. "I know today might suck. But I'm here if you need me. For anything." She placed a soft kiss on Alex's lips. They didn't deepen the kiss, but they did stay pressed against each other for another moment, and Quinn savored the feeling, knowing she might not see Alex again for a few days.

She finally broke the kiss and moved back but felt an overwhelming wave of emotion. Alex's pain felt like her pain. And perhaps she had never really been in love before, not even with Jenna, because she felt a longing to shield Alex from what was to come.

But she knew she couldn't fix this. And she couldn't tell Alex how she was feeling in that moment. Not when she was about to face Simon. Quinn cleared her throat and put everything she wanted to say but couldn't on a shelf in her mind. "I'll go make some coffee you can take with you."

"Thank you," Alex replied softly.

Quinn nodded and turned to her bedroom door, once again swallowing the thing she wanted to say.

CHAPTER THIRTY-ONE

Please, dear. Just sit for a moment."

"I don't want to sit, Janet. I want to know how the fuck something like this happened. How did it even end up in the *Post*?"

"I'm going to get to the bottom of this, but I can't until the editor at the *Times* is at the office, and it's not even nine on a Saturday. I don't even know if he's in today."

"They don't get email on their phones? They don't have phones? Call them. Email them. Get to the fucking bottom of this."

When Janet leveled a calm look at her, she took a deep breath and moved to one of the chairs across from her desk. "Thank you," Janet said when Alex was sitting. "I don't know what happened. The only thing I can think of is that Jeremy took the story elsewhere when he was told he couldn't print it at the *Times*."

"He can do that?"

"Not ethically. But it looks like he freelances for both publications. The *Post* gives more leeway to gossip, and he probably was able to sell it to them easier since that's his beat there."

"He's a gossip columnist?" Alex asked, sitting up straighter.

"Not at the *Times*. They don't have a gossip section."

"Well, that would have been good to know."

"I only found out after the fact."

"It's so bad. My father will never forgive me for this." She deflated. Everything she had worked for was crumbling down around her.

Janet moved around the desk to take the chair next to her. She gently put her hand on Alex's arm, but it didn't feel as comforting as Quinn's had. "I promise, it's not as bad as you think. Most of it is quite flattering. He doesn't even mention your sexuality until close to the end."

"It's in the headline, Janet. And it doesn't matter if the beginning is flattering. This is the exact thing that will set my father off. Someone else taking credit for the success of his theater."

"Your father cares that his shows are selling out. This certainly won't hurt that. In fact, it may even help. Even someone as obtuse as Simon will understand what happened here."

Alex knew that wasn't true but decided not to argue with Janet about that point when she needed answers. "He only included one of the quotes I gave him about the theater. And nothing from his interview with Quinn. Which is enough to showcase to my father that I did the interview but not enough to prove it wasn't supposed to be about me."

"I know," Janet replied in a patient voice.

"And half the things he claims aren't even true." Alex wanted to get up to pace again but forced herself to stay in her seat.

"I know that too, dear. Which is why I'm meeting with our legal team this morning. I can't undo the damage, but I can fight them on the article staying online, and I promise you, there will be repercussions."

Alex allowed her breathing to even out again. She felt like she was on a roller coaster of emotions that spun her from angry to defeated in the span of a minute. "Who do you think their source was?"

Janet let out a long sigh. "I don't know for sure, but it's not hard to guess."

"Sloane."

"She's the only one who has that kind of inside knowledge." Janet looked out the glass door of her office and motioned for someone to wait, but Alex couldn't see who it was from the angle of her chair. "My legal team is here, and I need to meet with them. But before I do, I need to know what is true and what's not from the article. I already know about Sloane. The other actresses he mentioned—"

"Why does it matter who I've dated?" Alex could feel her anger rising again.

"Because he wrote about it. And now we must address it."

Alex took another long breath and closed her eyes so she could calm her racing heart before she answered. "There were no other actresses. Just Sloane."

"Until Quinn Collins?"

Alex didn't reply. Denying her relationship with Quinn felt completely wrong and a betrayal to what they shared. She might not have been the reason Sloane didn't get cast by her father, but she had made the messy decision to enter into a relationship with a woman at work. And now she'd done it again, even though she knew the repercussions of it coming out would be detrimental to her career.

"I see," Janet said quietly. "And that's it?"

"I'm not some kind of lesbian predator."

"I know that. You are your mother's daughter. Now go. Talk to your father. I'll call you soon."

Alex reluctantly lifted out of the chair. "If you don't hear from me by five, send a search party."

"I will, dear," Janet said with a kind smile before Alex turned and left so she could face her father.

❖

Alex checked her phone again as she entered the theater. She hadn't received any communication from her father yet. On any normal day, that wouldn't be unusual, considering his disdain for even the smallest form of technology. She had never received a text from him in her life, but on urgent things, she at least got a call. Today, he had been eerily silent, and she couldn't blame the early hour anymore.

The administrative office was quiet when she got there, which was normal for a Saturday, but she could see light coming from under his closed office door and knew he was there. She thought about going to her own office first so she could have a moment before facing him, but she also wanted to get this conversation over with, so she knocked.

"Come in," he called from the other side.

Alex took one final breath before opening the door. He was sitting at his desk looking impeccably fresh in his expensive suit. He looked up casually, as if nothing was amiss. She knew him better than that and assumed whatever he was really feeling was simmering just under the surface of this fake facade. "Alexandra. To what do I owe the pleasure?"

She sat slowly in the chair across from his desk and stared at him. He was playing a game with her, and he had the patience to continue until she was squirming in her seat. To avoid that waste of time, she decided to be direct. "Have you read the *Post?*"

He casually leaned back. "What section?"

"You know what I'm talking about."

"Oh, I'm sorry. I assume you're speaking of the unsanctioned interview you did with Jeremy Hart?" His face, impassive only a moment before, took on a hard expression the moment his game was over.

"It wasn't supposed to be about any of that," she said, stumbling over her words.

"Tell me what it was supposed to be about. And then you can tell me why I had no knowledge of it happening."

She would have given anything to be transported out of that office and sent to literally anywhere else in the world. But she willed herself to keep her voice steady. "It was supposed to be a feature on Quinn Collins's show. And in the *Times*, not the *Post*. I told you about it. Janet thought it would be good for me to give a couple quotes on the winter series as a whole. I didn't mention it since it didn't seem pertinent. The larger story was supposed to be about her. Not me. And we had no idea he was freelancing. He took the story to a new outlet when the *Times* said no to printing it."

"So your intention was not to take credit for the success of my theater?" he asked in an icy tone.

"Of course not. You read the article. He didn't even have named sources."

"If it was not intentional, then it was unforgivably careless. You are the managing director here. Not the face of the theater. You don't give interviews."

"I know, but—"

"I can't for the life of me understand why you would ever be so clueless. Especially now that we've finally gotten past your last mistake."

"I didn't make a mistake. You know what happened."

"It doesn't matter. The fact is, it still happened. At least that one had kept quiet. Until now. Now, I have a PR disaster on my hands."

"Ultimately, he said that Horizon is leagues beyond the other venues in New York. That's not the worst thing." Alex knew she was grasping at straws, considering the other implications the article made.

"Yes, by your talented hand," he replied in a sarcastic tone. "And on the matter of Ms. Collins's show, I have no problem pulling it if it will embarrass my theater. Until it closes, I hope I don't see you even look her way. I will not repeat the past any more than you are already making me. Is that clear?"

Alex felt like a child again and could only nod. She hadn't felt this close to crying from her father's words in years, but she wasn't going to let him see her do that. She took a quick breath through her nose and forced herself to swallow it down.

"Now, if you will excuse me, I need to take care of this," he said.

"How?"

"I have a call with a PR consultant in a moment, and we will devise a plan."

She let his words sink in for a moment as her mind raced around their implied meaning. "But Janet handles our PR."

"Not anymore."

She didn't respond right away because her jaw had physically dropped. "You're firing Janet?"

"She no longer handles our PR. I need to make a call," he said and pointed to his door.

"You can't just fire Janet. We need her," she said in desperation.

"I can do anything I want. This is my theater. Go."

There was nothing she could do to reason with him when he had that stubborn look on his face, so she began to leave the office before she heard his voice again.

"And Alexandra?" He didn't continue until she turned. "I'll be the emcee at the winter gala. I suggest you focus on the behind-the-scenes needs for now."

"But the winter series is my program—"

"I think you've gotten enough unwarranted credit for one year. The series needs to be about these productions. Not your personal life."

She knew that if she opened her mouth now, she would say something that all but sealed her fate as Horizon's forever theater manager. At this rate, her chances of securing Rick's job were slim, but she didn't need to make things worse by saying what she really thought of her father.

When she didn't respond, he gave her a small smile. "That will be all."

She refused to react to his cloying smile, so she left without turning back.

As she returned to her office, she felt as if her legs might give out, and her breathing became ragged. She'd never had a panic attack, but she assumed it must feel a little something like this. She allowed her body to sag against the wall before she needed to slide down and put her head between her hands. Everything was too overwhelming. On top of the article, now she couldn't even lean on Janet.

The only thing that forced her to move from her spot on the floor was the fact that her father was just down the hall, and the last thing she needed was for him to see her like this. She picked herself up and moved to her office so she could shut herself in and be alone.

She needed to talk to Quinn and Courtney and most definitely Janet, but all she wanted to do was crawl into a hole until the gala was done, and she could finally breathe. So instead of calling anyone, she reached into her pocket, grabbed her phone, and turned it off.

CHAPTER THIRTY-TWO

"Fuck, fuck, fuck," Quinn screamed as she wiped her smeared makeup for the third time. She should have accepted Mikey's offer to help her get ready for the gala, but she knew he had dinner plans with Tim, and she didn't want to interrupt that. Besides, she was a model, or had been, and should have been able to put on some damn eyeliner.

She glanced at the clock on her nightstand. She only had fifteen more minutes before a car came to pick her up, but she already had her dress on and was just trying to finish putting on some makeup. But as she sat there looking at her reflection in the mirror, she felt very alone. Despite what Alex had said the day the article had come out about not disappearing, Quinn had only seen her in passing at the theater. Their only communication had been through text messages.

She was trying to be as understanding as she could. The article was obviously damaging Alex's place at Horizon, and within the theater scene at large, and it had most likely created more tension with her dad. But Quinn couldn't help feeling hurt by Alex's complete lack of attention. They still hadn't even established exactly what this relationship was, but right now, she felt more like a dirty secret than a girlfriend.

She took a long breath before letting it out slowly. She needed to shake herself out of the gloomy mood she was in. Ultimately, she couldn't imagine the stress that Alex had been under since the article had come out, especially with Simon watching her every move. But knowing that and stopping herself from being upset at their sudden distance were two different things.

She tried to push thoughts of Alex aside for the moment so she could focus on what was right in front of her. Tonight should have been special. This gala would be announcing her New York debut, and she had been waiting months for that. Once it was over, hopefully, they could figure things out. After all, her show opened in two weeks, and then there wouldn't be a reason to hide their relationship.

She jumped when the phone rang. She didn't usually have the sound on, but she was worried about missing a call from Alex, so she had turned it up. When she looked at the screen and saw that it wasn't Alex, she tried her best not to be disappointed. "Hey, Evie," she said as she picked up the call.

"Hey. Just called to say congratulations on the gala tonight. We're really proud of you."

Quinn felt an immediate rush of guilt for being disappointed. She could hear Will in the background shouting something about loving her, and she laughed. She needed to remember that she had people rooting for her. Her value couldn't begin and end with a woman again. She had done that once before, and it had left her alone and her confidence in the gutter.

"Thank you. And thank Will. I can hear him screaming."

"He says he loves you. Are you all dolled up and ready?"

"I am. I'll send you a picture so you can send it to Mom."

"Or you can just send it to Mom?"

"And get ten texts back about how to do my hair or makeup better? No, thank you."

Eve let out an airy laugh that made Quinn smile like it always did. She was the best at centering Quinn when she needed it. "Just have fun tonight. Mikey told me a little bit about what has been going on." She paused. "And I read the article."

Quinn's stomach clenched. "Oh. Right." She got up and walked out of her bedroom so she could gather her coat and purse.

"Forget about it. This is still your night, Quinney. I've always admired your courage and your talent. And you're going to take that city by storm."

Quinn slowed her steps and leaned against the hallway wall. She'd just finished getting her eyeliner right, so she closed her eyes to stop the tears pressing in. She wasn't sure if it was the words of support, the entire night as a whole, or the fact that she missed Alex with every fiber of her being, but she felt overwhelmed with emotions.

"Quinn?"

"I'm here. Thank you. I miss you so much."

"We miss you too."

She pushed off the wall when she heard the buzzer on her front door. "Sorry, Eve. Someone just rang my doorbell, and I think it might be the driver."

"Go. Have fun. Text me details, and I want a lot of photos."

"I will. Tell Will I love him." Once she hung up, she looked at the time on her phone. She still had ten minutes before the driver was supposed to be there, and she thought that she was meeting him at the curb.

When the doorbell rang again, she quickly made her way down her hall. She looked through the peephole. It wasn't her driver unless her driver was a beautiful woman who looked exactly like Alex Anders.

Nerves set off in Quinn's stomach, which didn't make sense considering this wasn't her first date with Alex. But something about the way Alex was standing in the hall looking so unbelievably sexy had Quinn's pulse quickening. No amount of deep breathing was going to calm her increased heartbeat, so she opened the door.

"Hello," Alex said formally.

"Hi," Quinn responded but didn't move out of the doorway as her eyes roamed up Alex's body.

Alex had on a black, double-breasted blazer and a pair of black slacks. But what really caught Quinn's eye was the fact that she wasn't wearing a shirt under the blazer. Quinn could see the smooth skin of her chest and the slight outline of her cleavage.

"You are the most beautiful thing I have ever seen," Alex said, her own eyes making their way down Quinn's bright red dress.

"Mikey picked my dress."

"But you're wearing it."

"I did choose the color."

Alex smiled, but an awkward silence settled around them. "Can I come in?"

"Oh, yeah. Come in." When Alex was about to pass her, she leaned in so their lips could touch. What started as a small, chaste kiss quickly turned deeper as their lips met. It wasn't as passionate as some of their others, but feeling Alex's lips against her own after so many days still made her body come to life with sudden want.

"I'm sorry we haven't been able to see each other," Alex whispered when they parted.

"Let's go inside." Quinn felt a mix of emotions. Her body was still vibrating from their kiss, but one show of affection wasn't enough for her. Alex's silence over the past two weeks couldn't be erased by one sexy pantsuit and a hot kiss. "What are you doing here? I thought you'd be at the restaurant by now."

"My father seems to have run out of menial jobs to give me. Last night, I was in charge of setting up chairs and cocktail tables. I'm not part of the run of show, so he doesn't need me, I guess."

Despite her annoyance at Alex's ghostlike behavior over the past few days, Quinn tried to remember that she was going through a lot right now. "He's taken over the entire night?" She moved over to a small bar in the corner of the room so she could pour Alex a glass of bourbon. She had bought it after she'd noticed that it was Alex's preferred drink. She couldn't be bothered to open a bottle of wine for herself, especially given their time constraints, so she poured herself one too.

"Thank you," Alex said when Quinn handed her the glass. She motioned for them to sit on the couch. "And not exactly. I still did all the work leading up to tonight. He's just taking the spotlight. Last night, we did a dry run, and I basically just stood in the back of the room watching."

"Have you spoken with Janet?"

Alex shook her head. "No. We spoke right after everything happened but not since. I think she might be home in Connecticut. She'll be fine. She has a lot of other clients."

"And you?"

Alex put her glass on the table and did the same with Quinn's. She gently took her hands. "I'm sorry. I know I've been distant. Things have just been hard at the theater with my father."

Quinn hadn't planned on talking about any of this tonight. Not with such a big event just an hour away. But with Alex sitting there looking open and vulnerable, she didn't want to miss the chance. "I get that. But if you never talk to me, it's hard to feel like we're in this together."

Alex nodded and stared at their joined hands for a full minute before she looked up again. "Everything feels like it's caving in around me. It's my default to just internalize everything and close everyone else out."

"I noticed. Courtney called it your 'Alex cave' or something."

"Courtney talked to you about it?"

"I'm not the only one you've been ignoring," Quinn said with more bite than she intended.

"Courtney is used to me by now. Don't worry about her."

"She shouldn't have to be used to it. She's your best friend. You can't just keep pushing people away."

"Courtney understands the stakes at the theater. She gets why this promotion means so much to me."

"And I don't?" Quinn pulled her hands away.

"That's not what I meant. She's just been with me through a lot of years of trying to please my father. She's seen all the work I've put into this theater. And that article all but sealed my fate. It gave my father every excuse not to promote me, and I think a lot of people would understand that decision after the way Jeremy portrayed me."

Quinn wanted to understand Alex's extreme desire to take over for Rick. To her, it just seemed like it would keep Alex handcuffed to Simon Anders indefinitely, and Alex had so much more to offer than to be working somewhere she wasn't valued. But she wasn't going to say that right before the gala Alex had poured so much of herself into. She laced their fingers together again. "Rick's job or not, look at what you've done there, babe. You've changed Horizon. You've honored your mother's legacy. And you've changed my life."

"I have?"

"In more ways than one."

A small smile finally spread across Alex's face, and Quinn softened. Alex might be incredibly frustrating with her emotional guardrails, but Quinn knew there was nothing she could do to change the way she felt about her. "Not to keep apologizing, but I'm also sorry we can't go to the gala together tonight," Alex said.

"I never assumed we'd go together. And I'm fine with that. But I do need to know what this is. I know the past two weeks have been hard. But it hasn't been easy feeling like I don't know where we stand. I need to know I'm not alone in this. What are we?" Her nerves spiked as soon as she asked the question that had been at the forefront of her mind all week.

Alex seemed to be searching her face for some answer, and the silence in the room was so thick, Quinn could almost hear her own heartbeat.

Alex didn't break eye contact until she pulled something from inside her blazer. A delicate silver chain hung from her fingers. Quinn's eyes widened when she saw a teardrop diamond hanging from the end. "We're everything, Quinn. Even if I can't have you on my arm tonight, I wanted you to have something that reminded you of how much I care about you."

Quinn didn't know what to say as her mind raced around the fact that Alex was holding out a diamond. She tried to focus on that and not the fact that Alex had said she cared about Quinn again instead of the words she really wanted to hear. "You got me a diamond?" she asked, still staring.

"Technically, it's just your birthstone. But that may have been coincidental. Mikey told me you don't wear bracelets or watches, so I opted for this."

"You talked to Mikey about getting me a diamond?"

"No, I told him I wanted to get you a gift to celebrate the gala," Alex replied and glanced at the necklace. "You don't like it."

"I love it," Quinn said quickly, putting her hand over Alex's. "I'm just surprised."

"You're not going to tell me you can't accept it, are you? Because I've already come up with a list of arguments for why you can and should."

"I don't think we have time for that list. So please. Do the honors," Quinn moved her hair away from her neck.

Alex moved behind the couch. She grazed her fingers down Quinn's exposed neck, and when she leaned down and placed a small kiss there, Quinn closed her eyes at the feeling.

"To be clear, you already look perfect, and even a diamond can't compare to you," Alex said. "But I will enjoy seeing you wear this tonight. Remembering how your skin tasted as I put it on."

Quinn kept her eyes closed as Alex's lips grazed the back of her neck again. A moment later, she felt the slight weight of the diamond on the base of her collarbone. Her hand automatically went up to feel the stone sitting there. She leaned back into Alex's lips as they made their way from her neck to her earlobe.

"May I see?" Alex whispered against Quinn's ear, sending an instant shiver down her spine.

She moved off the couch and turned. She noticed a slight rise and fall to Alex's chest and knew their quick moment of intimacy was also affecting her.

"Lovely," Alex whispered. There were more things Quinn wanted to say, but before she could, Alex was looking at her watch, and Quinn was reminded that her own car would be there any moment. "I should go," Alex said. "My driver is parked illegally, and I do need to get to the restaurant before my father has one more freak-out."

"I'll be right behind you. A car will be here soon for me," Quinn replied and moved from the couch to the doorway so she could walk Alex out.

She opened the door, but Alex didn't make any move to go through it. Instead, she turned so they were standing close enough to touch.

"Thank you for the necklace. It was very sweet," Quinn said.

Alex brought her hand up to play with the diamond. "What you said earlier, I hope you know that you've changed my life too."

"Sometimes, you're such a mystery. You guard your heart so fiercely and shut me out. But then, you turn up with diamonds and say things like that."

"I don't know why you put up with me."

"Maybe because I fell in love with you."

Alex's eyes snapped up. She slowly lowered her hand, and the silence that followed felt more significant than any they had ever shared.

Quinn waited for Alex to respond, but with every moment that passed, the silence seemed to ring louder in her ears. When her phone began to ring, blaring out into the apartment and entryway, she dropped her gaze. "My driver must be here," she said, allowing her phone to ring through to voice mail.

Her words from before still hung in the air between them, and even she was surprised by them. Maybe it wasn't the right moment to say them, but now they were out there, and she couldn't take them back, nor did she want to. She wanted Alex to admit the same thing.

But instead, Alex nodded as if in slow motion. "I should go," she said in a quiet voice. "I'll see you soon." She headed down the hallway, but after only a few paces, she turned again and seemed torn between going and staying. But when she opened her mouth only to quickly close it, disappointment ran through Quinn.

"See you soon, Alex," Quinn said, closing the door. She knew it was probably childish, but the tears she had kept at bay all night were threatening to fall, and this time, she knew she couldn't stop them.

Her hand went up to the necklace, but now the gift just felt hollow, and as she closed her eyes, the only image she could see was the scared look on Alex's face

Before the article had come out, she would have bet on the fact that Alex loved her. And maybe deep down, she did. But whether Alex would allow herself to acknowledge those feelings was something Quinn wasn't sure about. And now she was left with a diamond around her neck that made her feel empty and a sinking feeling of déjà vu. She had once thrown herself at another woman who hadn't returned her feelings. And obviously, Alex wasn't Jenna, but she didn't know how far Alex would push her away if it meant she had to be vulnerable.

The second ring from her phone was enough to break her out of her wallowing. She quickly grabbed her purse and coat and made her way down to the car. Tonight was going to be about her show. She could deal with her mess of a personal life tomorrow.

CHAPTER THIRTY-THREE

*M*aybe because I fell in love with you. Alex lost count of the number of times those words rolled around in her head as she sat in her office waiting for the gala to officially start. She had only minutes before she needed to be at the restaurant, but she wanted a moment alone after her trip to Quinn's. During the entire ride to the theater, she'd replayed her reaction over and over and couldn't stop thinking about how Quinn must have felt as she waited for Alex to respond.

While she was standing in the hallway, it had felt as if her brain was screaming the words back to Quinn, but she couldn't make them come out. It had been so long since she had said those words to anyone—the last person being her mom—that she'd panicked.

She couldn't shake the expression on Quinn's face as she'd shut the door. Alex had stared at that door for an entire minute, willing herself to knock so she could tell Quinn she loved her too, but ultimately, it was easier to walk away. The fact that she took that route caused a wave of self-loathing to hit her.

When she knew she couldn't wait any longer, she picked herself up from her chair and made her way over to the restaurant. The gala was in the back room, and when she entered, it looked the same as it did last night when she had been there for their final check. The mood lighting was now in full effect, and she could see images from Horizon's fall show flashing across the screens in each corner of the room. It was already packed, but seeing the men and women laughing as they ate, drank, and socialized in their formal wear did little to brighten her mood.

Not only had she royally messed things up with Quinn, but everything about this event was now tainted. She had worked for months to put this together, and it didn't even feel like hers.

She arrived right as the lights were dimming for the presentation, and she didn't have to talk to anyone. She saw Mikey and Tim across the room and went over to them so she at least had a friendly face next to her as her father took her spotlight. *Stole* her spotlight.

"Alex, good to see you," Tim whispered as she took the open space around their cocktail table.

"You too, Tim. Hey, Mikey."

He smiled and nodded as a spotlight hit the stage.

"I thought you'd be up there," Tim said, pointing.

Alex's eyes connected with Mikey's. She had a feeling he knew exactly why she wasn't up there, but he didn't say anything. "Not this year," she responded.

"I hope it has nothing to do with that rubbish in the *Post*. Don't even think about it, darling." Tim put his arm softly on Alex's back before turning his attention to the front of the room.

Alex was saved from having to respond by her father taking his place in the middle of the stage.

"Ladies and gentlemen. Thank you for being here to help us celebrate Horizon Theater Group's eleventh winter series." He paused dramatically as he allowed the audience to clap. "When I began this theater almost twenty-five years ago, I vowed to create a space for everyone. A place where we could cherish what has come before us and champion what's new. And nothing in our theater exemplifies that more than our winter series. It is the heart of what I was trying to create. This is my favorite time of year. When we get to welcome new artists into our community and experience the future of this beautiful craft. The winter series is about finding those gems that haven't yet been found. And this year may be one of our most exciting programs to date."

He paused again as he looked out over the audience. He never could resist the attention of a crowd, and tonight, he seemed to be in his element. Alex stopped herself from rolling her eyes at his theatrics. But more than that, she bristled at the fact that he didn't even mention her mom. That he had so casually erased her part in Horizon's legacy.

"But ladies and gentlemen, don't take my word for it," he continued. "To showcase the three amazing productions in this year's winter series, please turn your attention to the screens and join me in watching a quick video showcasing our exciting program. I present to you, Horizon's winter series."

He ended his speech by pointing to the large screens. A sizzle reel began on each, diving into the details of the three different productions. Right away, Alex could tell it had been reedited from the one she had last seen. The biggest change was that Quinn was featured far more than the other two shows, which Alex couldn't understand. Her father had never shown anything but indifference toward her show. She assumed this had to be the influence of the new PR firm he had recently hired.

Image after image of Quinn's modeling career flashed over the screen while the other two productions were merely mentioned in the reel. When the video finally ended, Alex joined the rest of the audience as they clapped but only because it would look odd if Horizon's managing director was sulking in the corner.

"An exciting program indeed," her father said as he walked back onto the stage. "Opening in just two weeks, we kick our program off with Quinn Collins's *Model Behavior*. A true hidden gem, Ms. Collins is here with us tonight, and I ask you to give her a very warm, New York welcome. I first saw Ms. Collins's show last year in a festival showing, and I am beyond honored to produce her show on the Horizon stage for her New York debut. Please join me in giving her a round of applause. Congratulations, Ms. Collins. We are lucky to have you."

He motioned to where Quinn was standing to the side of the stage. She turned to the audience and gave a quick smile and a wave, but Alex thought it looked forced. And that would make sense considering her father had just lied to the entire audience and made out like he'd discovered Quinn's show. She also wondered how Quinn felt about her modeling career being splashed across the entire sizzle reel when her show was about so much more than that.

Alex caught Quinn's eye as the crowd clapped, but all she saw was sadness there, and she hated herself all over again for being the one to put that expression on her face. The only silver lining was that Quinn still had the diamond around her neck. Maybe Alex hadn't ruined everything yet.

"Now is the time I would normally turn you all back to the delicious appetizers and cocktails. But before I do that, we have one more special announcement to make. I now turn you over to Horizon's executive director, Rick Weston." Her father moved to the side of the stage as Rick made his way onto it, and as they passed each other, they shook hands.

Alex couldn't understand what was happening. Rick never presented at these things. In fact, some years, it was hard simply getting him to attend.

"Thank you, Simon," Rick began, looking at her father, "for your leadership over all these years. But mainly for your friendship." He turned to the room. "I began at Horizon in 1996. That was just one year after Simon and Peggy opened the theater. And these have been the most enriching twenty-four years a man could have ever hoped for. I thank all of you for being a champion of my work. It has meant the world. But the time has finally come, and it is with great sadness that I announce to you all here tonight that I am retiring."

Alex's stomach dropped, and she straightened from the table she had been leaning on. Her father hadn't told her that they would be making Rick's retirement announcement at the gala. She didn't think they'd be making that until the spring gala or even after.

"Rick's retiring?" she heard Tim say, but her eyes were transfixed on her father, who was staring right at her.

She was aware that Rick was still talking, but she wasn't listening anymore. She couldn't tear her eyes away from the triumphant smile her father directed her way. She forced herself to look away. When her eyes met Quinn's, she could see that she looked as confused as Alex felt.

"But I won't be leaving this place without the best leadership New York City theater has to offer. And now, I will let Simon make our final announcement. I'm retired, after all," Rick joked and took a step to the side so her father could join him at the microphone again.

"Horizon is not Horizon without Rick. Thank you for your artistry and your friendship over the past twenty-four years. This place is as much you as it is me," he said to Rick before turning back to the crowd. "But he is right. Rick's departure marks a new day for our theater, and with it, we welcome new leadership."

The more he spoke, the louder the blood rushing in Alex's ears became. The sinking feeling that had settled itself in her stomach since the article had come out finally plummeted as realization began to hit her. Her father was about to announce Rick's replacement, and it wasn't going to be her.

"Some shoes can never be filled. But we have certainly tried with our choice of Horizon's new executive director. When choosing this replacement, I wanted someone who shared our love for theater. Someone who understood New York audiences and the way into their hearts. Someone who has been a champion of Horizon her whole life. And we found that woman. Tonight, we celebrate change. And as we welcome new, talented artists like Quinn Collins into the Horizon family, so too do we open our doors to a new leader. Please join me in welcoming a woman whose face may be familiar to Horizon Theater but is about to become the beacon of our future. Janet Jameson."

Everything seemed to move in slow motion as Janet appeared on the stage as if out of nowhere. And as she embraced Alex's father and Rick, Alex tried to wrap her mind around what was happening. But she couldn't. How could he be giving the job to Janet?

She was vaguely aware of Tim saying something, and her eyes found Quinn's across the room again. Hers were wide, and her mouth hung open slightly, and Alex had to assume her own face mirrored the expression.

Janet's voice boomed from the microphone, but her words sounded jumbled in Alex's mind. She felt paralyzed until she looked at her father. He wasn't smiling anymore. He simply raised one eyebrow at her before averting his gaze back to Janet and allowing a fake smile to spread across his face.

Alex had to leave. She could see Quinn making her way over, but she couldn't face her or anyone right now. She needed to get out of the room before she screamed. She cut through the crowd, not even worrying about pushing through the tight spaces to get out. Appearances didn't matter anymore. None of this mattered anymore. She just needed to be alone so she could drink and forget her father had just taken away her entire life.

CHAPTER THIRTY-FOUR

A lex looked around her office as if she had never been there before. Years of discarded programs and contracts piled high on cabinets that were pressed against walls covered in show posters. She used to look at the mess with pride. But right now, none of the reminders of her time at Horizon meant anything to her. As if her whole life had just been leading to this one disappointing moment, one final blow from her father that showed exactly how much she was worth to him.

More than anything, she was angry at herself. She should have seen it all coming. Right as her heart was beginning to open and trust, she was sent a cruel reminder that doing so just led to heartbreak.

Her eyes finally landed on the *A Streetcar Named Desire* poster in the corner. The same one she had caught Quinn staring at all those weeks ago when they'd first met. That one poster used to be the thing in her office she cherished most. But now, she couldn't stand the sight of it. She knew a piece of paper couldn't technically mock her, but it felt as if it was. It stood there, reminding her of all the dreams she'd let go without a glance back.

And maybe for the first time, she was truly admitting to herself that she could no longer blame her mom's sickness for it. She couldn't blame the fear of living in her mom's shadow. She couldn't even blame her father for telling her she wasn't good enough. She'd stayed in the theater out of loyalty and because she'd thought she wasn't good enough for anything else. The moment her mom had died, the place she had loved since she was a little girl had become her father's theater, and she should have left.

As she continued to look at it, all the anger and frustration with her father hit her like a tidal wave. She lunged over to the wall and ripped the poster off. When that didn't feel like enough, she grabbed the closest thing she could find and flung it as hard as she could.

"Fuck you, Dad," she shouted into the room as a glass award that the theater had won broke against the wall. She let out another scream as she threw the other award and watched its shattered pieces fall on top of the last one.

But as she stood there with her chest heaving and a mess at her feet, she only felt worse. The office felt hot and suffocating, and it was the last place she wanted to be. As she turned to leave, the moment got even worse when she saw who was watching her from her doorway.

"May we speak, or were there more things you need to smash first?" Janet's voice was calm, which only fueled Alex's anger.

Alex had trusted her like family and still had trouble grasping the betrayal. Janet had always been in her corner, especially when it came to the matter of her father. She had never hidden her dislike for him and had been a true and steadfast friend to Alex's mom. None of that matched with what had happened across the street tonight.

"You left your own party a little early, don't you think?" Alex was grateful her voice wasn't as shaky as her hands felt.

"You know I've never been one for a party. I just came to see how you are."

"I'm supposed to believe you care how I am? Just tell me how long this has all been in place."

Janet let out a long sigh, as if the whole conversation was already boring her. "Long enough."

"I think I deserve to know exactly what happened."

"Your father and Rick chose the person they want to lead this theater. That is what happened."

"And they chose you? You're a fucking publicist, Janet."

"Stop being so dramatic. I've been a silent investor here for years, among many other theaters. I'm a staple within the theatrical community. It's not a stretch."

"And my father? You don't even like him. Or was that all an act?"

"I didn't care for your father being married to my best friend. I would never deny he's one of the best theater directors in the city."

Alex laughed harshly at Janet's mention of her mom. "Your best friend? You're a nice friend to screw over her daughter."

"Alex, dear. Your mom passed years ago. We all need to move on. And that includes you."

There were so many things she wanted to say and even more things she needed to know. But she felt so overwhelmed that she could only stand and look at the broken glass strewn across her office. When her eyes fell on a framed *Time Out* article about Horizon sitting on her desk, some of her own questions began to answer themselves.

"The article," she said, her head snapping back to Janet.

"I must admit, I didn't know Jeremy would be quite so colorful."

"But you did know what it was going to be about. The interview was a setup."

"Your father can be an indecisive man. He needed a push. I gave him one. And you played right into it. The moment I saw a picture of Quinn, I knew you wouldn't be able to resist. Don't forget how long I've known you. Though I must admit, I didn't think it would all be quite so easy."

"My mom would never forgive you for doing this. This was her theater too."

"Your mom had everything in life handed to her. She didn't know what it meant to come from nothing and work her way up like I have. Nor have you, for that matter. I know you wanted the job. But today, nepotism lost. I wouldn't have expected Peggy to understand that, just like I don't expect you to." Janet's voice finally lost its sweet quality and took on and edge that Alex had never heard.

"You sound a little jealous, Janet."

"I'd rather be where I am than where your mom is."

Alex felt a flash of anger. It was as if Janet had finally let all false pretenses fall away, and Alex didn't know how she had never seen the venom right under the surface. "Don't ever talk about her again," Alex said with as much bite as she could muster. "You're a complete betrayal to her memory."

"That doesn't change the fact that I earned this. Over years of hard work and investment."

"Earned it? I'm the one who poured every ounce of myself into this theater for the past decade. All you did was place a false story in a gossip rag and use your dead husband's money."

"It wasn't completely false," Janet replied with a smile she didn't even try to soften.

Alex let that last statement sink in, which caused her to think back to the interview. "The source he kept quoting," she said as another realization dawned on her. "You're it."

"Nobody has heard from Sloane in years."

Alex nodded. Each revelation becoming less and less surprising. "And if I tell my father that you set me up?"

"He won't care. As you so aptly said, it gave him every excuse he needed. In fact, he may even thank me."

"That's it, then."

"It doesn't have to be. You're still an integral part of this theater. And you are a talented theater manager. I hope you will stay in your role and work with me. But I also understand if you decide to move on. I'll expect your answer soon."

Being talked down to like she was Janet's employee was the final straw. She gave one final glance around the office, but there wasn't anything she wanted. "You can consider this my resignation. Good luck, Janet," Alex said in an empty voice as she moved past, careful not to let their bodies touch.

"Aren't you going to speak with your father?"

Alex didn't even bother turning back as she continued toward the elevators. "As you said, he won't care. You tell him."

CHAPTER THIRTY-FIVE

Quinn ended the call the moment she heard Alex's voice mail again. She had been trying to call her since Simon's announcement at the gala but hadn't been able to reach her. The calls went straight to voice mail so quickly, she knew Alex had turned her phone off.

Her stomach clenched again as she thought back to the complete shock and devastation on Alex's face the second after Simon had called out Janet's name. She'd felt the same shock at the news, but she couldn't be even half as upset as Alex. In all their conversations about Rick's role, never once had Janet's name come up, and she still didn't understand what had happened.

As she walked down the cold New York street in her heels and dress, she felt a mix of emotions. On one hand, her heart ached for Alex and what this meant for her. But on the other hand, she was once again being shut out and was running around Manhattan trying to find her.

She could see the theater bar up ahead and pulled her coat closer to block out the cold night wind that had picked up since she'd left the restaurant. After Alex had rushed out, Quinn had called Courtney to tell her what happened. Courtney had told her that Alex usually came to this bar when she was upset.

The smell of stale beer and body odor hit her as she entered the space, but for some reason, it just made her think of Alex and the first time she was able to blatantly stare at her in this very room.

That seemed like so long ago now, even though it wasn't. She could have never predicted then that she'd be completely in love.

Her eyes roamed the bar, but Alex wasn't there. The place was busier than the last time, so she had to push around a group of rambunctious men singing some kind of showtune before she could make her way through the dingy seating area.

Alex sat at a table at the far wall. But the relief Quinn thought she'd feel upon finding her dissipated as she saw the curvy bartender from last time standing over her. Alex had a bored, detached look on her face as she stared into an empty glass, but the bartender had her hand on her shoulder and was giggling as if Alex had just made a joke.

When Alex noticed her approaching, she shook off the bartender's hand. "Quinn, what're you doing here?" By the slight sloppiness to her words, Alex wasn't completely sober.

"I came to find you," she replied, but her eyes were on the bartender.

"You should be at the gala. Go back."

Quinn tore her eyes away to look at Alex. "I should be here."

"Actually, Gabby, cancel that next drink. I'll pay now." Alex pulled a small wallet out of her back pocket and placed some money on the table.

"You sure?" the bartender asked.

"Yeah," Alex said, standing. She didn't give the bartender another glance as she pushed through the crowded room and toward the door, and all Quinn could do was follow until they were out of the bar.

"Seriously, Alex?" she said as soon as they were on the street. "You turn off your phone, again, I might add, and then come here to drink with her?"

"She's a bartender, Quinn. I wasn't drinking *with* her. And please don't make this about whatever it is you're making this about right now."

Quinn forced herself to take a steadying breath. She didn't like walking in and seeing a woman's hand on Alex, especially a woman Alex had slept with before, but Alex was right, and this wasn't about that. She once again felt stuck between protecting her own heart and supporting Alex through what had become a never-ending string of Horizon drama. "Then talk to me," she said more calmly.

"There's nothing to say. You saw what happened."

Quinn could see the pain on Alex's face but thought twice about touching her when she noticed the way she was half shielding her body. She took a tentative step closer but kept her hands at her sides. "I did see it. And that's why I want to talk. Let's go somewhere."

"I don't want to talk. I just want to go home. Alone."

"You don't have to be alone."

"But I am. My father just proved that once again."

"You didn't have your dad's support long before tonight. And I know what happened tonight was awful. But you're not alone. You have Courtney. And you have me." Quinn finally put her hand on Alex's arm.

Unlike all the other times she had touched her, Alex's body tensed under her hand, and she made no move to hold on to it like normal. She simply turned, forcing Quinn's hand to drop. "I quit," Alex said.

"You quit? When?"

"Janet followed me to the theater, and I quit. I also found out the entire article was a setup. Everything that has come out of her mouth since you met her has been a lie."

Quinn had already put that together while she had been looking for Alex. She knew that Janet's betrayal was just as hurtful to Alex. Because of the shock of it, possibly even more hurtful than her father's. "I can't imagine the kind of betrayal and hurt you feel right now. What they did was unforgivable. But in time, it may be a good thing."

Alex let out a quick, harsh laugh. "Please explain to me how this is a good thing."

By the expression on Alex's face and the short tone of her voice, Quinn was entering dangerous ground. Alex's glassy eyes were guarded, and she looked ready to bolt at any moment, so Quinn tried to choose her words carefully.

"You can start fresh. Get out from under your dad's thumb. Not worry every day that he'll pry into your love life."

Alex's eyes narrowed, and even though the step backward she took was small, it felt like a huge emotional divide between them. "You've never gotten it," Alex said in a quiet voice, shaking her head.

Quinn felt her own annoyance flicker at the icy tone. Courtney had called Alex stubborn, but that descriptor didn't even begin to cover it. This was like having a conversation with an emotionally stilted wall. "How can I understand anything when you pick and choose when you open up to me?"

"None of this is about us," Alex said in a much louder voice. "But you keep trying to make it about us."

"Of course it's about us, Alex," Quinn shouted, finally losing the patience she had been holding on to. "You wouldn't even be in this situation if you hadn't met me. Our entire relationship has been about your dad and you getting Rick's job. And I'm not sure if you noticed or not, but that article also mentioned me. You can't keep separating me from the rest of your life."

"And now what? You want to be with some out-of-work theater manager who only got her first job because of Daddy?" When Alex took another shaky step backward, Quinn wondered how many drinks the overly friendly bartender had plied her with before she had shown up.

"Stop it. I don't care about your job, and I never did."

"I don't know who I am without that theater. Why can't you get that?"

"Because there's more to life than Horizon." Quinn realized she was still shouting, but nothing else seemed to be working to get through to Alex. "Why is that place the only thing you care about?"

"Because it was my mom's. It was *her*. It's like I've lost her all over again."

Quinn didn't know what to say. When Alex simply looked at her feet with a defeated expression, Quinn took a few calming breaths before taking one small step closer. "You can't even see how special you are. How much you have to offer. I know you're upset, and that is totally understandable. But you don't need Horizon. You are so much more to me than that place." Quinn took a deep breath. "I know I never met her. I wish more than anything that I could have. But I'm certain your mother would have told you the same thing."

When Alex just continued to stare at the ground, Quinn knew her words weren't resonating. Alex was determined to be alone in this.

"Stop thinking about the theater for a second. What about us? What about *me*?"

"What's the point? You'll just be one more thing that I lose."

The reason behind Alex's intimacy issues hit Quinn like a brick. "You're not losing me." She gently cupped Alex's face. "Look at me. I'm not going anywhere."

But Alex pulled away. "I just want to go home," she said in a hollow voice. "I'm just sorry if my quitting has any negative impact on your show."

Quinn grabbed her chin so she was forced to look into her eyes again. She could see that the corners of Alex's eyes were wet, but she was breathing through her nose and seemed to be willing the tears to stay put. "I don't care about my show right now. I care about you."

"You should care about it. It's why you're in New York."

"It's not the only reason anymore."

"You deserve better than me, Quinn."

Quinn shook her head before she could get her mouth to work. She knew what Alex was doing, but she wasn't going to let her. "Don't do that. Don't throw this away because you're upset." She moved her hands down from Alex's face to grip her arms. "I know you're in pain. I can help take some of it away."

"No. Not right now. Just…just stop pushing." Alex shrugged out of Quinn's grip.

"Pushing? Alex, all I have done since we've met is be there for you. All I'm asking is for you to let me be."

"I've told you more than I've ever told any woman. I've never been as vulnerable as I am with you. What more do you want from me?"

"One trip to Coney Island isn't enough. Diamonds and smooth words aren't enough. Do you love me, Alex?"

"Yes, I love you," Alex shouted before taking a breath and another step back. The first tear fell down her face. "Is that how you wanted me to tell you? By badgering me into it?"

Quinn's entire body recoiled at those words, and Alex's eyes were wide too. "Oh, so we're back here, are we? Making hurtful jabs to push me away? Why is it so hard for you to say the words when you know you feel them?"

"Because my mom is the only person I've ever said them to."

"So she's the only one who will ever deserve them?"

"Is this what you did to Jenna?"

That name shot through Quinn's body like lightning. "Did you really just say that to me?"

"Quinn, I didn't mean—"

Quinn just shook her head and took two meaningful steps back down the street. "It's fine. You wanted to be alone. I should have listened." She turned and began to walk quickly down the street until she heard Alex call her name again. She didn't want Alex to see the tears streaming down her face, but the desperation in Alex's voice caused her to stop.

"Just wait, please."

Quinn stood there, waiting and hoping. Hoping Alex would finally say something—anything—that would show her that they had a chance. But like the rest of the night, Alex stood there staring. Quinn could tell she wanted to say something, but she was done "pushing," as Alex called it.

When the silence grew heavy, Quinn slowly nodded. "You know, Courtney said you'd do this. She said you'd push me away. You can tell her she was right." She finally walked away, not waiting to see if Alex had anything more to say. Perhaps she was being unfair, considering what Alex had gone through earlier in the night. But she needed to protect herself at some point, and if tonight and the past two weeks had taught her anything, it was that Alex Anders didn't need her.

Her feet were screaming at her in the heels. She waved a taxi down so she could get home and crawl into bed. There was no way she was going back to the gala now.

She needed to focus on rehearsals and her opening. Once her show was done, she could leave New York and the memories of Alex Anders. Quinn was done being *something* to the person she loved but not *everything*.

CHAPTER THIRTY-SIX

A lex threw down the controller and didn't even flinch as it clanged against the glass coffee table and fell to the floor. Usually, overly violent and mindless video games helped take her mind off whatever she was going through. But right now, nothing was working to distract her.

Despite that, staring at a screen was better than doing anything else, and it kept her from sleeping, which was when things got really bad. She couldn't remember the last time she'd closed her eyes and didn't see that final, devastated look on Quinn's face.

She had already made up every excuse for herself that she could think of. She had been drunk at the time. Quinn had pushed her too hard. That night was about more than them. She didn't care that much anyway. Ultimately, all her excuses were empty.

The fact was, she'd fucked up and probably lost the best thing that had ever happened to her. Quinn leaving an envelope with her front desk containing the diamond necklace Alex had gotten her only solidified that thought. Quinn hadn't included a note, and upon receiving it, Alex had shut it into a desk drawer that she didn't plan on opening anytime soon.

She was a coward and should have called Quinn, but she didn't know what to say or how to apologize. And mainly, she didn't know how to promise she wouldn't do it again.

Quinn might have been angry, but it couldn't compare with how Alex felt about herself. She had been on a road of self-loathing for a while, but how she'd treated Quinn that night made it almost hard to look in the mirror.

Instead of picking up the controller again, she leaned her head back and closed her eyes as she contemplated getting another drink. Not that drinking helped, but it was better than sitting there thinking about Quinn. She only had her eyes closed for what felt like a moment when she heard keys in her door. There was only one person who had access to her apartment, so she braced herself for the tornado that was about to enter.

When Alex opened her eyes, Courtney was standing at the end of the couch, staring calmly, with one challenging eyebrow raised.

"What're you doing here?" she asked, sitting up slightly so she could see better. "That key is meant for emergencies."

"You've had your phone off for five days. I think that counts. Why haven't you answered anything?"

"My phone is dead."

"Don't be an ass," Courtney responded and sat next to her. "I heard about the gala. I'm sorry. I can't imagine how much that kind of betrayal from both of them must have hurt." She gently placed her hand on Alex's leg.

It felt easier to look at the controller on the floor. She didn't know what to say about what her father and Janet had done. Quinn had been dominating her thoughts. Not Horizon.

"Have you spoken to anyone from the theater?" Courtney asked when it was obvious Alex wasn't going to offer anything.

"There's no point. They made their decision, and I no longer work for them."

"I talked to Quinn."

Alex lifted her eyes. "When?"

"The night of the gala. I called her yesterday too, but she didn't pick up."

"What did she say?" Alex's insides tightened in anticipation of hearing any bit of information about Quinn, and this was probably the first time she had felt anything other than numbness since that night.

"She didn't stay on the phone long. She sounded pretty choked up. But she said you needed to be alone and that it was over."

Alex shifted away. She didn't want to be touched when she felt like her heart was being clenched. She was the one who had pushed Quinn away, but hearing those words through Courtney felt like a huge blow. For five days, Alex had sat on this couch replaying that night but not allowing herself to really feel the devastation of losing Quinn. But with Courtney confirming her worst fears, she finally let herself feel the pain.

As the tears hit her cheek, she could feel Courtney's arms come around her, and she had no power but to sink into the embrace. Something about it felt so familiar. The last time she'd cried in Courtney's arms like this was when her mom died.

"Shh. It's okay. You're okay," Courtney said as she began rubbing Alex's back.

After a few minutes of crying, her breathing began to even out. As soon as she felt more composed, she pushed off Courtney and attempted to wipe her wet face with her hands. "Sorry."

"For what? Showing some real human emotion? Al, it's okay to cry and to be vulnerable. Especially after what you've been through."

"I'll get us something to drink," Alex said and went to grab a napkin and two glasses of wine. It was only midmorning, but she needed an excuse to leave the room for a moment. She took her time pouring so she could compose herself.

When she sat back down on the couch, Courtney's eyes were trained on her face as if studying her every expression. "What happened with Quinn?"

Alex took a sip and shrugged before setting it next to Courtney's untouched glass.

When she remained silent, Courtney rolled her eyes and looked around. "This is exactly where I thought I'd find you. Sitting in front of a video game with a drink."

"Apparently, you're right about a lot of things these days."

"What does that mean?"

"You told her I'd push her away. You were right." Alex didn't say it with any bite in her tone. She wasn't mad that Courtney had warned Quinn. Ultimately, Courtney had been right and probably should have told Quinn to run as fast as she could before it was too late.

"Tell me what happened," Courtney prodded again.

She wouldn't leave without actual details, so Alex took another sip of wine before leaning back against the couch. "What happened is that I'm an idiot. She told me she loved me, and I returned her words in a horrible way. And when she was walking away, I let her."

"She said she loves you?"

"Yes, and I accused her of badgering me into saying it back."

Courtney's face scrunched up in pain. "Okay, not the best. But *do* you love her?"

"Yes," Alex replied instantly. "I love her." Her feelings about Quinn had never been in question, and it wasn't until the night of the gala that she'd really understood how deep her own intimacy issues ran. She didn't know how to get over her fear of saying those words.

"You were going through a lot that night. Maybe you didn't say the right things, but she told you she loves you. That means something."

"No, it *meant* something. She told you herself. It's over."

"I heard her voice. She sounded heartbroken. This isn't over. You just need to fix it."

"I can't." Alex stood, not able to stay still. This time, she didn't walk out of the room. Courtney would only follow her. Instead, she walked to her window and looked out at the city as she worked on steadying her breathing. "I know what she needs me to be. I just can't give it to her. I can't lose one more person I love."

"Bullshit. That's such bullshit, Alex."

"You can go now."

"Oh, believe me, I will soon. This whole apartment reeks of self-pity. But first, you're going to listen to me." Courtney stood but didn't move any closer. "You're so scared of everything. You'd rather push her away than break down some of your walls. But I don't get it. You lose her either way."

"How can I not be scared of losing her when the person I loved the most in this world left me?" Tears began to prick her eyes again, but she was too tired to stop them, so when she closed her eyes, she let them roll down her face.

When she opened her eyes again, Courtney was standing in front of her with a soft expression. "She died, babe. She didn't leave you." She pulled her sleeve down over her hand and wiped away some of the tears coating Alex's face. "And we both know it's not just Quinn you've pushed away."

"What do you mean?"

"Why did you quit acting?"

Talking about Quinn was one thing because she could easily admit where she'd messed up. But she wasn't going to go down this road again. Performing had nothing to do with any of this. She moved back to the couch so she could sit and grab her glass. "You know why," she said. "And it has nothing to do with this."

Courtney crossed her arms. "It has everything to do with this. One day, you'll need to stop using your dad as an excuse."

"How can you say that after what he just pulled?"

"He only pulled that because you allowed him to. You stayed at a theater that has never valued you, and I understand why. With a man who has never loved you the way you deserve to be loved. *You* stayed there, Alex. When you could go do anything. You know how many people would kill for your talent and money?"

She glared at Courtney in her best effort to intimidate her, but that had never worked. She knew Alex too well and wouldn't let this go until she had said everything she'd come here to say.

"Quinn and performing are linked," Courtney said, ignoring the glare. "You're so scared of losing the things you love that you don't allow yourself to be happy at all. And I've never seen you happier than when you were onstage."

"When you've had the kind of rejection I've had, it's hard to trust anything."

"What rejection? You know Quinn loves you, and you just couldn't say it back. I tell you that I love you all the time. You never say it back. When's the last time you told *anyone* that? You're scared of saying the things you feel. Anything that might remind you of who you used to be."

Before Alex could even respond, Courtney walked down the hall that would take her to the back bedroom. Alex was too stunned by the words to follow.

A minute later, Courtney was striding back holding Alex's laptop open. She set it on the table in front of them, and when Alex looked at the screen, she saw YouTube and their production of *A Streetcar Named Desire.*

"Watch it," Courtney said, pointing.

Alex refused to even look. "Watching that will accomplish nothing. It was years ago."

"Watch it and read the comments," Courtney replied in a gentler voice, sitting next to Alex again. "Simon's opinion is wrong. You threw a dream away because he said you weren't good enough. See how many people disagree with him. But I think that if you are honest with yourself, you'll realize you threw it away because of your mom too. Because you don't want to lose one more thing. But you're the most talented person I've ever met. Doesn't my opinion matter more than his? Doesn't your mom's? Doesn't Quinn's? He's not a god. He can't control every theater and casting director in this city."

Alex was quiet for a moment before looking at Courtney again. "I don't know what to do."

"Start here," Courtney replied, pointing at the laptop. "Remember who you are. And then decide if you can open up your heart again." Courtney pushed Alex's hair behind her ear. "Not everyone leaves. But before you try to fix things with her, maybe try to fix things with yourself."

Alex grabbed Courtney's hand and squeezed. She felt a small smile grow on her face, which felt foreign after days of sulking. "When did you get so damn insightful?"

"Since I found my own reason not to be a fuckup. Indirectly, you can thank Paige. And these? You don't need." Courtney picked up the wineglasses on the coffee table, taking them into the kitchen. When she came back out, she leaned against the couch but didn't sit. "I'm going to go and let you think. I hope you watch that."

"Thank you for using your emergency key," Alex replied in a small voice. She hadn't even wanted Courtney there at first, but now she felt vulnerable at the idea of being alone again. "I'm sorry I'm such a mess."

"I get it more than anyone. You know that my mom was never around. But I met you and your mom. And you made me believe that I'm something special. You are too. Trust the people who love you."

Before she could even register what her body was doing, she was crawling over and pulling Courtney into a hug. The arm of the couch was between them, but she pressed in regardless. "I don't know what I'd do without you, Court," she said into her shoulder.

"See, that wasn't so hard to say, was it?"

Alex laughed before pulling back into her own space. "Actually, it was. But I said it. So progress?"

"I think there's hope for you." There was a beat of silence, and it looked like Courtney had something else she wanted to say. "Her opening night is coming up. Will I see you there?"

"Do you think she'll even want me there?"

"There's only one way to find out," she replied before leaning and placing a quick kiss on Alex's cheek. "Watch the video," she called as she headed to the door.

Alex sank onto the couch when she heard the door close. She closed her eyes as her mind replayed some of Courtney's truth bombs. There was so much to process, but the one thing Courtney was right about was that she needed to fix whatever was going on with herself before she could fix anything with Quinn.

When she opened her eyes, they landed on the laptop, and she knew what she needed to do. But she wasn't going to do it in her apartment. If she was ever going to break down some of her barriers, she needed to face what she hadn't allowed herself to face since her mom died.

Without letting herself change her mind, Alex rose from the couch so she could change and visit a place she hadn't seen in years.

CHAPTER THIRTY-SEVEN

Despite living somewhere as expansive as New York City, Alex rarely left midtown, given that was where Horizon and her apartment were located. Every now and then, Courtney would convince her to try some trendy bar or restaurant in Brooklyn or another area of Manhattan, but she had no interest in anything on the Upper East Side.

As her car continued down Madison Avenue, she couldn't remember the last time she had been in this area. After her mom died, she had gone to their family house a few times for dinner with her father, but those soon fell off, much to the relief of them both.

"I can get out here," Alex said to her driver as he turned on 69th Street and headed down the block towards 5th Avenue. "I don't know how long I'll be. I'll text you when I'm ready to go." Once the car stopped, Alex got out and walked the handful of steps until she was in front of her childhood home.

She had always liked the front of her parents' home. From the outside, it looked like a normal townhouse where someone would occupy a floor of the building. It wasn't until someone was inside that they were hit with obscene opulence. Her parents owned the entire building, six floors and fourteen rooms. The few times that she'd had friends over growing up, she was always embarrassed. Her father's taste could only be described as museum chic, and the entire house felt untouchable.

She always understood how lucky she was, especially when she walked just a few blocks uptown and saw how other people in Manhattan lived. But it didn't change the fact that she wished she had grown up a little bit more like other children.

As she used her key and walked into the giant entryway, she remembered the way her father had used money to appease her instead of expressing true love. A simple kind word from him would have gone further than another gift she didn't need. It hit her that maybe the diamond necklace she had given to Quinn had made her feel the same way. She had meant it to be a sweet gesture, but she could see now how it appeared to be a substitute for real intimacy.

The house was dark, and after she passed the long stairway, she took a moment to glance at the high ceilings that went all the way to the third floor. She could tell by the lack of lights and sound that her father was out, which was what she was hoping for. He was the last person she wanted to see right now.

She had spent enough time in this house that she didn't need lights and easily found her way down one of the first level hallways. Halfway down, she pushed against the wall, and a door swung open, letting her into the room. The secret door had been one of the only things she'd loved about the house as a kid, but that was mainly because of where it led.

As Alex crossed the threshold into the library, she wasn't prepared for the wave of memories that enveloped her like a flicker of dreams come to life. The room seemed to pulse with haunting nostalgia. Her mother's presence was palpable, as if time had folded back, transporting her to a realm where her childhood was still alive. The air was filled with the smell of lavender, as if her mom had just glided through it like she had so many times before. Sunlight streamed through heavy golden curtains, painting the room with a soft, warm glow.

As a kid, this library had been their haven. Her father had rarely entered here unless he was giving people tours and wanted to impress them. So the whole room felt like her special place to share with her mom. The room had transformed into a sanctuary, a stage for their shared stories, a magical place they had always been eager to experience together.

As if drawn from the very pages of her childhood, a ghostly image materialized in her mind's eye. Her mother and a seven-year-old version of herself appeared before her. The ethereal image of her mother pulled out costumes from a large chest in the corner, and they played out scene after scene from their favorite plays.

Tears streamed down Alex's face as she relived the moment, but she wiped them away as the memory slowly faded. With a pang in her heart, she continued toward the back of the library, the place she had spent the most time during her childhood and her mom's favorite spot in the whole house.

Her eyes were drawn to the blanket on the worn, cozy couch. It wasn't even folded, as if her mom had just stood and let it fall off her lap. Alex sat and stared at the blanket. Everything in the room felt like a time capsule, and it was obvious her father hadn't touched anything since her mom had passed. Maybe that was his way of being sentimental, or maybe he just never bothered to come in here. But something told Alex it was the former. He might have never shown her much affection, but he had been very much in love with her mom.

For years, she'd felt as if she didn't know how to cry anymore. As if she had spent all the tears she ever would on her mom's death. But ever since her conversation that morning with Courtney, she'd been in a perpetual state of either crying or trying not to. And when she finally picked up the blanket and pushed it into her face, a whole new flood of tears rushed in.

But for the first time, crying about her mom didn't feel as painful as it usually did. Something about sitting where her mom had sat so many times caused her to feel connected to the memory of her, and she hadn't thought that would ever happen again. She couldn't remember a time when memories of her mom had elicited anything but complete devastation.

As the tears began to slow, she looked to the side of the room where her mom had used the bookshelves to line up some of their favorite movies. Because that was what they'd mainly used this little room for, watching old classics that her father wanted nothing to do with. Her mom had set up a small TV in the corner of the alcove, and over time, the library had become more of a movie room.

Alex smiled at the movies lining the first shelf, all of which were on VHS. Her mom had insisted that buying DVDs was a waste when she had everything organized. Her favorite films included anything with either Hepburn, but she also had a soft spot for Grace Kelley since the actress reminded her of Alex.

The next bookshelf held her mom's real pride and joy: videos of Alex's performances. She walked to the shelf to see what was there. She had known her mom had kept these, but she had never spent much time going through them. As she read her mom's small, neat handwriting on each tape, she realized that there were two whole shelves dedicated to her theater work. Though "work" was probably a strong word, considering some of the videos were from elementary school choir performances.

Next to the shelf was a cabinet Alex had never bothered to open. In a way, she felt like a child again, going through her parents' private things, but she had a feeling her mom wouldn't mind, so she opened the drawer. She expected to see more videos, and when she saw how wrong she was, her mouth opened slightly.

Piled high were all kinds of items and mementos from Alex's life in the theater, everything from old show posters and programs, torn tickets from performances her mom attended, and photos she had taken of Alex backstage or after shows. Halfway down the pile, she even found a copy of the poster from *A Streetcar Named Desire* that she had torn up in her Horizon office after the gala.

She knew her mom had some of this, but she didn't know her mom had been so meticulous about saving everything from her past. One of the posters was for a show Alex wasn't even in. She had merely helped paint the set pieces.

She continued to sift with a small smile on her face. For so long, she had blocked out memories of that time in her life, and she was surprised how quickly and clearly they came back now.

After going through the pile, she gazed at the drawer in awe. It wasn't just that one of New York's greatest stage actresses had believed in her talent. Her *mom* had believed in her talent.

"Why did I believe him, Mom?" she whispered to the empty room.

She forced herself to close the drawer and turn back to the videos on the shelf, the real reason she'd come back to this house in the first place. After finding a few of the tapes that featured her most recent roles, she set them by the TV. She sat on the couch and pulled out her phone.

Before watching her older performances, she decided to go through some of the online videos from *A Streetcar Named Desire*. As she pulled up YouTube, she curled her legs under herself on the couch and pulled her mom's blanket across her lap. But she simply looked at the static image with her thumb hovering over the play button. She had decided to come here to watch the videos because it made her feel closer to her mom, her biggest fan. But she could still feel the hand holding the phone shaking in anticipation of watching herself onstage again.

She shook her head. Facing her fear started here. She needed to stop relying on everyone else's opinion of her, even her mom's, and decide for herself what her value was.

She pressed play on the first video. "Okay, Court. Here I go."

❖

Alex leaned back against the couch as the cast of *The Importance of Being Earnest* made their final bow on the screen. This was the third show she had watched, and it wasn't until she looked at her phone that she realized she had been there for hours.

She hadn't even known her mom had a tape of this show that was from one of the all-women productions she'd done at NYU with Courtney. Watching it brought back memories she didn't even know she still had. With every show, she began to feel things she had suppressed for years. Feelings of passion and fun and an ambition that were very different to the narrow-minded kind she had held on to since joining Horizon.

She could remember how happy she had been working on shows that maybe fifty people saw. Or working on musicals that were terrible but still offered her the chance to spend time with people who shared her love of theater.

She was proud of the work she had accomplished at Horizon, despite what had happened at the end. But watching herself onstage reminded her that she could do both. And she could finally admit to herself that she had the talent to do both. More than anything, she *did* miss performing. Even more than she realized.

Alex forced herself to get up and put the tapes back on the shelf. She had a strong feeling she wouldn't be back in this house for a while, if ever again. As she began to fold her mom's blanket, she made a quick decision and stuffed it into her bag. Her dad wouldn't miss it, but now that she had been reunited with it, she would.

As soon as she left the library and made her way back through the entryway, her stomach dropped. Standing just feet away, her father was speaking to one of the house staff. The look of surprise that crossed his face when his eyes found hers indicated he'd had no idea she was in the house. "Alexandra. I haven't seen you home in quite a while," he said with a fake smile. "I thought you forgot how to get to the east side."

"Well, I do try to avoid it as best I can. It's a bit too stuffy for my tastes."

"Ah, yes. You do live in such squalor. How is the view of Bryant Park these days?"

Alex had no interest in having another passive-aggressive back-and-forth with him. She should have just walked out. But something about the challenging expression kept her rooted to the spot. For once, she didn't feel remotely intimidated by him.

"Besides, this house has been in my family for generations, and one day, it will be yours. I wouldn't go criticizing it just yet."

"I won't hold my breath. After all, Janet may be looking for a third home."

"Is that why you're here? Did you decide to finally resign in person instead of doing it through someone else?"

"No, I'm sure you got that message. I came to watch some of Mom's old movies. But I'll be going now that you're home."

Something flashed across his face that looked like confusion, but just as soon as it came, he schooled his features into one of neutral stoicism, as he always did upon any mention of her mom. "We should talk about the gala. I understand you're upset, but—"

"You don't understand anything," she snapped, cutting him off for maybe the first time in her entire life. "You've never understood. And you don't care to. The only thing that has ever mattered to you is that precious theater. I was just a pawn to help you make it a success. Until I wasn't needed anymore."

"You left me no choice with that article stunt." He pointed at her. "That was selfish and stupid."

"I didn't pull anything, Dad. Your new shining star did." When the same confused look flashed across his face again, Alex let out a low, humorless laugh. "You didn't know? Janet orchestrated the whole thing. I'd keep an eye on that one if I were you."

"As I understand it, that article wasn't too far off the truth. Or are you going to stand there and deny you're in a relationship with Quinn Collins?"

She could tell him that she was no longer with Quinn, but she knew he would look at it the same way. They had been in a relationship, and she wasn't about to deny that to this man.

"Exactly," he said when she didn't respond.

"I think you wanted me to fall for her. I think you've just been waiting for the next thing you could use against me."

He sighed as if he were engaging with a toddler. "You always had a flair for the dramatic."

"Cut the crap. I saw your face at the gala. What kind of a father enjoys watching his daughter's heartbreak? Or skips every single one of her shows? Or how about the kind who has never once told his daughter he loves her?"

He was quiet as he looked at her. His intense eyes bored into her own, and for one small moment, his expression softened. "I saw your shows, Alexandra," he said in a quiet voice.

She was ready with her next retort, but his words were so surprising that they stopped her short. "What?"

Like every other time he had expressed anything real, the moment was fleeting. He straightened his already straight tie and cleared his throat. "I don't want to do this with you. The past is the past."

"You don't want to do what? Show any kind of genuine emotion? No wonder I don't know how to."

When he didn't respond, Alex pressed her hands against her eyes in frustration. She had no more tears to give, especially to this man, but she did deserve an answer from him.

"Why didn't you ever tell me you saw me perform?" she asked. She hated how small her voice sounded. As if she was a child again asking for validation.

"Why does that matter now?"

"Maybe it would show me you cared, even if just barely."

"I'm the artistic director of a theater. Of course I wanted to see if my only daughter could cut it."

Alex nodded. After the gala, she'd known her relationship with him was over. But for the first time, his cutting words didn't hit her as hard as they once did. "Right. And I didn't cut it."

"Very few people do. I was helping you avoid a very long and very heartbreaking career. I see people's dreams fail every day in this city."

"Yes, you are such a kind and considerate father. Thank you so much for that clarity," she replied sarcastically. "And on that note, I think I'll go." She pushed past him and started walking to the door before his voice stopped her.

"I never asked to be a father."

She turned, but he had his back to her. "Don't worry. I relieve you of all further duties."

When it became clear he was going to continue staring ahead, Alex opened the door. Before stepping outside, she took one last look at the entryway. Her mom had loved this house, but her mom wasn't here anymore, and as her eyes settled on her father's stiff back, she finally felt free of the hold the place had on her heart.

"Mom was the only good thing about you," she said to his back. "Now that she's gone, you're just a sad, lonely theater director. You may come home to a mansion each night, but the beds are all empty. And I'm guessing they always will be."

She walked out of it. It was probably the last time she would ever step inside her parents' house, and she was at peace with that. It was time to move on from that life and especially from the man inside.

She walked quickly down the block, needing to get away from this street as fast as she could. She finally slowed once she was two blocks over and could text her driver with her new location.

As she waited, she realized she wasn't nearly as upset with her father as she might have been. All these years, she had blamed her intimacy issues on losing her mom, but the sad truth was, once her mom had died, the only example of love she'd had to follow was her father.

Her mom died because of an unfair illness. But she had loved Alex, and nothing proved that more than the display of support in her alcove of movies.

Her father never cared to begin and obviously never grew to love her. And in time, she could learn to live with that realization instead of waiting around for declarations that would never come. What she couldn't live with was letting Quinn go. But she didn't want to be this scrambling, emotional mess for her. She wanted to be someone Quinn deserved.

For both of them, she needed to find a way to make herself happy that had nothing to do with her father, and for once, she had an idea of how to do that.

Chapter Thirty-eight

Quinn, where are you today? Miles from here, it seems to me," Diego shouted from the back of the theater.

With only one week until her opening night, Quinn was able to rehearse her show on Horizon's actual stage, but just like with every other run-through she had done so far, she felt detached from the work.

After Jenna, she had promised herself she would never let a breakup destroy her again. But ever since she'd walked away from Alex on the night of the gala, she had vacillated between crying uncontrollably and feeling numb. The creative spark she had felt ever since arriving in New York had dissipated that night, and she hated that she was again allowing a woman to have that kind of effect on her. But with Alex, it felt different than Jenna. It meant more.

With more time to reflect on everything that had happened that night, she knew that Alex loved her. And she knew how much Alex was probably hurting. But that didn't change the fact that she valued herself too much to be with someone who was going to run or push her away every time things got tough. She wasn't convinced Alex would ever let herself be as vulnerable as Quinn needed her partner to be.

"Come, sit," Diego said, motioning to one of the seats.

She plopped down in it with a frown. She couldn't blame Diego's frustration with her. She hadn't been giving rehearsals her all, but at this point, it was as good as she could do with everything that was running through her head.

Diego moved down and sat right next to her. He held up her script. "This is why I'm here. It's why I thought you were here. Do you not believe in it anymore?"

"I do believe in it," she replied, not looking at him.

He gently put two fingers under her chin and directed her gaze toward his face. "Then tell me. Where has the passion gone? And can we get it back?"

She wasn't about to tell him that she was having trouble at work because of a woman, so she nodded.

"We finish lighting tomorrow. And it will be a very long and grueling day," he said, letting his hand drop. "Go home and do something that makes you smile. Come back tomorrow ready to work."

"Thanks, Diego. I'll be ready."

"Good. I've seen you do every one of these scenes to perfection," he said, holding the script up again. "Whatever it was that created that raging heartbeat? Find it again. Honor your work." He placed a quick kiss on her head before moving out of the row. "Tomorrow, we begin again," he shouted as he left the theater.

She sat back and let out a frustrated sigh. She desperately wanted to be alone, but she wasn't going to find that in the busy theater where the production team was still setting lights and working around the stage. She picked herself up and walked to the front row so she could grab her bag. Being in the theater didn't feel as good as it once did anyway, and she couldn't lie to herself about why that was.

So far, Simon and Janet had steered clear of her rehearsals, but she couldn't avoid them forever. They'd be at her opening, and Mikey already warned her that she wasn't free of them even then. Luckily, he had taken all the meetings Janet had scheduled so far, which made sense, given her rigid rehearsal schedule, but she had never been so grateful for his presence as her manager and not just her friend.

When Quinn was heading out of the lobby, the very person she had just been thinking about was standing at the bottom of the stairs. She was used to him waiting for her post-rehearsal, and most of their business conversations now took place on her walk home. Ever since the morning after the gala, when Mikey had come over and seen the state Quinn was in, he had been more attentive and less pushy on the business side of things. As she bounded down the steps, he had the same wary look on his face that he had been directing her way all week.

"Are you coming from a meeting, going to a meeting, or just stalking me again?" she asked.

"You wish. I think you're going to need to wait until your show opens before you get stalkers."

"No, thanks, I think I'll pass on that," she responded as they began walking down the street.

"Well, you may not get a choice. To answer your question, I was coming from a meeting. With Janet. Apparently, your show has already sold out and has a waiting list. She implied that's quite unusual for a winter series production."

Quinn scoffed. "How would she even know? She was a publicist until a week ago."

Mikey turned to her, but she kept her gaze forward. After the gala, she had said that she didn't even want to do her show at Horizon, given everything that had gone down, but he had quickly talked her off that ledge. Giving up this opportunity for any reason wasn't worth it, but she also didn't want to talk about Janet or even hear her name.

"How was rehearsal?" he asked.

"Fine."

He must have been able to tell she wasn't in the mood to be pushed because even though she could feel his eyes on her again, he didn't say anything. For the next several minutes, they transitioned into an easy silence as they got closer to Quinn's apartment.

"There's one more thing," he said as they got to the steps. "Janet wants to discuss an extension."

"How? There's a show right after mine."

"It wouldn't be an official extension. They would bring you back as their fall show for a full run."

"Simon and Janet haven't even sat in on one of my rehearsals. The only person there who's seen any version of it quit. Why would they be talking about a full run?"

"I think it has something to do with how fast you sold out and some of the early buzz."

"I hope you don't mean the *Post* article," she said with more bite than she meant for Mikey, who was purely the messenger.

"That article may have been intended to hurt Alex, but it had other effects as well. Namely, everyone in the city seems to be talking about your opening night."

"Not exactly the kind of success I was going for."

"I know that, Q. Once your show opens and people see how amazing it is, none of that will matter."

"What if it's not amazing?" she asked in a much less combative voice.

He put his hand on her shoulder with a familiar look of support that had gotten her through so many hard times before. "Don't go there again. I know how proud you are of this work. You know how good this show is. Don't let another breakup make you think any different. We can talk about the extension later. Just something to think about."

He was right. She had let Jenna tear her down so far that she'd forgotten who she was. But she was in New York City for a reason that had nothing to do with a woman.

"You have people in your corner," he said when she simply nodded. "Go upstairs. One of them is waiting."

"What do you mean? Who's up there?"

He squeezed her shoulder and gave her another soft smile. "Better go find out," he said before walking down the steps. "See you tomorrow."

She didn't even say good-bye as he walked down the street and disappeared around the block because her stomach was a mess, and her mind was racing too fast to give him a proper farewell. Before she could even process her movements, her legs were taking her up the final steps and into her apartment building. She was self-aware enough to admit that part of her hoped Alex was waiting there. Even though she was still so upset with her and didn't know what she would say, she couldn't lie to herself. She was desperate to see her again.

As she pushed her door open and rushed in, the person who rose from her couch was a happy sight, just not the one she was hoping for. "Eve," she said as she looked at her older sister.

"Hey, Quinney."

Quinn felt frozen to the spot. It wasn't that she wasn't happy to see Eve, but she was still coming down from the surprise that it wasn't Alex.

Eve didn't seem to notice the conflicting emotions because she pulled her in for a tight hug. The second Eve's arms went around her, all the emotions that had been simmering just under the surface all day came crashing down on her.

As Quinn's tears began to fall, she shook in her sister's arms, and if Eve hadn't been holding her up, she would have fallen into a heap.

"This was supposed to be a good surprise," Eve said as she continued to hold her.

"It is," Quinn tried to say through her tears, but her words came out garbled. "It's the best surprise."

"Okay, well that helps my ego a bit." Eve pushed Quinn away so she could look at her. "Come here," she said, guiding her to the couch so they could sit. "Now, tell me why you're crying. I know your happy tears, and these aren't them."

Quinn pressed her hands into her eyes, trying to stop the flow that didn't seem to want to let up. She wanted to talk but didn't want to be choking out tears as she did.

"Is it Alex?" Eve asked. "Mikey didn't tell me much, but he implied something happened."

"Is that why you're here?"

"I'm here for your opening. Will couldn't get the time off work, but he sends his love."

"You came for my opening?"

"Of course I did. I would never miss this. And from the looks of things, I'm glad I'm here." She rubbed her hand down Quinn's back. "What happened?" Eve was always gentle in the way she approached things and never pushed. It was something Quinn had always appreciated.

She wanted to confide in her, but as she opened her mouth, she didn't even know how to articulate what had happened. She didn't know how to explain the extreme fear in Alex's eyes that night. She didn't know how to explain that Alex would never truly let her in despite how she might feel.

"She won't allow herself to be vulnerable with me," she said in an attempt at an explanation. "Her dad betrayed her in a pretty terrible way, and instead of letting me in so I could help, she pushed me away. Her go-to is to shut down and snap at anyone who shows her any kind of love. And I don't know how to move forward with someone like that."

Eve continued to rub her back as she listened. For a moment, she didn't say anything but nodded her head thoughtfully. "Does she know you're in love with her?"

"Yes. I told her that same night."

"Do you think she loves you?"

"I know she does. She told me she does. But you should have heard the way she said it. She basically shouted it in anger. All because I was asking her to let me in."

"All this happened the same night her father betrayed her?"

Quinn shifted on the couch. She had thought about the timing of everything over and over again since that night. She had pushed Alex on a night she was struggling with something significant, but it didn't change the result. Alex would always shut down when pushed, and Quinn didn't want to be with someone who ran. "Yes. I found her drinking at a bar, and we got into a fight shortly after," she replied, knowing already what Eve would probably say.

But instead, she got up and moved to the kitchen. When she came back, she was holding two beers as she sat back down. "You know, Will broke up with me the first time I ever told him I loved him," she said right before taking a long sip.

"Will is obsessed with you. I don't believe it."

She laughed. "He is, but God, when I met him, he was an out-of-touch frat boy who was almost flunking out of college."

"How did I not know this?" Quinn asked, sitting up.

"Because I didn't want you, Mom, and Dad to hate my new boyfriend. I knew we'd probably get back together."

"What happened?"

"We did get back together. And then it happened again. But I believed in him. I knew who he was deep down. Back then, he was a product of his environment. Nobody had ever told him that he could succeed at anything. You know how his parents are."

"When did things change?"

"Well, after a few useless breakups, he started to trust that I wasn't going anywhere. And I learned the kind of communication that worked best with him. Soon, all that fell away, and we were just Will and Eve. But it wasn't always easy. Our parents aren't perfect, but we always knew we were loved. Will didn't have that."

Quinn took a sip of beer as she listened. She couldn't help but think about Simon and some of the things Alex had told her about their relationship.

"I'm not saying it's your job to teach Alex how to be in a relationship," Eve continued. "I'm just saying that everyone is different in how they deal with their emotions. And not everyone wears their heart on their sleeve like you do. I love that about you, but I could see it being scary to someone who isn't like that naturally. Sometimes, it takes time to break out of what we know. Do you still love her?"

"I can't turn that off just because she broke my heart."

"Then your heart is still open to her. Maybe give it some time."

Quinn was grateful she had Eve there. The next few days would be beyond stressful with final rehearsals and opening night. It would be nice to have someone who knew her so well by her side. "I'm really glad you're here," she said.

Eve smiled widely. "Me too. Mikey told me Horizon wants to produce a full run of your show. How do you feel about that?"

"I haven't processed it really. I don't want to work with those people. But I also don't feel like I can turn something like that down."

"You have a lot to think about, Quinney."

"What do you think I should do?"

"About the possible extension?"

"No." She knew Eve would understand the larger meaning behind her response.

Eve leaned back on the couch and motioned for Quinn to put her head on her shoulder, which she did. "Maybe focus on your show. You're just days away from opening. And then figure things out. Maybe break the ice and call her."

"Why should I be the one to break the ice?" She knew she sounded petulant, but her point remained.

"We are who we are. The key to love isn't trying to find someone who meets all your needs. It's about finding someone whose faults you can live with. And in time, you learn how to work through them and navigate life together. But being stubborn never made anyone happy. It may be that you need to make that first move."

Eve always had good advice, and Quinn would think about her words, but right now, she was too overwhelmed to make any decisions. And Eve was right. She had an opening coming up, and she needed to focus. "Are you hungry?" she asked

"I only came here because you keep raving about the pizza. Please tell me it's somewhere close."

Quinn laughed and pushed off the couch. "Come on. This is New York. You're never far from a slice."

CHAPTER THIRTY-NINE

Quinn sat at the mirror in her dressing room and gave her reflection one last glance. She could hear the rising pitch of the audience filtering into the theater and knew she needed to get into costume soon. She just wanted a moment to sit alone in the quiet without Mikey and Eve hovering over her.

Not that she hadn't loved having Eve in town the past few days. She only got to see her in the morning and late at night, but her sister's presence still calmed her and allowed her to focus. But having someone in her apartment, plus the time spent with Mikey outside of rehearsal, meant that there had been very little time for herself.

The lack of alone time was probably good, all things considered. Alex was still constantly on her mind, but she was able to push those thoughts aside as her world barreled toward this one important moment. One that didn't include romantic angst. And Diego appreciated the difference in her performance. Each rehearsal had improved upon the last, and the show was ready for audiences. But as she sat at the mirror alone, the excitement she should have felt about her New York debut was muted. All of it felt dim without Alex.

She needed to shake herself out of her melancholy before she walked on that stage. After taking a long breath, she put on her simple costume of jeans and a T-shirt, her act one outfit. The noise from the theater became even louder, and she wondered how many people she would even know out there outside of Eve and Mikey.

She wished Alex was one of them. But she hadn't heard from her since the gala two weeks ago and figured she'd be staying as far away from Simon and Horizon as she could. Quinn couldn't help the way her stomach tightened at the thought of doing this show without Alex watching.

She was about to take her top off when she heard a knock at the door. "Come in," she said, putting the shirt back on. She heard Janet before she saw her. The clanging of her bracelets was as pronounced as ever, and soon, she was moving swiftly into the room as if she owned it, which Quinn guessed she sort of did now.

"Quinn, dear. I came to tell you to break a leg and congratulations."

Now that Quinn had seen her true colors, Janet's easy, charming demeanor felt smarmy. Even though Quinn was mad at Alex, she still felt an incredible defensiveness over her, and being in Janet's presence made her entire body tense. "Thank you." She turned back to her clothes rack, pretending to sift through it. She didn't want Janet to stay, but it also wasn't the best idea to mouth off to her. She did run the theater now, after all. Quinn hoped ignoring her might get her to leave.

"I understand you're close with Alex, dear," Janet said after a few beats of awkward silence. "But I hope you can understand the opportunity here. And will be able to move forward professionally."

The condescending tone grated, and Quinn pulled the rack aside so she could look at her. "If I had trouble being professional, I wouldn't be here right now. What you did to Alex was despicable."

If Janet was surprised, she didn't show it. She simply folded her arms into the scarfs hanging from her neck and gave Quinn a small, patronizing smile. "Simon made the decision he made. And I hope you know that we both respect your show greatly. I expect big things from you if you play your cards right."

"And what exactly does that entail?" she asked, folding her own arms.

"Simon Anders is one of Broadway's most important investors, as am I, I might add. This show could go far. What can Alex offer you now, Quinn?"

"My relationship with her is none of your business."

"Of course not. But you're too young to choose love over success."

There was so much more she wanted to hurl at Janet, but as the noise from the theater grew louder by the minute, she was reminded of where she was and what she was about to do. Now wasn't the time to burn a bridge with the executive director of Horizon. But she also wasn't going to listen to career advice from someone who'd only gotten to where she was through duplicity.

Janet took one look around the dressing room and dropped her hands to a less combative stance. "Anyway, dear. Let's see how tonight goes and then figure out the future. Horizon Theater is going to soar if I have anything to do with it. Alex ran this place like a moody teenager, but I plan to see it live up to its legacy."

Quinn's anger rose again, and she didn't even try to hold back the bite in her tone. "Thank you for stopping by. Now, if you'll excuse me, I need to change. I don't want any photos to end up with your friend at the *Post*."

"Careful," Janet said with a smile that Quinn didn't interpret as friendly. "I like you. And I think your show could do well long-term. But don't for one moment think that I need you. And don't forget who I am in this city. Someone we both know already made that mistake. Don't follow her lead, Quinn. You're too good for that."

"You mean too good for her."

"Perhaps both," Janet replied with the same smile. "Break a leg tonight, dear.

❖

It felt strange for Alex to be standing so close the theater but not actually in it. This was the first opening night in as long as she could remember that she wasn't front and center. But as she leaned against the building across the street, she was anything but front and center. Tonight, she was just another audience member.

It felt especially strange not being involved in this production, considering how instrumental she had been in bringing it to Horizon.

But she was happy Quinn would still get her moment and that whatever her father and Janet did to Alex, it hadn't affected Quinn's show. She deserved a stage, and Alex was thankful she still had one.

As she stood there looking at what had been her second home over the years, she wasn't as upset or sad as she'd thought she'd be. In fact, ever since the visit to her parents' house, she had felt freer and more determined than she had in all the time she'd spent at Horizon. For once, she was excited to experience a piece of art as a fan and not as someone who had to count the dollars afterward. And it wasn't just any piece of art. She was going to get to watch the woman she loved have her New York debut.

"Not that I'm trying to rush whatever ruminating roller coaster you're on right now, but it's fucking cold out here. Can we please go inside?" Courtney asked from beside her.

Alex's stomach exploded in butterflies. And not just at the prospect of seeing Quinn. She knew her presence at the theater was unwelcome, considering her recent conversations with both Janet and her father, and the last thing she wanted to do was to make this night about her. She had asked Courtney to wait with her until most of the crowd had entered the lobby, hoping it would decrease her chances of running into anyone she knew. "Okay, let's go," she said, and they pushed off the wall to head across the street.

As they walked up the steps, Alex clutched a small package to her chest. She had no idea how Quinn would react to it, given how her last attempt at a gift had gone, but she wasn't scared of trying anymore. She was going to try and try until Quinn gave her another chance. And this wasn't just a gift. She hoped Quinn could see the sincerity behind it.

As they waited for the sole person in line to get his ticket, Alex again reflected at the turns her life had taken. As managing director, she'd often watched the flow of the box office, but it felt surreal to be waiting for her own ticket.

She knew everyone who worked at the theater, so when it was their turn to step up to the counter, she said, "Hey, Talia."

"Alex! Hey," Talia said, but Alex could tell she was surprised to see her. "Hey, Courtney. How are you guys?"

"Fantastic. There should be two tickets under my name," Courtney said with a smile.

"Unfortunately, the box office is closed," an icy voice said from behind them. "We had to release those tickets for some important members of the press. I'm sure you both understand."

Alex tensed as Janet spoke. Talia just gave her a quizzical look and a shrug. Alex took a deep breath so she could steady her emotions before she turned. Courtney, however, did not seem to possess the same kind of control.

"Oh God, Janet. Does Simon have you running the box office too? The whole bouncer thing would be more intimidating without the scarfs." Courtney waved at the myriad of flimsy scarfs hanging around Janet's neck.

Janet didn't even bother to look at her. "Or I just had a feeling you'd turn up."

Alex looked at Janet, someone she had once trusted. She couldn't even remember a time when Janet hadn't been a core part of her life, and in some ways, she had always thought of her as the antithesis to her father. But now, Janet's easy flamboyance and gentle authority seemed like a mask for a much more sinister persona, one so like her father, she couldn't believe she'd never seen it before. "Courtney is a paying customer. You can't bar her entry."

"We'll be sure to refund her tickets, and she has our deepest apologies for the inconvenience," Janet replied. "Courtney, we'd be happy to see you at another show."

"And I'd be happy to tell you where you can put that apology," Courtney responded.

Alex loved how protective Courtney was, but she could feel the tension vibrating off her and knew that if she wasn't stopped, she'd take things too far. Tonight wasn't the night for that. In fact, as she looked at Janet again, she didn't feel any of the same rage she had felt the night of the gala. She was done with this place and everything that went with it.

She put a gentle hand on Courtney's shoulder before stepping slightly in front of her to face Janet. "It's okay, Court. She's not worth the energy."

"If you care about her, you'll go," Janet said. "There's an entire roomful of critics in there. Don't make tonight about you."

She could argue that Janet was the one who'd created the original mess with the media, but out of the corner of her eye, she saw more people coming up the theater steps, and she wasn't going to make a scene on Quinn's opening night.

"Quinn would want Alex in there," Courtney said from behind her.

She wished that was true. She wished she could be sure that Quinn *did* want her there tonight. But she wasn't going to throw a tantrum in front of Janet. "Let's go," she said. "We all know this place can't afford another media scandal."

"Neither can Quinn," Janet replied.

Those words caused Alex to turn again, and she took one step closer so she could keep her voice low. "Quinn is the best thing to ever cross this theater's stage. I'll be interested to see what you do once you're not riding the coattails of the programming I chose or artists like her."

"That's rich coming from a girl who rode her parents' coattails for all these years."

Alex nodded and returned Janet's cold smile. "Perhaps I was. But I'm not anymore."

"No, now you're just unemployed."

"Not for long. Good luck. You're going to need it." She walked back down the theater steps. She vaguely heard Courtney say something to Janet, but she couldn't bring herself to care what it was. She had spent the last two weeks shedding herself of all the toxic parts of her life, and walking away from Horizon for what was the last time felt like the final piece.

And while she didn't really wish luck on Janet or her father, she wasn't being sarcastic in what she'd told her. They were going to need all the help they could get. Alex was finally beginning to understand her worth, and she knew how influential she had been in the success of Horizon. She had little faith that Janet would continue that trend.

None of that mattered anymore. She had her own future to worry about. The only thing still at Horizon that she cared about was the woman about to take its stage. Quinn's show would close in three weeks, and they'd both be free of her father and Janet Jameson. She just hoped Quinn would eventually see her.

Once they were down the block, passing the alleyway entrance to Horizon's stage door, Courtney put her hand on Alex's arm and stopped them. "Are you okay?"

"I should have seen that coming," she replied. "I shouldn't have even tried. Quinn doesn't deserve to have her show monopolized by this drama."

"Quinn would want to know you tried your best to see her show. You did the right thing."

"Thank you. I know you get a lot of work out of Horizon, and that interaction with Janet probably didn't help."

Courtney let out something that sounded like a mix of a snort and a laugh. "Please. Like I'd ever step foot on their stage again. Now, give me that," she said and reached for the package still in Alex's hand.

"Why?"

"This isn't the Pentagon, Al. We were breaking into this theater long before you got the codes. I can get this to her if you want her to have it."

Alex looked at Courtney's mischievous smile and couldn't help but return it. She desperately wanted to be in the audience when Quinn debuted but not at the expense of the show itself, and that was what her presence would do if Janet had her way. She wasn't going to give that gift to Janet. She would go another night. After all, Janet couldn't be at every show, and Alex highly doubted they'd hire security to watch out for her. "I was planning on giving it to her afterward," she said.

"What's the difference?"

She looked at her watch. "She goes on in ten minutes. Janet was right about one thing. Tonight is about Quinn, and I don't want to do anything that will mess that up."

Courtney was practically bouncing on her feet. "I'll sneak in once she's onstage, and I'll put it in her dressing room."

"You look entirely too excited about this."

"I feel like a spy. I should have worn all black," Courtney replied, looking down the alley like she was on a mission.

"I think it's the hair that's the giveaway more than anything."

"True. Okay, I'm off. If you don't hear from me again, tell Paige I went out bravely."

"Just please don't get arrested for trespassing."

"Why? That would make a good story. And my best friend can afford my bail."

"Not anymore. Don't forget that I've spent my money. Now I'm just a starving artist like you."

"And I've never been prouder," Courtney said, but there was no sarcasm in her tone. She was looking at her softly, and Alex could tell she meant what she said. "Where are you off to now?"

For years, it had seemed as if the only answer Alex ever had for that question was her apartment, a bar, or Horizon. But the realization that she had somewhere new and exciting to go caused her to smile widely.

"Back to work."

CHAPTER FORTY

Quinn tried to shake off her interaction with Janet, but now that she had her makeup fully done and her costume on, she had nothing in her dressing room to distract her from her rising anger.

Janet had only ever shown an interest in her because of her name, and since joining the theater, she hadn't shown one ounce of interest in her show. The fact that neither Simon nor Janet had cared to attend a rehearsal showcased to Quinn just how much they really supported her. Perhaps they wanted to extend her show, but it wasn't because they believed in it. They believed in what it could do for their theater.

She stopped pacing when she heard another knock on the door. She closed her eyes for a moment and said a silent prayer that it wasn't Simon. She didn't think she could take both Horizon leaders in such quick succession.

When Courtney peered around the door, Quinn let out a breath. "Can I come in for a sec?" Courtney asked.

"Yes."

Courtney looked a little flustered, but she often had that kind of energy, so Quinn didn't read too much into it. Mainly, she felt bad as she faced someone whose texts and calls she had ignored for the past two weeks.

"I'm sorry I haven't gotten back to you."

Courtney waved a hand. "We don't have time for that. Besides, it's totally fine. I get it. I'm the best friend. And that's why I'm here."

Her stomach did a flip when she realized Courtney was talking about Alex. "Is she here?" she heard herself asking before she could stop herself.

"No, she's not. But she tried."

"What do you mean?"

"Janet wouldn't let us into the theater. But Alex was here, and she really wanted to see your opening, but she didn't want to make a scene that drew attention away from you."

Quinn leaned against the makeup counter, not feeling like she could hold herself up. The anger she had felt right before Courtney entered the room only grew. "Janet sent her away? But she came? She was here?"

Courtney took the few steps and put her free hand on Quinn's shoulder. "I know you've been upset with her. And you have every right. She's been a total idiot. But she came. And I have a feeling this isn't the last time she'll try."

"To see my show?"

"Not just that," Courtney said softly. "Just try."

"What's that?" Quinn said, looking at the package in Courtney's hand.

"Oh! That's the reason I came. Alex was going to get this to you after the show, but now she can't. And I had explicit instructions not to disturb you before your show, but I never listen to Alex. And I guess if you're anything like me, I'd want to know that the woman I love was thinking about me. It's never good to go onstage sad." Courtney set the package down on the counter. "Now I need to go before NYPD finds me lurking back here."

"Did Janet call the police?" Quinn asked, looking horrified.

"No, but this whole breaking and entering thing makes me feel more badass if I think she did."

Quinn offered Courtney a smile, but her head was still spinning from the revelation of what Janet had done. At this point, she didn't know if the butterflies in her stomach were from the impending debut or the fact that she now knew Alex had tried to attend.

"Anyway, I'll get out of your dressing room." Courtney looked at Quinn tentatively before she pulled her in for a hug. "I'm sorry we can't be there tonight. I assume Mikey's in the audience?"

"Yes, and my sister flew in from Seattle," she replied, attempting to control the shakiness in her voice.

"Good." Courtney moved over to the door but turned back. "Alex told Janet tonight that your show is the best thing to ever cross Horizon's stage. I know it's killing her that she can't be here. I hope you'll give her another chance." She stood there for a moment and looked like she was trying to decide on something. "She'll be at 22 Thomas Street later if you want to find her. Break a leg, kid." She gave Quinn one last smile before walking out.

Quinn continued leaning against the counter. Her breathing felt erratic, and she needed to steady herself before she went onstage. But she was livid. It was her show, and Janet had no right deciding who could and couldn't attend it.

She looked at the package Courtney dropped off and sat in the same chair she'd used to put on her makeup as she unwrapped the brown paper. Sitting inside was an envelope on top of something else that was wrapped. But unlike the brown paper on the outside, this wrapping paper had little rainbow fish all over it. She couldn't help but smile at the thought of stoic Alex Anders searching through a store for fish wrapping paper.

Her hands shook as she opened the envelop. She unfolded the single piece of paper inside and read a handwritten letter from Alex:

Quinn,

I hope I get to say all this in person, and this note becomes redundant. But in the chance that I don't get to see you tonight, please read this.

Congratulations on your New York debut. This isn't how I pictured saying that on your opening night, but I know I've made a mess of things. Seeing you onstage for the first time changed me. The rawness of your stories mixed with your beautiful delivery caused something to stir in me that I still haven't let go of, and I now know I never want to.

As I read your script all over again this week, it's your bravery that calls out to me most. Your bravery shines through every page, and it goes well beyond your writing. Every moment I've spent with you has shown me a woman unafraid of being herself.

I'm sorry I didn't show you the same kind of bravery. Until very recently, I didn't know how to find it. I will never forgive myself for letting you walk away that night. Or the things I said to you. Every day that has passed since has only proven to me how much I want you in my life.

If you'll let me, I know I can be brave for you. And I'm going to keep trying to show you that until you believe me. There's so much more I need to say. I hope in time, you'll hear me.

To many more openings.

Always yours,

Alex

Quinn's heart hammered against her chest. Alex's words reverberated through her head as her shaking fingers held the package. She blinked rapidly a few times to keep the threatening tears at bay.

She tore through the fish paper and looked at the two-paneled frame now sitting in her lap. On one side, Alex had framed the first page of her script that had the title and her name on it, and on the other side was a page from one of the final scenes. Mostly stage directions but halfway down, there was a paragraph Alex had put a small dash by. She read the familiar words:

We're taught as children not to lie. But what that really means is don't lie to each other. I had been lying to myself for years. Because it was so much easier to believe I was happy than to face the broken person I had become. The part of me I thought of as the logical part had her arguments: people didn't leave a successful modeling career. People didn't give up that kind of money or glamour. But one day, I woke up and realized that it wasn't logic. It was fear. Because when you spend your life as one thing, it's hard to remember all the other things you can be. All I knew that morning was that I was going to find out what those things were.

Quinn stared at the section of script. She knew those words like the back of her hand, but reading them through Alex's eyes was like reading her own writing for the first time.

After doing this scene repeatedly for the past few weeks, the meaning had lost significance. Her departure from modeling felt like so long ago that it was hard to put herself back there. But as she read her words again through a new context, she could remember the debilitating fear she had felt all those years ago. And she knew it must have been similar to what Alex had felt the night of the gala.

She set the frame down and picked up Alex's letter again, reading her words another time. She was in the exact spot she was supposed to be. Backstage waiting to debut her show to Manhattan. She had been waiting for this moment for over a year now. But as she looked at the dressing room, she felt empty without the one person she needed.

She didn't want her show to be for Janet or Simon. Getting through tonight was one thing, but how could she come in here night after night after what they'd done? The beauty and mystique Horizon held when she'd first arrived in the city was gone. Alex was Horizon for Quinn, and Alex was no longer there.

Someone knocked on her door, and Mikey stepped into the room. "I saw Leah coming down the hall, so I told her I'd give you the five-minute call. So, five minutes," he said, but when his eyes met Quinn's, his brow furrowed. "What's up?"

"Janet wouldn't allow Alex in to see the show."

Mikey nodded but didn't seem surprised. "I was wondering when I didn't see her anywhere. Janet's turned into a real piece of work."

"I can't do this show here, Mikey," she said shakily.

He pulled one of the chairs from the makeup counter over to where Quinn was sitting and sat so their knees were touching. In a very un-Mikey-like move, he pulled her hands into his lap. "Tell me what you want to do. It's your choice, Q."

"It's not just mine. This affects you too. I don't want to make a mess of things all over again for you."

He squeezed her hands and waited until she was looking at him. "You've never made a mess for me. And even though talking all mushy like this makes me feel like my skin is crawling, you should know that I'd go anywhere with you. So make the call, and we'll figure it out. Like we always do."

"There are critics out there tonight."

"There are."

"Pulling out won't make the theater look good. But it also wouldn't make me look good." Quinn had minutes to make a decision, but for once, Mikey waited and didn't rush her. Before she could say anything, there was another knock on her door.

"Places, Quinn. It's time," her stage manager said as she popped her head into the room.

"Thanks, Leah. Coming."

Leah gave her a quick thumbs-up and left again.

"What do you want to do?" Mikey asked, standing.

Quinn stayed seated for just one moment longer. She knew what she wanted to do. And slowly, a mischievous thought took hold. "I want to fuck this place up."

CHAPTER FORTY-ONE

Quinn watched the city pass by as her taxi zipped downtown toward the Tribeca address Courtney had given her. Now that she was alone, she tried to catch her breath, but the inside of the cab felt dry and suffocating. She rolled down the window so she could suck in some of the cold night air.

After the air hit her face, she looked at her phone to see if Mikey had texted again, but the last message on the screen was the one he'd sent a few minutes after she'd left the theater. She knew it wasn't fair to leave him to deal with the mess at Horizon, but she needed to get to Alex, and she didn't care to hear what Janet had to say.

She didn't regret her decision, but the adrenaline from it and her subsequent departure had her buzzing with energy. She hadn't felt like this since the day she'd quit modeling, and maybe that was the best indication that she had made the right decision. She had already spent too much time in an industry that used and manipulated her. Even if it meant she would never work in New York again, Quinn was proud of the decision she'd made.

She didn't have much time to dwell on it. When the cab began to slow, her mind transitioned from her show to thoughts of Alex, who was somewhere on this street. As the cab came to a stop, Quinn got out and looked at the tall brick building in front of her. It didn't have a sign out, but she could see a small metal number beside a run-down door and knew she was in the right place.

Now that she was here, she realized she wasn't going to be able to just walk into an unknown building, but when she pushed against the large door, it opened easily. The immediate entryway was dark. But after walking through some plastic paper that acted as a doorway, she was in a large bright room. It took her eyes a moment to adjust, and the first thing they landed on was Alex sitting at a table in the middle of the room with her back to the door. She was wearing a pair of charcoal slacks and a black button-up, and it was obvious she had been dressed to go somewhere nice, but right now, she had her shirt untucked and the sleeves rolled up.

She didn't seem to hear Quinn come in, probably due to the music blasting from her laptop, but she also seemed focused on something in front of her. Quinn took the moment to look at the rest of the room, but all it looked like was a warehouse under construction.

The table was the only piece of furniture, except for two stools placed around it and a ladder leaning against a wall. Along the other wall were some diagrams and drawings, but beyond that, the room was empty. "Alex," she said loudly.

Alex whipped around with wide eyes. "Quinn," she said and quickly turned off the music. "What are you doing here?"

"Courtney gave me the address. What is this place?"

"It was a wholesale clothing distributor, but they moved to Brooklyn. It's been sitting here empty for a couple of years. And, well, I bought it."

Quinn's eyes widened too. "For what?"

Alex looked around before walking closer. "I'll show you," she said tentatively. She held her arms up. "This is the lobby." She pointed to a long piece of tape that went along the ground. "This tape marks where that ends." She walked along the tape until she was at the other side of the room and motioned for Quinn to follow.

"Lobby for what?" she asked, but Alex's obvious excitement caused something in her stomach to stir, and she followed without getting an answer.

They walked through a doorway at the far end and were standing in what was seemed to be the main part of the warehouse. "These will be glass doors instead of a solid one," Alex said. "Once you're through, you can go either left or right. Each side will have a staircase leading to the top rows." She almost skipped as she guided them farther back into the space. Quinn had never seen her so young and excited. "It won't have a balcony, but I still want an incline that goes down to a thrust stage. The stage will be about here." She stopped walking once she got to another piece of long tape. "And the back of the space will obviously hold the green room and dressing rooms." When she was done waving her arms around, she turned to Quinn with an expectant expression.

"You bought a theater?" Quinn asked, her head spinning.

"Kind of. I bought the space. I need to build the theater."

Quinn opened and closed her mouth before anything came out. "I know you have money, but do you have that much money?" She had to assume building something from scratch would take hundreds of thousands of dollars.

"I'm not doing it alone. I have some investors. Including Tim."

"Delvin?"

"I swore him to secrecy. So Mikey doesn't know yet," Alex replied with a soft smile.

"I can't believe you bought a theater." She was still trying to wrap her head around it. "What made you do it?"

Alex walked over to a bench set against the far wall. "Will you sit with me?"

Quinn sat, but she made sure their legs weren't touching. She needed a clear mind while they spoke, and touching Alex had the opposite effect on her.

"You were right about so many things that night, Quinn. But one of the things you were most right about is that there's more to life than Horizon. Losing that job to Janet was one of the best things that could have happened to me. I was holding on to that place so tight because it was my mom's. But it isn't anymore. I just wish I had figured that out sooner. Because I pushed away the actual best thing that has ever happened to me."

"Alex—"

Alex put her hand on her leg. "Wait. Please, let me say this to you." She continued to hold on, and now that they were touching, Quinn didn't want to stop. "I love you. I'm so desperately in love with you. And I'm sorry for the way I told you last time. I haven't said those words since my mom died, and that's not an excuse, but for so long, it seemed easier to just let myself be scared. But I pushed away the two things I love most: performing and you. I'm just hoping it's not too late to fix either." She looked behind her at the empty room before returning her eyes to Quinn's. "That's what this place is. A mix of what I loved from Horizon and my own stage to create whatever I want. I was hoping it could be whatever *we* want."

Quinn looked around in disbelief. "You built yourself a stage."

"Do you think I'm crazy?"

"I think it's wonderful. But it doesn't erase how much you hurt me. I need to understand what got you to this point. How do I know you won't just run again?"

"You got me here," Alex responded and grabbed her hands. "Your show did. The love and support you've shown me did. Courtney did. My mom did. And for once, I stopped hiding behind the excuse of others and did it for myself."

Tears rolled down Quinn's face, but she didn't want to move her hands, so she just let them fall. Alex gently wiped them away. "I don't want to just be the person who teaches you how to be in a relationship," Quinn said. "I need more than that. Who's to say you won't snap at me next time I try to dig a little deeper? Or that someone new won't come along who will be able to teach you something else about yourself?"

"I didn't open up because you pushed me to. It's because of who you are. Nobody else could have done that because nobody else is as perfect as you. And it's my fault that you don't know all the reasons I love you. Because I've been an idiot, and I haven't told you."

Alex slid to the ground so she was on her knees. "I love you. I love how unabashedly you laugh when you find something funny. And how it bubbles out of you effortlessly. I love your soft smile that seems just for me. I love how random and silly you are and how you make me sillier. I love how excited you get over snacks or pajamas and your weird obsession with fish.

"I love your sounds. The way you hum when you eat or the cute little sounds you make when you're waking up. I love how you find something positive in everything, even when I can't. I love the way you always find my hand when we're in bed falling asleep. I love how sweet you are to everyone you come across. I love the way you kiss. I love the way you taste."

She moved higher on her knees. "Everything I learn about you just makes me fall more and more in love with you. And I should have told you that the second I felt it. Because I've felt it for so long, Quinn. I think my mom would finally be proud of me. Because I won't run from this. Any of this. I will never run from you."

As Quinn gazed at Alex's face, which looked soft and open, the last remnants of her anger floated away. She pulled on Alex's hands so she could interlace their fingers. "I love you too," she whispered, not able to stop more tears from falling. "I was so heartbroken. But I couldn't stop loving you."

"I will never hurt you like that again. I can be everything you need me to be. And I'll add some more on top of that." Alex opened her mouth to say something else, but Quinn cupped her face so she could lean down and bring their lips together. She had heard enough, and at this point, she needed to connect with her in a different way.

It had only been two weeks since their last kiss, but it felt as if their mouths had never touched before. Their lips were tentative as they pushed against each other. When Alex's tongue lightly pushed against Quinn's lips, she opened her mouth. As soon as their tongues connected once again, all newness evaporated, and their mouths began a familiar exchange. Quinn wanted to feel more of Alex against her, so she opened her legs and pulled her between them. Alex threaded her hands through Quinn's hair.

Before Quinn was even close to ready to have the kiss end, Alex pulled away. "I never want to go that long without kissing you again."

"Stop talking," Quinn replied and pulled her back in.

Alex laughed into her lips, but just as soon, she slipped her tongue back into Quinn's mouth. Her hands returned to Quinn's hair, and when their tongues began to flick against each other, Quinn couldn't help but moan.

Alex kept her mouth on Quinn's as she moved off the floor and put her legs on either side of her. They continued kissing for what felt like minutes until Alex pulled away again. "Wait," she said, breathing heavily.

Quinn let out a frustrated sigh. "For someone who said that they love the way I taste, you seem very chatty."

Alex let out a sexy, low laugh, and the sound vibrated through Quinn's body. "Believe me, sweetheart, I plan on getting you home as soon as I can. But..." She paused to look at her watch. "Shouldn't you be at your opening night party?"

Quinn had been so caught up in the moment that she had completely forgotten. She laced their fingers together. "There is no party. There is no show. Janet posted a closing notice. I'm sure the reviews in tomorrow's papers will be colorful."

Alex's face morphed into simmering rage. "She did what? She can't do that. Why would she do that?" She tried to get up, but Quinn didn't want to lose the feeling of her there, so she pulled her down again.

"Stay. It's okay. I expected her to do something like that after what I did."

"What did you do?"

"Well, since the final scene of the show ends with me discussing my decision to leave modeling, I decided it was time for a new ending scene." She attempted to make her face look innocent.

She saw the realization hit Alex's face. "And what was the new scene about?"

"My new life in New York and everything that happened. You, the *Post*, the gala, Janet, your dad. I told our story. I can't say it was my most eloquent writing, but I think it had the desired effect." Quinn remembered the shocked look that had crossed Alex's face after Simon gave Rick's role to Janet, but that was nothing compared to the look of pure disbelief currently frozen there.

"What happened after? Did you see Janet or my father?"

"I left the moment I got backstage. I texted Mikey and told him I was leaving to find you. He's the one who texted me that Janet posted the closing notice. I guess she was pretty pissed. No word on how your dad reacted yet."

"You know all the critics were there tonight and likely saw that, right?"

She nodded and gave Alex another smile. "And so does Janet."

There was a moment of silence as Alex continued to look at her with her mouth hanging open. But unexpectedly, she threw her head back and laughed loudly. "I can't believe you did that."

"You're not upset? I kind of outed us in a big way."

Alex put one hand on Quinn's cheek and leaned closer. "We don't need to hide anymore. I will never hide you again. The only thing I'm upset about is that I didn't get to see Janet's face when you did it."

"I guess I kind of screwed up my New York debut."

"One of the things I've realized is that New York is a big city with a lot of theater. Come with me."

Alex lifted off Quinn's lap and put her hand out. Her smile was one Quinn had never seen on her face. The shadow in Alex's eyes was gone, replaced by a youthful glimmer.

Alex pulled her to where the stage was meant to be. She stood behind her so their bodies were barely touching. "You know, when I was first talking to your team about your show, there were a handful of other theaters in the mix. You won't have trouble finding a new home in this city." She placed her hands on Quinn's shoulders. "But I was hoping I could throw my hat into the ring. I know it won't be as big and fancy as Horizon, but I promise, there will be other benefits."

"What are you saying?"

"Close your eyes," Alex said and when Quinn complied, she put her hand under her elbow and guided her forward. "You'll walk out as the lights are off and stop here. Centerstage. Now, take a breath." She paused. "You can feel the audience in front of you, even if you can't see them yet. Everything feels intimate and real. You own their anticipation. And their excitement. Then, the lights slowly come up, and it's just you everyone can see. And you're free, Quinn. Free to create whatever you want, night after night. This stage is yours. A canvas for whatever you want to put on it. Now, open your eyes."

Quinn took in a deep breath. She could feel Alex against her back, and when Alex's lips grazed her earlobe, she sucked in a sharp breath. After a moment, she opened her eyes.

"I'll be there," Alex said next, pointing in front of them. "Center section. Front row. Every night."

Quinn loved the feeling of Alex's arms around her, but she also wanted to be able to see, so she turned. "You want to do my show here?"

"I would be honored. But I also know how many offers you're about to get, so I won't be offended if you go with an established theater. I don't even have a name for mine yet."

"Alex, you don't have to give me a stage just because I got fired from Horizon. You should choose shows that—"

Alex put a finger on her lips. "You don't need to finish that sentence. I fell in love with your work before I ever fell in love with you. Now I get both. I was going to make the offer anyway. Your show deserves a full run. And I can do that here. Maybe not for another ten months, but I can't think of anything I'd rather have than a new theater with your show as the opener."

A smile broke across Quinn's face, but she schooled her features quickly. "Well, I guess I'll have to consider your proposal," she replied, doing her best to sound serious. "If the competition is as steep as you say, how will you differentiate yourself, Ms. Anders? You mentioned something about additional benefits?"

Alex directed a playful smile her way. "Oh, yes. There are many benefits that I'd be happy to outline for you."

"A sample might be good so I know what we're working with."

Alex leaned down but didn't kiss her lips. Beginning at Quinn's collarbone, she brought her lips up the length of her neck, making sure to kiss and lick every spot. She swiped her tongue over Quinn's ear before bringing her mouth back down so she could sensually swipe Quinn's lips. When Quinn tried to flick with her own tongue, Alex pulled back with a smug smile.

"Just a sample," she whispered.

"I can't imagine another theater beating that. The show is yours."

"That was a much easier sell than I was expecting."

"It helps that the artist in question in desperately in love with you."

"That certainly helps. And I love you too," Alex said before placing a soft, chaste kiss against Quinn's cheek. "Does this mean you'll stay in New York?"

"As long as my fish are invited, New York is my home," Quinn replied. "You're my home."

Alex took a long breath at her words, and as she let it out, tears fell down her face. And now that Quinn wasn't mad, she could see just how beautiful Alex was when she cried. "I would never exclude those ninjas," Alex whispered.

"You're not scared about being a fish mom?"

"I told you, I'm not running. Not even at the prospect of raising some aquatic teenagers."

"Good," Quinn said with a smile. "Now take me to get pizza and take me home."

Alex leaned back in for another kiss. Kissing her always felt passionate, but now more than ever, it also felt safe. Because now Quinn knew there were so many more moments like this to come. As they opened their mouths, she tasted the slight salt from Alex's tears, and she brought her arms around her so she might feel as safe as Quinn did.

But when Alex's fingers left Quinn's face and grazed her sides, barely touching her tits, she didn't want steady or safe anymore.

She broke her mouth away from Alex's to see the same fire she felt inside reflected on her face. "Actually, how about home and then pizza?" she asked in a breathy voice.

"Anything you want, sweetheart."

EPILOGUE

One Year Later

"'Tonight, all eyes are on The Olander, the hot new theater taking Tribeca by storm,'" Courtney said as she barged into Alex's dressing room without knocking and read off a newspaper in front of her. "'The Olander came onto the scene earlier this year with their smashing debut of Quinn Collins's *Model Behavior*, and tonight, the theater celebrates the opening of the much anticipated, gender-bending version of *A Streetcar Named Desire*. Founded by Alexandra Anders, formerly the managing director of Horizon Theater, The Olander...' blah, blah, blah."

"Courtney—"

"Wait, let's skip to the good part," Courtney said, waving Alex off before she turned back to the page in front of her. "'Ms. Anders got her start working at Horizon Theater, a company founded by her father, well-known theater investor, Simon Anders, and renowned stage actress Peggy Anders, who passed away in 2011. Even with her dramatic departure from Horizon, with two sold out runs under her belt for The Olander, Ms. Anders has bucked off the inevitable calls for nepotism and proven that she is a force in her own right in the New York theater community.'" Courtney looked up and smiled before looking back down. "Oh, and this part is good too," she said. "'Given Horizon Theater's recent struggles sans Ms. Anders, perhaps we're witnessing that the maternal apple didn't fall far. Tonight, like her mother before her, she's taking her own turn across the stage and will be starring as Stanley Kowalski in the theater's production of *Streetcar*. Perhaps her father and Horizon should take some notes. The Olander is here to stay.'"

"I read it already," Alex said when Courtney finally set the newspaper down, but she couldn't help her smile.

"You know who else probably read it?" Courtney said with a mischievous smile as she plopped on the couch against the wall of the dressing room.

"After the year they've had, I wouldn't be surprised if my father canceled his subscription to the *Times*."

"That's their own doing. With a little help from Quinn. And whoever recorded her opening night and put it on YouTube."

"For the record, I told them not to do that god-awful David Coe play. I'm just glad I got out before I had to deal with the press from that one."

"But then we wouldn't have gotten to read the *Times* review that claimed your father's theater was an affront to feminism. That was a really fun day."

Alex agreed, but she wasn't about to vocalize it, so she smiled and turned back to the mirror to apply her makeup. Tonight wasn't about the failings of her father and Janet. The article Courtney had read from meant more to her than accomplishing some vendetta. She was proud of what she had created at this theater, and for once in her life, she felt validated outside of anything that had to do with Horizon.

She reached for the hat on the counter and put it on, carefully pinning her hair under it so it didn't look long. "What do you think?" she asked so Courtney could evaluate her. "Manly enough?"

"The best I'll give you is slightly butch. You can't get around that face. But I'm sure you'll have all the ladies swooning."

"All I care is that one of them does."

"Yeah, yeah," Courtney replied with an eye roll.

They were both in the habit of teasing each other about their respective relationships, but ultimately, Alex couldn't be happier that Courtney and Paige were going so strong. And she knew Courtney felt the same about Quinn.

As if on cue, Paige popped her head into the dressing room. "Fifteen minutes, ladies," she said. "Alex, you know you can kick Courtney out if you need to focus."

Courtney let out an exaggerated scoff. "Why do you assume she needs to focus, and I don't?"

Paige leaned down so she could place a quick kiss on her head. "Because, my love, you're in her dressing room. If you wanted to focus, you'd go to your own."

"I share my dressing room with two other women. Alex gets her own," Courtney argued as she pulled Paige into her lap.

Paige let out a laugh before hopping off her lap and moving back toward the door.

"Perks of owning the theater," Alex said from her chair. "But don't worry, Paige. I'm used to Courtney annoying me in my dressing room."

Courtney pouted. "You only wanted a private one so you could fuck your girlfriend in it. The least you could do is let us borrow it."

"I'm on the clock, babe. There will be no fucking," Paige replied in the stern voice she did so well. "And you need to go put on the rest of your costume. We're now"—she looked down at her watch—"thirteen minutes until curtain."

"Fine, fine. I'll go. But just know that I'll be thinking about you with that sexy stage manager stopwatch around your neck."

Paige rolled her eyes. "I'm going to check on the rest of the cast. Behave, baby."

As soon as Paige was out of the room, Courtney moved over to the makeup counter and began looking at her own reflection. "God, Paige is such a tease when she's in work mode. I can't handle that tight little bun with the pencil through it. How am I supposed to perform Tennessee Williams with that strutting around backstage?"

"Well, she's the best stage manager I've ever met. I'd fire you before I'd fire her. So I guess you'll need to deal with it."

"I see how easily you flip sides. But that's fine. I prefer Quinn to you."

Alex could feel a small smile as soon as Quinn's name came up. Something that happened a lot. "I can't blame you for that."

"Speaking of which, I have to assume she's the reason there's now a fish tank in the lobby?"

"She is. She said life always brightens up a room."

"Or makes it look like a dentist's office."

"Sometimes, you make concessions for love, my friend."

"Whoever you are, will you just make sure that Alex Anders is getting fed and watered?"

"I'm mere minutes away from going onstage again. The Alex Anders you're referring to is a distant memory." She felt Courtney's hand on her own, causing her to lower the mascara.

"I'm so proud of you," Courtney said in a much more serious voice. "I know this is a big deal, and you're pretending like it isn't. But I've been rehearsing with you for weeks now. This is where you belong."

"It feels good to be back onstage with you. And it's only slightly annoying that your Blanche DuBois is better than mine ever was."

"Yeah, well, nobody can pull off Stanley's white T-shirt look like you. Your mom would be proud too."

"You think?"

"I mean, I still think you should have called this place The Lesbian Sexytime Theater, but I'm sure it would have meant a lot to your her that you used her family name."

"Thanks, babe." Alex smiled. "Now get your damn costume on so we can go out on that stage and yell at each other all night."

"Is that why I'm playing Blanche this time?"

"You were born to play Blanche. Plus, Quinn likes the white T-shirt look on me too."

"Is there anything Quinn doesn't like you in?"

"Nothing I can think of," a voice said from the doorway. Quinn stood there looking like a vision in red.

Alex almost forgot Courtney was sitting there until she heard her voice again. "Well, I have a costume to get to, and apparently, you two have a staring contest to conduct, so I'll be out."

That seemed to shake Quinn out of the moment. "Can't wait to see you onstage again, Court," she said with a warm smile.

"Thank you," Courtney replied, leaning in to place a quick kiss on her cheek. "And you look hot. Alex would probably say the same thing, but I'm not sure she's capable of language anymore."

Alex would have rolled her eyes, but she was busy staring at Quinn's red strapless dress and heels. She was holding something, but Alex was too distracted to pay it much attention.

"I'll make sure she gets onstage with her verbal faculties intact," Quinn said.

"I know you will. See you onstage, Al," Courtney said before leaving.

"Hey, you," Quinn said to Alex as the door closed, her eyes roaming up Alex's body.

"You look unbelievable, Quinn. You're so beautiful." She stood up so she could step closer.

"You just like me in red."

"I like you in anything." Her eyes caught the necklace around Quinn's neck, and she moved closer so she could touch the stone resting there. "You're wearing the diamond."

"It's mine, isn't it?" Quinn asked with a playful smile.

"I'm glad you're wearing it."

"I know you don't have much time, and your girlfriend coming backstage beforehand is probably bad luck, but I just wanted to see you."

"You're always welcome back here. Seeing you could never be bad luck." Alex leaned in for a quick kiss, but she didn't want to ruin her stage makeup, so she pulled back before either of them could deepen it.

"Well, things will be a little chaotic after the show. Especially with all your adoring fans clamoring for attention. So I thought I'd stop by before you went onstage for a little opening night gift."

"I don't think we have time for that kind of gift, sweetheart," Alex said with a raised eyebrow, even though she knew Quinn was referring to the package in her hand.

"At least until after the show. I wanted to give you this." She held up the package, and Alex took it. She couldn't remember the last time someone had given her a gift. "Open it," Quinn said with a small laugh when Alex continued to stare at the paper.

She started to unwrap it slowly.

"My God, woman, you go onstage soon," Quinn said in an exasperated tone and grabbed the package so she could rip the paper off herself. "Here." She handed Alex a black box, and because Alex didn't want to get scolded again, she quickly moved to the makeup counter so she could set it down and lift the lid.

She touched the beautiful wood inside. "A chess set," she said, lifting the board out.

"I still can't believe you don't have your own. The computer version is just sad. I thought you could use one."

"This is beautiful." Alex inspected the pieces. Each looked hand carved and unbelievably detailed. "Where did you get it?"

"I had it made for you.."

"It's perfect," Alex said, swallowing the intense emotion she felt. "You're perfect. Thank you so much." She gently put the board back in the box and grabbed hold of her hands. "Does this mean you'll play me at strip chess after the show?"

"We have a party to go to after the show."

"How about an after-party?"

"Always. Though it will be a very short game. There's not much to take off me tonight," Quinn replied with a suggestive expression.

Alex eyes snapped down Quinn's body as if she might be able to see what was under her dress. "Meaning?"

"Meaning panty and bra lines didn't go with the dress."

Alex let out a frustrated groan as she thought about all the things she'd like to do in that moment. "Do I really need to go onstage right now?"

"Yes, you do," Quinn said, putting a finger under Alex's chin and bringing her eyes up to a safer area.

"I should have cast an understudy for myself."

"You'll have me tonight. And tomorrow night. And all the nights."

"And some mornings?" Alex replied with a small smile.

"Those too."

She knew she only had a moment, so she leaned back in for another soft kiss. Quinn rested her hands lightly on Alex's waist as their lips pressed together. But when Paige's voice came over the backstage intercom, Quinn pushed Alex back slightly:

"Places, everyone. This is places. Have a great show tonight. Once again, we're at places."

"I better go grab my seat," Quinn said. "I don't want to miss Stanley's entrance."

"Thank you for coming to see me."

Quinn gave her another smile and walked out. In the hallway, Alex saw a few cast members heading to the wings and green room, but her eyes were still on Quinn, who had turned again.

"Break a leg," she said softly. "I love you."

Alex would need to school her features very soon since her huge smile didn't exactly fit with her character. But as she looked at Quinn, she felt overwhelmed with happiness, and a small, unexpected laugh bubbled out of her mouth.

"What's funny?" Quinn asked.

"Nothing. Those are just the best six words I've ever heard."

About the Author

From an early age, Shia Woods enjoyed writing and became an avid reader of literature. Those passions prompted her to earn a degree in journalism. But after years of devouring every queer story she could find, what started as a desire to chase headlines diminished, and she decided to indulge her dream of writing her own stories of love, lust, and passion. When she's not writing novels, Shia can be found hanging out with her family and three high-maintenance chihuahuas in the Pacific Northwest.

Books Available from Bold Strokes Books

Language Lessons by Sage Donnell. Grace and Lenka never expected to fall in love. Is home really where the heart is if it means giving up your dreams? (978-1-63679-725-0)

New Horizons by Shia Woods. When Quinn Collins meets Alex Anders, Horizon Theater's enigmatic managing director, a passionate connection ignites, but amidst the complex backdrop of theater politics, their budding romance faces a formidable challenge. (978-1-63679-683-3)

Scrambled: A Tuesday Night Book Club Mystery by Jaime Maddox. Avery Hutchins makes a discovery about her father's death that will force her to face an impossible choice between doing what is right and finally finding a way to regain a part of herself she had lost. (978-1-63679-703-8)

Stolen Hearts by Michele Castleman. Finding the thief who stole a precious heirloom will become Ella's first move in a dangerous game of wits that exposes family secrets and could lead to her family's financial ruin. (978-1-63679-733-5)

Synchronicity by J.J. Hale. Dance, destiny, and undeniable passion collide at a summer camp as Haley and Cal navigate a love story that intertwines past scars with present desires. (978-1-63679-677-2)

The First Kiss by Patricia Evans. As the intrigue surrounding her latest case spins dangerously out of control, military police detective Parker Haven must choose between her career and the woman she's falling in love with. (978-1-63679-775-5)

Wild Fire by Radclyffe & Julie Cannon. When Olivia returns to the Red Sky Ranch, Riley's carefully crafted safe world goes up in flames. Can they take a risk and cross the fire line to find love? (978-1-63679-727-4)

Writ of Love by Cassidy Crane. Kelly and Jillian struggle to navigate the ruthless battleground of Big Law, grappling with desire, ambition, and the thin line between success and surrender. (978-1-63679-738-0)

Back to Belfast by Emma L. McGeown. Two colleagues are asked to trade jobs. Claire moves to Vancouver and Stacie moves to Belfast, and though they've never met in person, they can't seem to escape a growing attraction from afar. (978-1-63679-731-1)

Exposure by Nicole Disney and Kimberly Cooper Griffin. For photographer Jax Bailey and delivery driver Trace Logan, keeping it casual is a matter of perspective. (978-1-63679-697-0)

Hunt of Her Own by Elena Abbott. Finding forever won't be easy, but together Danaan's and Ashly's paths lead back to the supernatural sanctuary of Terabend. (978-1-63679-685-7)

Perfect by Kris Bryant. They say opposites attract, but Alix and Marianna have totally different dreams. No Hollywood love story is perfect, right? (978-1-63679-601-7)

Royal Expectations by Jenny Frame. When childhood sweethearts Princess Teddy Buckingham and Summer Fisher reunite, their feelings resurface and so does the public scrutiny that tore them apart. (978-1-63679-591-1)

Shadow Rider by Gina L. Dartt. In the Shadows, one can easily find death, but can Shay and Keagan find love as they fight to save the Five Nations? (978-1-63679-691-8)

The Breakdown by Ronica Black. Vaughn and Natalie have chemistry, but the outside world keeps knocking at the door, threatening more trouble, making the love and the life they want together impossible. (978-1-63679-675-8)

Tribute by L.M. Rose. To save her people, Fiona will be the tribute in a treaty marriage to the Tipruii princess, Simaala, and spend the rest of her days on the other side of the wall between their races. (978-1-63679-693-2)

Wild Wales by Patricia Evans. When Finn and Aisling fall in love, they must decide whether to return to the safety of the lives they had, or take a chance on wild love in windswept Wales. (978-1-63679-771-7)

Can't Buy Me Love by Georgia Beers. London and Kayla are perfect for one another, but if London reveals she's in a fake relationship with Kayla's ex, she risks not only the opportunity of her career, but Kayla's trust as well. (978-1-63679-665-9)

Chance Encounter by Renee Roman. Little did Sky Roberts know when she bought the raffle ticket for charity that she would also be taking a chance on love with the egotistical Drew Mitchell. (978-1-63679-619-2)

Comes in Waves by Ana Hartnett. For Tanya Brees, love in small-town Coral Bay comes in waves, but can she make it stay for good this time? (978-1-63679-597-3)

Dancing With Dahlia by Julia Underwood. How is Piper Fernley supposed to survive six weeks with the most controlling, uptight boss on earth? Because sometimes when you stop looking, your heart finds exactly what it needs. (978-1-63679-663-5)

Skyscraper by Gun Brooke. Attempting to save the life of an injured boy brings Rayne and Kaelyn together. As they strive for justice against corrupt Celestial authorities, they're unable to foresee how intertwined their fates will become. (978-1-63679-657-4)

The Curse by Alexandra Riley. Can Diana Dillon and her daughter, Ryder, survive the cursed farm with the help of Deputy Mel Defoe? Or will the land choose them to be the next victims? (978-1-63679-611-6)

The Heart Wants by Krystina Rivers. Fifteen years after they first meet, Army Major Reagan Jennings realizes she has one last chance to win the heart of the woman she's always loved. If only she can make Sydney see she's worth risking everything for. (978-1-63679-595-9)

Untethered by Shelley Thrasher. Helen Rogers, in her eighties, meets much-younger Grace on a lengthy cruise to Bali, and their intense relationship yields surprising insights and unexpected growth. (978-1-63679-636-9)

You Can't Go Home Again by Jeanette Bears. After their military career ends abruptly, Raegan Holcolm is forced back to their hometown to confront their past and discover where the road to recovery will lead them, or if it already led them home. (978-1-636790644-4)

A Wolf in Stone by Jane Fletcher. Though Cassilania is an experienced player in the dirty, dangerous game of imperial Kavillian politics, even she is caught out when a murderer raises the stakes. (978-1-63679-640-6)

One Last Summer by Kristin Keppler. Emerson Fields didn't think anything could keep her from her dream of interning at Bardot Design Studio in Paris, until an unexpected choice at a North Carolina beach has her questioning what it is she really wants. (978-1-63679-638-3)

StreamLine by Lauren Melissa Ellzey. When Lune crosses paths with the legendary girl gamer Nocht, she may have found the key that will boost her to the upper echelon of streamers and unravel all Lune thought she knew about gaming, friendship, and love. (978-1-63679-655-0)

The Devil You Know by Ali Vali. As threats come at the Casey family from both the feds and enemies set to destroy them, Cain Casey does whatever is necessary with Emma at her side to bury every single one. (978-1-63679-471-6)

The Meaning of Liberty by Sage Donnell. When TJ and Bailey get caught in the political crossfire of the ultraconservative Crusade of the Redeemer Church, escape is the only plan. On the run and fighting for their lives is not the time to be falling for each other. (978-1-63679-624-6)

Undercurrent by Patricia Evans. Can Tala and Wilder catch a serial killer in Salem before another body washes up on the shore? (978-1-636790669-7)